have you got anything stronger?

Also by Imogen Edwards-Jones

Babylon series
Hotel Babylon
Air Babylon
Fashion Babylon
Beach Babylon
Pop Babylon
Wedding Babylon
Hospital Babylon
Restaurant Babylon

Others
The Taming of Eagles: Exploring the New Russia
My Canapé Hell
Big Night Out (with Jessica Adams,
Maggie Alderson and Nick Earls)
Shagpile
The Wendy House
Tuscany for Beginners
Ladies' Night (with Jessica Adams,
Maggie Alderson and Chris Manby)
The Stork Club
In Bed With . . . (co-edited with Kathy Lette, with Jessica
Adams, Maggie Alderson, et al.)
The Witches of St Petersburg

imogen edwards-jones

have you got anything stronger?

WELBECK

First published in 2023 by Welbeck Fiction Limited,
an imprint of Welbeck Publishing Group
Offices in: London – 20 Mortimer Street, London W1T 3JW &
Sydney – 205 Commonwealth Street, Surry Hills 2010

A CIP catalogue record for this book is available from the British Library

Paperback ISBN: 978-1-80279-566-0
Ebook ISBN: 978-1-78739-915-0

Printed and bound by CPI Group (UK) Ltd., Croydon, CR0 4YY

FSC
www.fsc.org
MIX
Paper | Supporting
responsible forestry
FSC® C171272

10 9 8 7 6 5 4 3 2 1

To the Book Club Queens:

Assia, Brigitta, Claire, Emma, Emily, Jenny, Justine, Kate, Phoebe, Pippa, Yasmin and elusive Charlotte!

I love you. Life would be so very dull without you all.

September 9th

6.30am: There's nothing wrong with an Indian summer, but you just don't need one quite so early in the morning when you're nursing a hangover and hovering over a toilet trying to pee on a stick. In fact, the sun is shining so brightly I'm wearing shades.

Squatting here, wearing sunglasses, I'm trying very hard to see an upside to this situation. I'm either pregnant at the age of forty-six. Or I've slid silently and unwittingly down the hormonal drainpipe and into menopause. It could be either. With my luck it'll be both. A menopausal pregnancy? Is that actually possible? Isn't that what happened to Cherie Blair, I wonder, staring at the Clearblue Pregnancy stick I found at the bottom of one of my many drawers full of tights I don't wear, scarves I've forgotten I had, knickers that no longer fit and bikinis that lie there, ever hopeful that, one day, they'll see the light of day.

I sit and wait and cross my fingers. Although quite what I'm crossing them for I've no idea. Either outcome is pretty appalling. I've got two children already. I couldn't possibly cope with a third. A third? I retch slightly. Two is *definitely* enough.

So fingers crossed for the menopause then.

6.31am: One minute's gone. I take off my Ray-Bans and look at the stick. Nothing. It says on the packet to wait for three minutes. Three whole minutes? I thought we were in an Instant World. Instant messaging, instant cameras, instant payday loans, instant coffee, instant death. Insta-bloody-gram. I wouldn't wait three minutes for a Mocha Latte in Starbucks – why do I have to wait three minutes to see which particular bit of shit Fate's chucked at me this week? It's one of these new-fangled digital predictor things – one that simply proclaims "Pregnant" or "Not Pregnant" on a small grey screen. I shake it to hurry it up. Back in the day when I spent many a tense Saturday morning in various girlfriends' flats watching the thin blue line spreading down a porous bit of cotton pad, we could see the score. We could watch our fates and futures seep out in pee and turquoise in front of our eyes. But now I'm staring at a blank screen. A bit like a calculator. It's doing my hormonal maths.

6.32am: Two minutes and counting. This is fun. Barren? Or up the duff? I shake the thing again. I drank quite a lot of wine last night. Maybe there aren't enough hormones in my five hundred per cent proof urine for it to register? Maybe I am pregnant but the Pinot/pee ratio is just too toxic?

6.33am: NOTHING is happening. Nothing. No announcement. Zip. I look a little more closely. Could I have possibly used this stick before and put it away? Could I? Really? Was the cellophane perforated, I can't remember? Was I/am I really the sort of person to piss on a stick, then pop the lid on and leave it in a drawer? I sit back on the loo seat and frown. A little too deeply for my liking. I must sort that out. I definitely need Botox. Frowning, as everyone keeps saying, is very overrated.

Finally, after ten minutes of sitting there, listening to my husband snoring away like a trucker with an adenoid problem, I pick up the box. *Use by March 2010.* Shit! This stick, much like my ovaries, is seriously out of date.

"Damn it!" I shout, throwing the thing into the bin with a loud clatter of plastic on plastic.

"What?" barks my startled husband from the bedroom.

"Nothing, dear, go back to sleep."

Forty-six today! Happy Birthday to me!

* * *

The early-morning bed invasion starts at about 6.45am. The first to wake is Pig. (Not his real name, he's actually called Sam, but no one bothers with that. What is the use of a name like Sam when he answers, happily, to Fat Pig or just Pig). So Pig, aged nine, is the first to wake. The noise he used to make while waking was so loud and distressed (like a stuck Pig, even) that it sounded like he was being tortured by a playground of peers. The heart-lurching scream was followed by the endless wailing of "Mu-u-u-mmy," which used to end in vomiting if not immediately attended to. Now he simply slopes into the room, stretches, yawns and demands I cough up another twenty quid for an extra skin on *Fortnite*. Somehow I am nostalgic for vomit.

"Not now."

"Why?" He folds his arms, practically cross-eyed with fury. "That's *so* unfair. *You're* so unfair. I hate you. You're the worst mother ever!"

"Because it's not even 7am and you're already asking for stuff."

"I only need your face," he says, like it's a totally reason-able request at 6.55am. "Up against the screen."

"I know, but it's my birthday and I don't want to . . . and . . . "

"What's your birthday got to do with anything?" he shrugs. He has a point. "And who cares about your birthday, you've had one hundred and fifty of them already. You don't need anything when you're nearly dead."

"I've got presents!" declares my husband, standing in the doorway naked but for a pair of very large, white, slightly see-through baggy pants, waving a depressingly small carrier bag. Sam looks at the bag and then at me. "When you're dead, I'm cutting off your face and keeping it in a jar and then I can buy whatever I like." He marches out of the room. I'm definitely nostalgic for the puke. Maybe I am pregnant?

Next to arrive is Ella who, even at the age of fifteen, looks like she's spent the night out on Martinis and Rothmans followed by a cosy lie-down in a skip, which she could easily have done as I went to bed before her last night, as I do most nights. There are only so many reruns of *Dance Moms* I can sit through, the days of me and Husband drinking wine and watching a box set are long gone. It's now back-to-back *Real Housewives of Beverly Hills* or some weird US Goth drama where girls with suspiciously thick lips look meaningful, with a perfect blow-dry, and discuss why all their friends want to commit suicide. Slopping into the room with attitude and bed-hair, Ella says neither "hello" nor "good morning" but immediately launches into the same conversation she was having last night without even missing a beat.

"Why haven't I got Buffalos?"

"Hi."

"Why am I the only one in my class not to have Buffalo trainers?" The stare is intense, the lip is curled, the braces glint in the sun.

"Morning."

"I need Buffalos."

"Need?"

"Yeah, need."

"You don't *need* need Buffalos, you want them."

"No! . . . Need . . ."

And so this goes on until, finally, the apotheosis of the argument is reached and she finishes in more or less the same way as Pig. "You are the *worst* mother in the world EVAH! I H-A-T-E you!" She then marches back out of my bedroom again, slamming the door so hard that a drizzle of dust covers the carpet.

To which I yell, "I hate you SO much more . . . Now do you want porridge? Or a fried egg?"

Breakfast is normally something of a poorly run restaurant where everyone, I repeat, everyone, will have something different. Ella will only eat eggs, Pig will only eat something covered thigh-deep in chocolate, and Husband absolutely has to eat in accordance with whatever diet he is attempting at the time.

The current favourite is *The Wild* which consists of food only hunted, gathered or gleaned on the savannah which is considerably hard to do on Ocado. So he's tweaked a vegan diet and called it *The Wild* and now takes a bowl of wallpaper paste in the morning (fat-free almond milk and oat bran) followed by endless plates of vegetables throughout the day and nothing much else. He usually manages to stick to his veg-only regime until about

9.30pm when his resolve, weakened by three glasses of wine, will suddenly snap and he'll demolish one bag of Haribo, five Werther's Originals, a packet of Oreos, plus a bar of cooking chocolate sourced from the back of the fridge. He'll then groan, yawn, fart and go to bed, only to wake up the next morning, weigh himself and loudly pronounce, "This diet is SHIT!"

So he sits at one end of the table eating paste and catching up on important overnight emails, fascinating repartee on Twitter, and which C-List Sleb has managed to 'debut their bump/curves/cankles/side boob/under boob/double boob' on dailymail.com. Meanwhile, Pig is dragged moaning and yawning into the car for the school run and Ella is pushed out of the front door.

However, as today is my birthday (oh, hip, hip, hooray!) it is slightly different. I am to be treated, in the words of Ella, "like a celebrity" (the apparent height of luxury) so I get given my cup of coffee in bed. I am not quite sure how it's been made but it arrives tepid and the consistency of a Covent Garden chunky soup. Undeterred, I gamely sip away only to hear my kidneys cry out in pain moments before my eyeballs flip back in my head. Whatever she's done to it, I'm not sleeping for the rest of this decade. Next, I'm handed two slices of toast and Marmite, as thick as a bonkbuster which someone, I think Pig, has forgotten to butter.

"Delicious!"

"Can I open all your presents?" asks Pig, elbowing his way into the middle of the bed.

Before I can reply, he's tearing at the brown paper with "Happy Birthday" written all over it in jolly neon writing. It's from WHSmith, it's £3.99 a roll. I know, because I was the one who bought it.

"Oh," he says, rejecting the first present. "A cookery book."

"It's that baking one, with the pretty girl on the front," chips in Husband. "She used to be a model, you know."

"She clearly doesn't eat her own food."

Husband laughs in hearty agreement. "No . . ." I watch as he slowly strokes the photograph on the front.

Pig attacks present number two. "Oh – a whizzing thing!" He holds it up to the light, gives it a whizz and then dumps it on top of present number one.

"A blender," corrects Husband. "We need one of those and it was on offer at Lidl."

"How could you refuse?"

"I know." He clears his throat, gets off the bed and walks across to the bathroom, looking pleased with himself.

"What's that?" asks Ella, feigning interest from the corner of the bed.

"Dust," dismisses Pig, tearing the paper off the last present. "Little boxes of dust." He curls up his top lip and throws the boxes across the bed. "Boring," he adds for good measure.

"Herbs," yawns Husband from the bathroom.

"Sumac," I read the label.

"You see . . . everything! Happy Birthday, darling."

Now, when you've had as many birthdays as I have (forty-six), you cease to suffuse them with any sort of joy or expectation. But I have to say even *I'd* been hoping for a little more than a book, a whizzer and some dust. It's the age-old adage of hope over experience and I fall for it every time. It's not that I'd like a brass band with bunting and a town crier following me around all day, proclaiming the joyous day of my birth to everyone. But some sexy knickers? Some heels? Or a handbag would be nice.

As my friend Sally always says, "If he gives you anything with a plug on it you're fucked." But then Sally is very opinionated about presents. Actually, she has lots of opinions on anything and everything, but particularly presents. "The day he gets you anything with an elasticated waist is the day you shoot yourself," she often shares with her lips clamped around a fag. "And if he buys you diamonds you have to ask who he's been screwing, because diamonds have guilt written on every fucking facet."

Along with opining, Sally also likes to swear. A lot. Then again, she has three boys under the age of six so she has plenty to swear about. I check the whizzer. It doesn't have a plug. It is a handheld one with a wheel and small wooden handle. No wonder it was on offer at Lidl; it went out with the washboard and the mangle. But still, there is no actual plug point. So my marriage might just about be OK. Ish.

Birthday celebrations over, I embark on the breakfast and the moaning and the shouting, bag-losing school run, which we manage to do without slipping in dog shit. Something both Pig and I achieve on at least a twice-weekly basis.

Children finally deposited, I head off to the chemist to try and ascertain if I am going to have any more of them, or if I'm going to spend the next five years complaining how hot it is.

Buying a pregnancy test at my age is almost as embarrassing as purchasing Anusol. How anyone ever decided to call a cream something that resembles the garbled mumblings of "arsehole" is quite beyond me. But it appears to be regularly stocked in all fine stores. Although, personally, I'd rather suffer from haemorrhoids than have to ask for "arsehole" over the counter, but each to their own. Anyway, in order to minimise any collateral damage regarding the pregnancy test purchase, I decide to choose a nice out-of-the-way chemist where the man in the white coat has no chance of knowing my name, or ever seeing me again. Mumbling like a teenager buying contraceptives, I direct the well-nourished woman behind the counter towards the Clearblue section and fork out £14 on a test. £14! Christ, they've gone up.

Fleeced, I turn and bump slap bang into Sally, who has a blond child in each hand and one strapped to her front like a starfish. She'd look like something straight out of *Shameless* where it not for the vastly expensive papoose she'd been regifted by her patronisingly rich younger sister, who managed to bag a banker back in the day when people pretended to tolerate them.

"Hi!" I smile. "What are you doing here?"

"Lice," she replies with a quick itch of her crotch. "What the actual fuck?" she suddenly shouts extremely loudly. The whole chemist grinds to a halt. The large bingo-winged lady at the till lets her jaw slowly hang open. Sally stares at my bag and the pregnancy testing kit poking out of the top. "Has Ella been having sex?"

God, I need a fag.

September 11th

"Is it wrong to wish for a mild concussion?" asks Sally two days later at my delayed birthday lunch.

"Concussion?"

"I'm just desperate for a lie-down. I'm so goddamn tired I'm longing for a really good illness to put me out of action for a while."

"What? Like flu?" asks Kate, looking up from her phone.

"Something *so* much better than flu," replies Sally. "You can battle through flu. You can bravely keep on fucking going with flu. People expect it. And I have zero interest in being brave, or fucking battling on anywhere. I need a lie-down. A proper lie-down. I'd like something that involves a non-fatal hospitalisation and some really good drugs."

"Who wants drugs?" asks Claire, as she scurries in with wet hair and what appears to be her life in a couple of Sainsbury's bags.

Claire likes a drug. Anything that can be rolled or smoked and stuck in a Rizla is right up her street. She used to do plenty of Class A, back in the day, when she'd dance on a podium all night, wearing nothing but a push-up bra and red dungarees. Now she won't go near anything she can't grow herself, or forage on a summer's eve in the Forest of Dean. "Ofph," she exhales dramatically as she sits down, dumping what still looks like her life at her feet.

We are in one of those irritating, high-concept restaurants that combine popularity with a no-booking policy. The end result being you have to queue up to spend your own money. An idea which I find a little rude, to say the least. But Kate was insistent. Kate's choice. And indeed Kate's shout (thankfully). Kate chalks up restaurants like other single girls do one-night stands. She's an early adopter, a tastemaker, an influencer in her own lunchtime. Anything new on the scene has to be sampled immediately, given a test ride, analysed, photographed, posted and then ticked off the list. She is a glamorous, single girl-about-town so if *she* didn't want to queue up for a cramped corner table and an overpriced sweetcorn fritter, how else would half of these destination restaurants ever stay afloat?

"Who wants drugs?" asks Claire again, looking puzzled.

"I was just saying," explains Sally, "that I am so shagged I'd happily be knocked unconscious, run over at the bus stop and put out of my misery."

"But you never take the bus," says Kate.

"Only because I never fucking go anywhere. Have you tried to get three children on a bus?"

"Do you exercise?" suggests Claire.

"Exercise!" Sally inhales with indignation. "Exercise! When the fuck do I find the time to exercise? How long have you known me, Claire? Ten years? OK, in those ten years have I ever once exercised?"

"You did pregnancy yoga?" tries Claire.

"We *all* did pregnancy fucking yoga! We all mooned around in that frigging cold church hall in Willesden with that skinny cow teacher because we all thought it would make a difference. Little did we know, no matter how many downward dogs you did, you'd still end up with a fifteen-foot episiotomy and low-level incontinence. And don't ask me if I'm hydrated either. You tell someone you're tired, they immediately ask you if you're hydrated. It's going to take more than a fucking glass of water to make me feel better. A pint of wine, maybe. But a glass of water . . ." She sighs. "All I want is a couple of days in hospital. Is that too much too ask? Gallstones? Kidney stones? A urinary tract infection? I could read a whole book from cover to actual cover, imagine that? Or frankly stare at the wall with my mouth hanging slightly open. *That* would make me happy."

"I think Michael Jackson had the right idea," I say. "Propofol sounds brilliant. One night's sleep is never enough. He'd be out for a couple of days at a time."

"Except it did kill him," says Kate.

"There is that," I concede.

"Although it's a risk I'd happily take," says Sally, snapping off a breadstick and rapidly munching it like a carb-starved chipmunk. "I don't think I've slept through one night in five years."

"We all know sleep is for the weak," says Kate.

"If you're going to tell me how Margaret bloody Thatcher only needed five hours' sleep a night, I am going to yawn in your face," replies Sally, offering her the bread basket. Kate looks horrified.

"Bread?" A shiver of revulsion shoots right through her. "I'm gluten intolerant."

"You're just intolerant," I reply.

"Gluten is the Devil's work," she continues. "Everyone knows that."

"They don't seem to have a problem with it in France. No one is lactose or gluten intolerant over there," says Sally. "They seem to be perfectly capable of finishing off a baguette and a whole fucking wheel of Brie without anyone being violently ill or blowing up like some giant flatulent helium balloon."

"*And* they're thin." I stand up from the table.

"Where are you going?" asks Claire.

"To have a cigarette."

"Smoking?" says Claire.

"But I thought you were pregnant?" proclaims Sally as loudly as she can.

Everyone in the surrounding section puts down their devices. This is clearly much better than Twitter and photographing their starters. Lips pursed, they all stare. Half of them, I can tell, are thinking, who'd sleep with *her*? And the other half are looking slightly stunned that I still might be ovulating at all.

"A. I'm not pregnant," I say, nodding towards Sally. "And B. I'm a big girl. I'm forty-six. It's all going tits up. So I may as well smoke while the ship is slowly sinking."

"Brilliant idea," agrees Kate, getting up from her seat. "I'm going to join you."

Outside, the pair of us light up like a couple of car thieves out on bail. The wind has an autumnal chill but fortunately it is not raining. The last time I properly lit up you could still smoke at the back of a plane and restaurants competed for the most nickable ashtrays, so this whole cowering on the street thing is new to me. It certainly makes you bolt your fag quickly and chug down another chaser, just in case.

"Ooh, I'm feeling a little rough today," admits Kate, touching her marble-smooth forehead.

Kate works in advertising, so hardcore drinking is part of the job description. Tall, slim and working jeans, a leather jacket and her favourite knee boots, her short, choppy, textured haircut is being blown flat by the wind and she's clearly slept in her eyeliner. I have to say I've seen her looking better.

"Work?"

"No, pleasure, well, not really pleasure. Old mates from school."

"Christ. When did you last see them?"

"Years. But it's one of those invitations you can't say no to. Particularly if you're single as, you know, they might have a brother, or an ex-husband, or a father I can grab as he comes out of the divorce courts." She takes a long drag, her right eye half closed in the smoke. "It's either that, or a bottle of wine and *Succession*."

"I dream of that."

"Quite odd," she muses. "There were a couple of single City girls. Plenty of cash and no one to spend it on. Apparently, it's all still about handbags."

"The ones with girls' names?"

"Yup," she flicks her ash. "Handbags, shoes and cocaine. What they don't put up their noses, they put on their feet . . . It's very sad, really." She nods reflectively, staring into the window of Zadig and Voltaire.

"Mmm . . . really very sad . . ." I nod. We both look at each other. "Although . . ."

"Well, obviously . . . I've never seen so many Louboutins in my life . . . But are they *happy*?" Kate expertly flicks her fag end halfaway across the road, narrowly avoiding a slim yummy mummy trotting behind a pushchair. Fortunately, she's too busy barking into her mobile to notice.

"Probably a fuck of a lot happier than both of us," I sigh. "Shall we go in?"

Back inside, the bread basket has gone and there are two types of water to choose from. It makes me long for the days of a three-bottle Sauvignon lunch. Sally and Claire are still staring at the menu trying to work out what to order, when Katie and I sit back down, accompanied by a waft of fag smoke.

"How does this work?" asks Sally.

"You basically order a salad or something and add the bits you want to it," explains Kate.

"Really?" Sally looks exhausted by this idea. "You mean, I actually have to put together the ingredients of what I'm eating? Isn't that the chef's job?" She lets the menu gently fall from her hands and sighs massively.

"What would you ladies like?" asks a waiter with five hoops in one ear and a couple of Celtic symbols on his forearms.

Everyone orders some variation on leaves and Sally, who appears to have lost the will to decide, asks for "whatever's popular". The tip of the waiter's tongue escapes his mouth as he struggles to write it all down on his small pad of paper; he is clearly between modelling contracts.

"What's the betting we don't get what we ordered," says Kate as she watches the waiter's backside weave its way through the tables. "He doesn't even look like he can send a text message."

"Even Nathan can do that and he's six," says Sally. "So you're not pregnant then?"

The table turns to look at me.

"No."

"Did you want to be?" asks Claire. She has always been the most emotionally literate of us all, in touch with her inner and outer self, her chakras, her yin, her yang and her yoni, but then again, she was a trained counsellor, so you'd kind of hope that were the case.

"No." I say that rather too firmly. I can see Claire's thin eyebrows rise slightly. "No, really I don't."

"Anyway, doesn't that require sex?" declares Kate.

"Someone was fucking listening in biology." Sally grins. "You're not the only one who's getting it, you know. You, with your single life and your filthy weekends away and your sex toys and your butt plugs and your anal beads . . ."

"Anal beads?" Kate looks appalled.

Sally always takes things a little too far. "Us married old cows do occasionally get laid."

"Very occasionally," I add.

"Very, very, very, very, very occasionally," agrees Sally, looking down and picking fluff off her jumper. We stare at her. She looks back up. "Birthdays, Christmas, that sort of thing . . . right?"

"And maybe a Friday?" suggests Claire, putting on a concerned face.

"No one does it on a Friday," I say. "They're far too tired."

"Unless they are completely plastered," Kate mutters, looking down at her phone.

"But you and Will do have sex?" asks Claire.

"Sometimes." Sally is sounding shifty.

"It is important," continues Claire. "Very important. I always used to give Rob a good milking, especially if he was about to go away on business. It gets it all out, you see, and then he's much less likely to stray . . ."

"A milking!" shrieks Sally.

"A MILKING!" I agree, struggling not to vomit in my own mouth.

"You know what I mean," Claire's cheeks pink slightly. "Like a cow. Once or twice a week. It's got to be done."

"Milk him like a cow! Please," says Kate, her eyes closed and her hands in the air like she's about to be shot. "I am so fucking glad I'm not married."

"Ladies!" grins the waiter, his forearms loaded with plates. "Who's for lettuce?"

The salads arrive with a selection of avocado, crispy bacon and chicken side orders, only half of which we asked for. Not at all surprisingly, Sally's 'popular' lunch appears to be the same as mine, so we tuck into our guilt-free food with all the gusto of a brace of rabbits.

"Rob and I are getting a divorce," announces Claire, not looking up from her food.

"What!" I say.

"You?" adds Kate.

"What the fuck do you want to do that for?" Sally is so cross she half gets out of her chair in fury.

"So much for the milking," mumbles Kate.

September 12th

It's 11pm and I'm trying to discuss the break-up of my friend's marriage but Husband can't hear me. It is like I am speaking Whale, or perhaps a special high-pitched language that only dogs can understand. Growing up, my father was always selectively deaf; any mention of money, or bills, or needing new shoes, and he literally couldn't hear a thing. Whisper the word "whisky", however, and he was suddenly all ears. But with Husband, irrespective of subject, financial or alcoholic, he genuinely actually doesn't hear me anymore at all. I'm white noise. Then again, I am trying to compete with that old slag.

You see, there are three of us in this marriage. Husband, Me and that slut iPad – I am definitely Diana, the wronged party – because the way he touches that screen, the way he drags his fingers across its surface, the way he tweaks the button. I swear that button has had a thousand times more action than mine in sixteen years of marriage. But it's the swooshing noise I can't bear. I'll ask a simple question like, "Do you want more carrots for supper?" To which I'll get no response. I then stand and wait, and wait, only to hear the little swooshing aircraft-taking-off noise as his email flies, very urgently, off into the ether.

"So Claire and Rob are getting divorced," I try again, putting some toothpaste on my brush.

"Mmmm." Swoosh.

"I never saw that coming." I start to brush my teeth.

"Mmm."

"Where are they going to live? Who's going to have custody of Jade?"

"Mmm." Swoosh. Swoosh.

"Are you listening to me?" I spit.

"Of course I am." He puts the tart down and looks at me. "Rob and Claire are getting divorced. He told me last week."

"He told you *last week*? And you didn't tell me?" I drink some water from the tap and spit again.

"I didn't think it was very important."

"Not *important*!"

"Yeah, it's not that big a deal."

"Really? My best friend is getting divorced and you didn't think it would be interesting to tell me?"

"You've got lots of friends."

"But she is my best friend."

23

"I thought Sally was your best friend?"

"I've got lots of best friends."

"How is that possible?"

"She is getting divorced and you didn't think I'd find that important?"

"I thought she would have told you."

"Told me!"

"Seeing as you're best friends . . ."

I turn back, spit one more time and look at myself in the mirror. My hair needs dyeing, my eyebrows need shaping and I should buy some more expensive face cream rather than the body butter I'm currently slathering on my face. I narrow my eyes. What are you supposed to do if your moustache is already blonde? Bleach it more? Shit! Are those smoker's lines around my mouth? Already! God, that's depressing! Six packets of fags and I've already got a mouth like a cat's arsehole. And now my best friend is keeping secrets from me. Another thing to add to the shitlist.

September 15th

Guitar, tennis, drums, swimming, cricket, rugby, coding. Football, remedial maths, remedial English, remedial science, remedial French, parties, "gatherings", "motives": my children have more bloody appointments than the Foreign Secretary and I'm the chauffeur. I did have a life and career once, but now I simply drive up and down the Kilburn High Road, my shoulders rounded, my mouth ajar, listening to Magic or Tragic FM as my children call it. All I need is a nodding dog and a mustard-velvet-covered box of tissues on the back shelf of my car and I could start charging.

But it is not so much the driving, which I obviously hate, but it is the hanging around outside the class, lesson, boot camp, remedial centre that really pisses me off. What are you supposed to do for those forty-eight minutes of freedom? Send emails? Text people? Google famous people? Read a newspaper/book? Phone Radio 5 Live and join in the heated debate?

Or wander aimlessly around the shops, not spending any money because you no longer have any. I did, once, have some money. When I had a full-time job. I used to have a desk, as well. It had drawers and a telephone and computer where, as well as working, I could perve on frocks on Net-a-Porter. I sometimes long for that desk. But I've quit marketing, that's my story at least. And since then I have taken up minicabbing, unfortunately I'm just not getting the fares.

"Can you believe she is bloody getting divorced?" says Sally for the fifth time in the last ten minutes. She is waiting for her son, Nathan, who is at the same street dance school as Ella, who I am only collecting to make sure she's actually gone to sodding class in the first place. Poor six-year-old Nathan is being forced to dance now, in order that he might be more attractive to girls later in life. However, according to Ella, who has seen him once or twice, he appears to have no aptitude for the discipline and spends most of the class swinging on the door handle, waiting to go home. Not that Ella is, truth be told, much better. I am just hoping that some exercise after school will mean she's got less time to vape. Although she swears blind that the Juul and the twenty-five vanilla-flavoured pods that I found in her bedroom the other day belonged to someone else. She was just "keeping them safe" apparently. And not smoking them on the way to school. At all.

"I mean, what's she going to do? Where's she going to live? They'll have to sell the house."

We are both walking around a small furniture shop where we occasionally pick up a photo frame and mumble something along the lines of "that's nice" as it is a cheaper way to waste forty-eight minutes of our lives than sitting in a café, and just as warm.

"She could move up near you," continued Sally. "It's much cheaper where you are."

Sally used to be a lawyer with clicky shoes, a twenty-five-inch waist and painted, clicky nails. Now the only thing that clicks are her hips, since baby number three, and she hasn't taken on a case in over two years. She keeps promising she'll return to the Bar but she's delayed her maternity leave three times and now she's not quite sure there is actually a job for her to go back to.

"Oh! You've got to get that!" she says suddenly. Sally likes shopping almost as much as she likes swearing.

"Yes," I nod, pretending to be interested.

"No, seriously," she says seriously. "They're seriously good." She also seems to have a bizarre encyclopedic knowledge of all products and their uses.

"What?"

"A thermo mug!" she grins, nodding away. "They're perfect for the car on the school run. They keep your coffee warm for ages. You'll save a fortune at Starbucks."

"I don't go to Starbucks. It costs a fortune."

"You can't be a school-run mum without a thermo mug," she states.

"I don't want to be a school-run mum."

"BUY IT!"

September 20th

It's 8.42am and against my better judgement I am using the mug. And I have to admit, Sally was right. It is quite useful. I can make a cup of coffee at home and it is still hot by the time I reach the school. (If there's not seventy-five miles of traffic crossing the Harrow Road). I only wish everything else worked so well. As usual I'm late, and as usual I spend ten bloody minutes trying to find somewhere to park. Eventually I spot a space about large enough for a Smart Car but I am undeterred: I braille-park my clapped-out Golf, bouncing off the other bumpers, tapping my way in. Just as I am about to congratulate myself on a job well done, I see a flicky blonde approaching the school gate on a scooter, her slim leg peddling away, followed by a mini-me with equally blow-dried hair.

As I stare at her, I realise that nothing is wobbling. I know her because she had a child at nursery with me. And she has another two children at senior school and NOTH-ING is wobbling. The sun catches her silk shirt and shining right through, I can see her perfect silhouette. She is braless; her in-profile boob points north rather than south. Suddenly I hit the car behind, spill my thermo mug of coffee in the crotch of my trousers and leap out of the car screaming. Clever Sally, the coffee is certainly still hot.

While I am standing, staring, distraught, down at my trousers, an Ab Dad walks past. He glances across at me. There is a semicircular stain seeping down between my legs. I have very definitely pissed myself.

"It's coffee," I say too quickly. "Coffee." He looks sorry for me. "It is not my pelvic floor," I insist, with a slightly manic laugh. "I can cough *and* do star jumps. In fact, I can cough, sneeze and do star jumps and shoot ping-pong balls . . ." He puts a protective arm around his whey-faced son and slowly moves away. "I promise you!" He gathers pace. "It is COFFEE!" I shout after him. "Very hot COFFEE!!" He's disappeared around the square.

I turn back to see Pig still sitting in the car with his head in his hands.

"Mummyyyah." I can always tell when he is pissed off as the "y"s go on forever – and then the word appears to end on an "ah". Mummyyyah. Daddyyyah. Grannyyyah. But mostly Mummyyyyyyah.

"What?"

He gets out of the car and slams the door. "You are *such* an embarrassment!"

"No, I'm not." I know I am, but I'm not letting him know that I know that I am.

"I am walking to school without you."

He starts to march off down the street, his huge square rucksack bouncing against the backs of his short legs. I trot along after him.

"I'm pretty sure you're not allowed to do this." He ignores me. "Technically, it is illegal for you to be walking along the street on your own . . ." And finally I yell. "Stop walking on your own!"

"I am not on my own." He turns and puts his hands on his hips. "I'm walking to school. Which is, like basically, just around the corner."

"Yes but, like basically, you need to be accompanied by an appropriate adult."

"Except you're not."

"What?"

"Appropriate. You're inappropriate."

"No I am not!" He stares at my crotch. "Where did you learn that word, anyway? Have you been on the internet again?"

"Personal Skills Development Class – talking about paedos!" He marches off ahead of me, and I follow rather like his stalker. He stops and turns around. "Five steps behind me," he says, looking at the pavement, waiting for me to obey. "Five!" I duly step back five steps. "I don't want to be 'associated' with you." I draw breath. "And before you ask," he continues with an imperious wave of his hand, "For'nite."

"Fortnite!" I shout after him. "It's got a T in it! ForT niTe. OK, go and get murdered! See if I care!"

"Everything alright?"

I turn around to see Erica, PTA princess, looking all washed and sporty, encased in elastane and sporting a super-swingy ponytail.

"Fine. You?"

"I'm off to Pilates." She smiles. It doesn't reach her eyes. But I suspect those muscles have long since been paralysed.

"Oh, I should do that."

"Yes," she agrees, trying, and failing, not to glance down at my crotch.

"It's coffee."

"I know," she nods sympathetically and gives my stiff shoulder a little pat. "We're all ladies here. I have a very good doctor friend who specialises in tightening vaginas – I'll email you."

"There's really no need."

She starts to power-walk away, pumping her arms, her ponytail swinging, her trainers squeaking down the street.

"My vagina is fine!" I shout. "It's absolutely fine!"

I turn back to see Ab Dad running back down the other side of the road. He looks across, pity written across his face.

"It's coffee. And I don't want to sleep with you anyway," I say weakly, before getting back into the car.

September 21st

I have so much filler in my top lip, I can't actually smoke. This is a little annoying as I had the filler to combat the signs of the smoking and can now, obviously, no longer continue with my new hobby. I clearly hadn't thought this through. Vicky, who runs the local Botoxeria, was Sally's recommendation. "She does fucking everyone," apparently. So, I thought, in order to combat "cat's arse mouth" I should collect all the change down the back of the sofa and my birthday money from my mum (I know, don't ask) and get as much shit pumped into my lips as possible. The full Kim K. Or Liz H. Kylie M. At least, that's what Sally booked me in for.

So, I sit in the white leather waiting room and flick through the magazines advertising fifteen-thousand-pound dresses worn by girls with urchin haircuts wearing wellington boots, and I wonder: "Why am I here? What am I doing? I'm not a fan of the sink plunger mouth, this is madness . . ." And as I break out in a sweat, Vicky appears. She's slim, with brushed hair and glossy lips, dressed in a pair of white jeans and looks about twenty-five years old.

"I'm fifty," she reveals as she indicates for me to lie down on the paper-covered bed. A tiny bit older than me and she has better skin than Ella. Actually Ella's skin is appalling. But she, Vicky, has the skin of a vitamin-chugging, exfoliating fourteen-year-old who's never stepped into the sun. A trained facial surgeon, Vicky's a little bit more qualified than the usual Tango-tanned, needle-wielding beautician, but perhaps with a little less bedside manner.

"What facial expression do you want?" she asks, snapping on her rubber gloves.

"I'd like to be able to smile," I suggest.

"Really?" She picks up her syringe and taps the plastic for bubbles with her white latex index finger.

Oh, maybe a smile's too much? Maybe a smile's a little last century? "Um, what do you think?"

Asking a slim, glamorous, fabulous woman in charge of a lot of injectables what's wrong with your face is not, let me tell you, the road to happiness.

"Well," she starts. "You have lines, here, here and here. Open pores here and here. Do you drink a lot of alcohol? You have the classic barcode across the top lip from smoking. You're losing volume in your lips, particularly the bottom one, which is common in the over-forties, especially if you are a white Caucasian. You've got bunny lines either side of your nose from wrinkling up your face and, of course, you've got the tramline frown. As well as crow's feet here and here. Some hound-dog drooping here and, oh dear, some more drooping there."

"Can you fix it?"

"Yes, I can."

Much like Bob the Builder, Vicky reaches into her toolbox and brings out the glue, the cement and the Polyfilla. It takes about twenty-five minutes of bleeding agony – literally agony with blood – before she finishes.

"There," she says, handing me a mirror. I am Bob De Niro in *Raging Bull,* with smears of blood all over my face. "It'll be fine once it's calmed down a bit."

"It looks amazing. Thank you so much," I lie, handing over my credit card to feed the machine. "How long before it actually calms down?"

"Oh, by this evening it should all be fine."

And she is/was right. By 7pm the blood washes off and the swelling has gone down and I am now channelling a Minogue forehead and Kim K lips (sadly/fortunately not the arse). None of which are moving. Well, the Botox-head has yet to kick in, but the lips won't pucker up properly. No matter how many times I try to shove in a Marlboro Gold, I just can't get purchase. I can't feel it. It's no wonder all these women are so thin, with their lollipop heads and their shiny, immobile features – they can't actually eat, let alone drink. The irony is, of course, that when they dribble their lunch down their chin, they can't even show surprise.

September 24th

Christ. My head feels thick and my eyelids are straining to stay open. Not only have I got one of those stinking, streaming, snotty eye-weeping colds, where you end up with red-rimmed mole eyes and nostrils as raw as Stevie Nicks's roadie, but I also think I've got a bit of a Benylover – a Benylin-induced hangover.

It's been a while since I've had one of those. Well over twenty-five years, I think. When I was a "schtudent" I developed a bit of a taste for the stuff. I remember, after a busy evening of smoking dope, listening to Blur's *Parklife* while seeing how long my friend Cath (who's since gone on to become a JP) and I could last, sitting (fully clothed) on a vibrator without laughing. Then I'd walk home, and I'd slip between the dank sheets in my bedsit (which had been condemned by Environmental Health for its stagger-ing ability to grow an immense variety of mushrooms in the corner of the living room) and hack myself stupid until I drank enough Benylin to knock me out cold. It usually took about a third of a bottle, sometimes a half, but I'd wake up the next morning feeling completely awful. I'd have a dung mouth, dung breath and a vampiric fear of daylight. I'd shuffle to lectures still dressed in my pyjamas, clutching a cup of viscous coffee, dragging down a Rothmans Blue – which was probably the originator of said troublesome cough in the first place. And there I'd sit, half-eyed, staring at the whiteboard, straining to see/hear what the old bloke, stinking of tweed and naphthalene, was banging on about. No wonder I got a Third.

Anyway, so there I am, quietly nursing my Benylover, shuffling my way along in the queue to drop off Pig, when I am accosted by one of the power yanks who run the Parents' Committee. It's the scooter blonde with the pert north-facing boobs.

"Hey you!" She greets me like we're both in the cast of *Friends*. I notice she has matching eye and teeth whites, and while she carries on talking at me, I find myself idly wondering if she's done her a-hole the same colour. "So you will?" she finishes.

"Er, yes," I sniff, feeling she's after a positive response. I pause. "Will what?"

"Join the Parents' Committee."

She lobs the hand grenade at me, in conjunction with a killing-with-kindness smile, and steps up into her blacked-out four-by-four. I would retaliate, but I'm still semi-sedated and I can't even express surprise due to my recently Botoxed forehead. So I simply stand and take it like a sweaty, overweight, lobotomised Barbie.

*   *   *

"Tell them to fuck off," yells Sally, which is her *de facto* answer to everything. She's driving and hasn't got any of those hands-free devices so, in the name of health, safety and three points on her licence, she's prone to popping her phone on her crotch and shouting at her own fanny while speeding through the traffic. "I mean, let's be frank here: there are some women who want to do that shit. They get off on the bossing, the organising of others, and making pretty signs, and painting other kids' nails; they series-link *Bake Off* and actually know the difference between bicarb and baking fucking powder. And you, my love, you are *not* one of them."

"You're right," I nod, a little too vigorously and regret it immediately. "What is the difference?"

"What?"

"Between bicarb and baking powder?"

"I've no fucking idea. One is good for cutting coke and the other is not – how the fuck do I know? But you should step down, fall on your sword and let those who want to, do it."

"D'you think?"

"I *know*. You're actually doing *them* a favour by not getting involved. You're freeing up the space for someone who truly wants it. And anyway, you'll only disappoint. Trust me. I am not a doctor but I am on my way to one now."

"Gastric band?"

"Health insurance. Will's been too terrified to drink or smoke all week in case they want to take his blood."

"He should lay off the smack as well."

"Ha ha. Anyway, you should definitely back down. Say you don't want to do it. There are people who really do like decorating cakes, don't deprive them of the opportunity . . . When's the first meeting?"

"Tonight." I sniff.

"Well, go tonight and hand in your resignation."

"Good idea."

"I'm full of them – SHIIIT," she shrieks, then there's an alarming screech of brakes.

* * *

It seems odd to be wandering around Pig's school, trying to avoid tripping over the red plastic chairs and low blue tables, toting an alcoholic beverage. But fortunately, I am not alone in this – there are some ten other women, all of whom are exuding fragrance, all of whom are chatting pleasantly together and all of whom are ignoring me like I'm some sort of macrobiotic fart. I waft slowly over to the boxed wine section to refill my paper cup. My eyes are still porcine and my head remains a little thick, so I'm hoping a fistful of Twiglets and a second glass of room-temperature white will go a long way to dispel my Benylover. A few sips later, and finally the rest of the room gradually pulls into focus.

"Hello," says a voice so decidedly male that I jump.

A bloke? I try not to stare and keep my slightly puffy mouth shut. A bloke? There's something rather dubious about a bloke wanting to join a Parents' Committee. I know it says "parents", but really it should stop posing as an equal opportunities employer and call itself the Mothers' Committee instead. Because blokes, well, I can't help thinking they must somehow have tumbled back through the teeny-tiny hole the sisters have chiselled in the glass ceiling only to find themselves stuck in a small plastic school chair, rather by mistake. When most of us are running a mile, or only accepting the job of organising the Christmas Fair out of guilt, I can't understand why any bloke would actively seek to join the competitive cake makers and glitter-card queens. But maybe that's just me.

"Um, good evening," I reply, taking a rather large gulp of box wine; only a small splash dribbles down my front. It's the Ab Dad from the school run. I can only hope he doesn't recognise me with my dry crotched trousers.

"I think I recognise you from somewhere."

"I can't think how."

"Do you go to the gym?"

"No," I say, shaking my head. "This doesn't just happen, you know." I point out my well-lagged hips. He looks at me, trying to work out if I am joking, or if it is actually OK to laugh at a reasonably plump lady to her face.

"I find counting crisps as part of your five-a-day also helps," he smiles, plucking a few cheese and onion from a nearby bowl.

"I agree, and the lemon in your vodka and tonic."

"I do draw the line at the olive in a Martini," he states. "I am David, James's dad." He offers me his hand.

"I am Sam's mother. And most definitely not a person in her own right."

"Excellent," he nods. "I'll call you Sam's mum. Shall we sit?" He indicates a red chair. "I think the meeting is about to start."

"Hey, guys, thank you for coming." Power Yank claps her hands together as I settle back into my uncomfortable seat and sip a little more box wine.

Before I know it, I am four glasses of tepid Chardonnay down and volunteering for everything – set-up, clean-up, the mince pie stall. For some reason, and I suspect it is the alchemy of cheap booze, an over-the-counter sedative and the proximity of James's dad's warm, sturdy thigh, but I have suddenly come over all Mrs-fucking-Christmas.

There's not a festive opportunity that I am not embracing with every rather drunken bone in my body. I even offer the services of Husband as the meet-and-greet Father Christmas on the door.

"You did what?" he asks, shoving a nasal hair trimmer up his right nostril and giving himself a quick buzz cut. A small lump of snot-clumped hair falls into the basin. I quickly remove my toothbrush, but the snot's already attached. Do I cry? Do I scream? Do I retch copiously into the nearby toilet? No. I simply wash it under the tap. This has happened before. I'm used to it. Married life doesn't get sexier than this.

September 26th

"I was the one who had an affair," says Claire, staring out of the large, steamed-up, plate glass window of the half-empty café at the traffic jam outside.

I don't know why she's chosen to meet here, as if our conversation weren't depressing enough. The walls are dark brown. The cream tables are tacky with decades of spilt drinks and the coffee machine sounds like a steam engine with emphysema. It makes so much noise we have to stop talking while they brew the sort of bitter coffee that makes your whole body quiver when you first sip it. Fortunately, there are not that many customers.

"You did?" I sit back in my wooden chair. "Wow!" Lucky cow is all I can think. "You kept that quiet."

"You're supposed to keep them quiet," replies Claire, fiddling with the pink and white packets of sugar in the chrome bowl in the middle of the table. She's not looking me in the eye. She's fixated on the sugar, flipping it back and forth. It's annoying.

"Um . . . anyone I know?" I venture.

"Oh, just some idiot at work, he doesn't want to leave his wife, he told me, not that I wanted to leave Rob anyway, but you know . . ." She looks up. "He found out anyway."

"Rob? How? Did he read texts or something?"

"Much worse." She sighs. "We were planning a weekend away in Madrid, I said I was going for work but . . . anyway he opened my emails and there were two boarding passes . . . one for him and the other for me . . . I'd checked us in . . ." She's now vigorously flipping a pink packet of sweetener between her thumb and forefinger.

"Shit."

"You could say that," she nods. "Anyway, he said he didn't want to leave his wife, but Rob decided he didn't want to stay with me."

"Shit."

"I know."

"Shit."

"I know. But he had it coming, really. Rob. We hadn't been getting on for a while. We were moving in different directions. Him, forever tap-dancing to the tune of consumerist capitalism and me, well, you know me, I'm more interested in exploring the spiritual side of things."

"He does work in insurance."

"And he voted Leave," she whispers across the table. "Imagine . . . I slept with him!"

"You're married to him."

"That too."

"What's going to happen to Jade?"

"Oh FUCK!" she shouts as the pink paper bag bursts and the white sugar-substitute crystals scatter all over the table. "Fuck," she repeats, scooping all the crystals up with one hand and pouring them into the other. "I don't know, I don't know," she mumbles. "I think I might get a little flat near you, it's much cheaper than where I am."

"Yes," I nod. "So they say."

"Quite a lot cheaper," she continues, scooping and scraping. "And then who knows? I can't go back to my work, that's for sure."

"I suppose not . . . It was rubbish anyway."

"What was wrong with it?"

She stares at me, her dark eyes questioning. Her thin lips are pursed. Her thin eyebrows are raised. She is clearly biting the inside of her mouth in annoyance.

"Oh, you know . . ."

I stare at her, thinking of the many times she's marched into my kitchen and thrown her bag down on my diminutive breakfast bar and demanded a pint of wine in an IV just to remove the stress of her awful day. Turns out that the post-partum job she'd got in "publishing" was

actually selling advertising space in the local through-
the-letterbox free glossy magazine and was not quite the
dream she thought it was going to be. There are only so
many minutes of your life that you can be on hold to
Jason at Fuxton, Arse and Leatherface, waiting for them
to approve their annual advertising budget for the NW6
area without wanting to crack open a Porn Star Martini
from Marks and Spencer at your desk as you slowly slide
off your chair.

". . . It was a little stressful . . ." I try.

"Nothing I couldn't handle," she replies, running her
hands through her dark shoulder-length hair.

"You were overqualified for it . . .?"

"That's true," she nods. "Not quite the ex-therapist's
dream. But every woman is overqualified for every job
they do over the age of forty. Except perhaps being a
parent." She shrugs. "But you're right. I hated it. *And* I
was overqualified."

"You should go back to counselling, the therapy."

"I haven't done it for over fifteen years, not since Jade
was born, and frankly things have moved on so much since
then."

"You could reskill? Upskill? Whatever it's called.
Retrain?"

"I could," she nods. The remaining sweetener is now in
a neat pile in front of her. "Or I could do something else."

"Like what?"

"I see they need someone in Mystique. There's a sign in the window."

"The tarot shop!" I didn't see that coming. "Oh," is all I can manage.

"They sell more than just tarot, they have crystals and books and cards and . . ." She smiles weakly as she runs out of things to add.

Mystique is one of those aged high street shops that smells of spilt incense and stale patchouli oil. In drastic need of a Farrow and Ball makeover, it has a couple of white plastic spinning card racks at the front, a few sparsely filled bookshelves in the middle of the room and some large, flat, faded-navy mirrored scatter cushions to relax on at the back. It's manned by stoned students in progressive states of veganism and its bestselling item is a solar-powered, paw-waving Chinese Lucky Cat. It's a wonder they ever pay the rent, let alone branch out and employ someone else.

"Oh, I know it," I say. "I bought a tiger's eye bracelet there once."

"It's got shelves packed with birthstones," agrees Claire. "Anyway, I have an interview on Monday."

"An interview?"

"I know!" she rolls her eyes. "God knows what they'll ask me."

God knows what's happening to Claire. She seems to be unravelling before my very eyes. She carries on talking about a little flat she's found over a pub off the Kilburn High Road. I don't know whether she is in shock or entirely relieved to be out of her marriage, but she doesn't seem to be wailing or bawling her eyes out. She's merely obsessed with practicalities, lists and logistics and, of course, money. I didn't think their marriage was in trouble. She and Rob were always so polite to each other. Maybe that was the problem. You're never supposed to know what goes on behind closed doors, in other people's marriages. Perhaps I should have just bloody asked.

September 30th

Husband has gone away on business. I forgot to "milk" him before he left – not that it seems the basis for keeping a marriage together, judging by what is happening to Claire. But the thought is playing slightly on my mind as I shove a packet of Marlboro Gold into my bag and shout at the children that I won't be long and that they should do their sodding homework before I get back, otherwise I am banning them from ever leaving the house, or picking up an electronic device ever again. Ella is legally allowed to babysit, and Pig is illegally allowed to play *Call of Duty* (Cert 18) and anyway, I am only around the corner.

Every other Tuesday I go and visit Mrs Rees at number seventeen. I signed up to "Visiting the Elderly" after bursting into tears during some advert about "Geoff" being so lonely and miserable since his wife died and not seeing a friendly face for the past fifteen years. And I wasn't even drunk. I'd had two glasses of red. Clearly, it was the beginning of the menopause. A year ago? I should really see someone about my growing anger and sudden weeping and my inability to sleep, ever.

So, every other Tuesday, I walk two streets away to see Mrs Rees. Her first name is Pamela, not that I would ever dare use it. I presume someone must have once called her Pam, sometime in the last century. But she has never asked me to call her anything other than Mrs Rees. I have to say, originally, when I first turned up, with a basket of food and some flowers in my hand and a benevolent, patronising smile on my face, ready to "help," I could not have been more shocked and surprised. Mrs Rees was not delighted to see me. She thought my basket of goodies was shit and that my patronising attitude and my beatified smile could disappear firmly up my slack arse cheeks. I thought she'd be grateful for my company, enchanted by my chat. But she wasn't. Actually, I think she finds me boring. Mrs Rees may not be able to sprint for the bus anymore, or jog swiftly up and down her own stairs, but her eighty-two-year-old brain is sharp as a tack. She has opinions, plenty of opinions, which is something of a rarity these days. *And* she lets me smoke inside.

In fact, we both do. She sits in the fat pink floral chair facing the telly, sucking down her JPS Superkings, while I perch on her white leather sofa, tucking into my Marlboro Gold and between us sits the cat, Winston, who frankly looks old enough to have been a contemporary of his namesake.

"You're looking skinny," she says as she opens the door. She's dressed in an orange floral tabard, thick support tights and brown easy-on shoes. She has candy-pink nails, which I know she gets done every week in "Swanky" and her thick, grey, curled hair never moves.

"Oh, thank you!" I say. I haven't been called skinny since 1993.

"Not in a good way," clarifies Mrs Rees. "Haggard, I'd say."

"Right," I smile. "You look well."

I kiss her on the cheek. She recoils slightly; she's never been fond of me doing that, but it's habit. I've tried to stop myself, but I can't. It used to be reflex but now I do it just to annoy her. She smells of talcum powder, lipstick and fags.

"How are you?" I ask, walking into the narrow hallway, which is the same width as mine, just a whole lot more cluttered. Who knows why Mrs Rees needs five umbrellas in a stand.

All the houses in the streets around here are the same. Some have been divided up into flats with multiple doorbells, but the majority are still four-up, three-down, redbrick Victorian terrace houses with small bay windows at the front and a garden at the back big enough to kick a football over next door's fence, or possibly squeeze in a trampoline from Homebase.

"I can't complain," she says, before spending the next twenty minutes doing just that.

The litany of aches and pains gives way to a long conversation about the length of Holly Willoughby's hair. Mrs Rees apparently prefers it longer. And Holly's had the temerity to have it cut. I have no alternative other than to agree with her. I make tea and we eat the biscuits I'd brought on my previous visit and I tell her about Claire's separation.

"That's the problem with your generation," she says, taking a drag on her fag and exhaling through her nostrils like a dragon. "You've got no staying power."

"I don't know about that . . . plenty of us stay at things. Maybe she was just unhappy."

"Unhappy?" scoffs Mrs Rees. "Whoever said us humans are supposed to be happy?"

"That's the general aim, isn't it? Happiness. Wellness. Mindfulness. Thriving, not just surviving."

"Self-entitled nonsense." She flicks her ash into an already full ashtray. "In my day it was keeping on going and loyalty that counted. You lot could do to learn a bit of that." She leans back in her chair. "You're all soft, that's the problem. Everyone's offended by everyone else. Everyone's human rights have to be catered for. Except when you're over sixty-five. If you're over sixty-five no one cares about you, or your human rights. If you look at those forms it says: 'Are you over sixteen?' Then it's twenty-one to thirty. Thirty to forty. Forty to fifty. And then sixty-five plus. You could be sixty-six or one hundred and ten, for all they care. You're old. You're over. You don't matter. You are dust!" She stubs her fag out very determinedly in her ashtray. "So that's why I voted UKIP. Shake things up a bit. No one cares what I think, so I may as well." She smiles. She's still got most of her teeth. "Do you want another cup of tea?" she suggests, waving her empty mug at me and not moving from her seat.

"Oh, let me, Mrs Rees," I say, getting to my feet.

"Two sugars," she says after me.

"I know."

"And—"

"Milk in first."

She lights up another cigarette. "So is she happy now, your friend, now she's put herself first? Is she thriving and not just surviving?"

"I don't know," I reply from the kitchen.

"Well . . ." I walk back into the sitting room, just as she blows a grey plume of smoke at the telly. "Be careful what you wish for, is what I say."

"Right." I sit back down on the sofa.

"Once you've rocked the boat, you can't get back in there. No matter how hard you try."

October 1st

"Fuck!" is how Sally's text message begins, but then there is nothing unusual about that. "I need to see you." She's usually quite needy and demonstrative, so that's fine. She is always "desperate" for something, or "has" to do something else "immediately" or "now" which is another one of her favourite words, along with the swearing. "This is serious."

She never says that.

Perhaps she wants to talk about Claire. I certainly want to talk about Claire. It's weird how someone doing something so radical makes you start to question your own life. I mean, I always quite liked her husband, Rob. He was a nice guy, he is a nice guy, in so far as I knew him, I suppose. We've been on holiday together. We once shared a villa in Greece, and we got on extremely well. He's generous with the wine, he's got some good jokes and he's very handy with the barbecue tongs. I am not sure what else Claire wants.

Why did she have the affair in the first place? She is forty-seven years old. Surely it would have been easier to take up Spanish lessons? Or become obsessed with cold water swimming? Or just plain swimming, as it was once called before Instagram, and women started swimming in woollen hats. She could have taken her frustrations out during a 10K slog in the freezing River Dent. Anything. Instead, she's shagged someone at work, got found out and Rob's divorcing her. She's thrown the baby out along with the bathroom, the sink, the fridge and the Nespresso machine. And now she and Jade are looking for somewhere to live, only to bump into Rob in six months' time to find he's lost two stone, gone to the gym and is propping up a bar with his toned thigh wrapped around someone Younger, Blonder, inner who is laughing hysterically at his super-funny jokes. And in a few years' time, Rob will be having another baby with YBT and Claire will be slapping on patches of HRT.

I knock on Sally's shiny black front door. She lives in one of those pretty London side streets, where the houses have been torn limb from limb as the owners have dug down and back and out and across in an attempt to make what was essentially a Georgian cottage into something they've seen in a magazine. The result is a litany of skips, beeping lorries and builders, all leaning against the railings, smoking roll-ups and drinking tea, wearing heavy boots, hard hats and high-vis jackets. There are usually a few gangs of rats rattling around too, having been disturbed from their cosy basements; they are now loose on the streets, staring at passers-by with indignant irritation.

Sally answers the door. She's barefoot, in leggings and some zip-up athleisure top. She looks like she's going to the gym but will not move beyond her sofa and sitting room for the rest of the day.

"Hi," she says. She has Alfie, three, on a hip and Ben, eighteen months, is crawling along the limestone floor towards the pile of wellington boots that were once placed together in neat pairs, but now resemble a giant pick 'n' mix of various colours and sizes in the corner of the hall.

I've known Sally for about twenty years. She was the younger sister of a boyfriend of mine, but I preferred her to him. So in the end I ditched him and added her to my SIM card and we've been best friends ever since. I was there at her wedding to Will, I read a poem at the service in Maida Vale, and I am godmother to Nathan who is in the same school as Sam, although a few years younger. Not that I ever see her in the morning, for despite appearances, Sally is the first one through the door. She hates a queue, she doesn't want to talk to anyone and she's desperate for the childcare. She's been up since 5.30am. The fact that the doors open at 8.15am is not early enough in her books.

"So I saw Claire," I start as soon as I cross the threshold. "And it's her fault, she was the one having an affair. Rob found out, and that's why they're getting a divorce. I got the full rundown. She doesn't look great, by the way. She was acting weird, thinking of moving near me, as it's cheaper . . ." I pause. "Are you OK?"

Normally, Sally would have hurled Alfie off her hip and shrieked with enthusiasm at my level of gossip and information. I would have to rewind and tell the whole story from the beginning while she shoved *Peppa Pig* on the TV to get rid of the children. But she's very quiet.

"Do you want anything?" She waves distractedly towards the large stainless steel kitchen sink. "Tea? Coffee? Water?"

"No, thanks." I frown. My forehead thankfully doesn't move. "What's the matter?"

"It's Will," she says softly. "You know the medical. The other day?" I nod. "Well, they found something. A lump. In the testes."

"Oh, God, really?" I sit down on a nearby bar stool.

"Anyway, apparently it is what you think it is. I'm not saying the word in front of the children, am I?" Her voice goes all sing-songy. "Because everything's fine. Isn't it, Alfie?" She kisses his forehead and ruffles his blond hair. "Come on, you two." She scoops Ben up off the floor. "It's telly time."

"Are they sure?" I follow her over to the sofa as she places Alfie and Ben side by side and turns on CBeebies.

"You guys sit here and have a nice time while Mummy goes over here." She turns the volume up as she turns around and stares at me and slowly shakes her head. "I mean, Jesus Christ," she whispers as she walks back over to the kitchen. "What are we going to do?"

"But he has actually got . . . it?"

"He's waiting for the results of the biopsy." She stares hopelessly out of the window and sighs. She looks exhausted.

"When did he tell you?"

"Last night." She turns to look at me; her dark brown eyes are filled with tears. "He could die!"

"I'am sure it won't come to that." I rush over and give her a hug. "I promise, they can do amazing things these days. It's no longer what it was."

She starts to cry for a second, sobbing, her shoulders moving up and down as she rests her head against my neck. Then she breathes in deeply and suddenly pulls away and, sniffing, wipes away the tears from under her eyes, glancing over her shoulder at her two boys sitting on the sofa watching *Chuggington*.

"He said he could have one of his balls removed." She looks at me; a wry smile plays on her lips. "Typical!" She laughs. "A nice Jewish girl like me being married to a man who's got as many bollocks as Hitler!"

"It'll be fine," I say. "*He* will be fine."

"He better bloody be," says Sally, trying incredibly hard not to cry. "I love him, you know."

"I know."

"I really do."

October 2nd

What is it about schools and their obsession with tech? They appear to love it, like grubby adolescents locked away in their darkened rooms. I don't get it myself. As far as I'm concerned, there was nothing wrong, or indeed as effective as, a nice newsletter, a pamphlet at the beginning of term, or even an email (if we must) between you and your children's teacher. Type. Send. Done. And don't reply to them for a few weeks. Simple. But now there's a "portal", and we have all to subscribe to the "portal", log in to the "portal" and worship at the altar of the "portal" in order to get anything done. They even want us to pay bills through the "portal". Who on earth wants to seek out, actively, things they have to pay?

And does this portal, like all good portals, take you to another world? Narnia, for example? Yes, it does! It takes you to a whole new world of pain, where you click and search and squint and have no idea what the fuck you're doing for hours at a time. Do I want to look at Ella's time-table? No. Do I want to know what she thinks of her own progress? No. Do I want to see what she had for lunch? Oh, stop it, now! When is the school play? And what fucking time is the Harvest Festival and do they want some out-of-date tins of tuna?

Anyway, through a portal-like email (or is it just an email with portal trimmings?), I find out that Ella has missed six homeworks in a row. I'm not sure if that is entirely true as I distinctly remember doing at least three of them myself. Maybe she cares so little that even after my doing the maths, French and geography for her, she simply forgot to hand them in at all.

So I have to report to the deputy headmaster, Mr Gilbertson, this morning, which means that Husband has to take Sam to school.

Ella and I are shuffling along the street, kicking the leaves, avoiding the shiny brown bags plump with dog turd. Both of us have our heads down. Neither of us is in the mood for talking. She is furious that I insisted on walking with her, cramping her style and ruining her life by my very presence, my mere breath, and I am furious that I have to come at all. My phone goes. It's Husband.

"Where's Sam's school?" He isn't shouting but his voice is high-pitched and strained.

"What?"

"He's refusing to get out of the car. He keeps insisting that he doesn't go to this school."

"What do you mean?"

"I can't make it any clearer! Listen—"

He is shouting now and I can almost hear the steam being expelled through his ears. "He won't get out of the goddamn CAAAAAR!"

"Pass him over—"

"Mum!" It's Sam. "Dad's got the wrong school. He's at the juniors."

"Tell him to go round the corner to the other building."

"He won't listen to me."

"Put Dad back on."

"What?" he barks. "He's at St John's, right? Last time I paid the fees?"

"He's around the corner, in the senior bit."

"The senior bit?" he pauses. "When the fuck did he move there?"

"Two years ago."

"No one tells me anything!" He shouts and immediately hangs up.

*　*　*

The only difference between the smell of an old people's home and a senior school is the ever-present aroma of Lynx. Walking down the lengthy grey lino corridor of

Ella's school, there is the usual high stench of ammonia that emanates from the urinals, plus the heavy back note of industrially boiled cabbage and, of course, the Lynx. I am pretty sure the girls douse themselves on a daily basis too, yet the sweet, sticky odour of Daisy by Marc Jacobs doesn't seem to last the short vape trip to school.

I follow Ella down the corridor as she slaps and slops her feet along the plastic floor, like every other teenager in the place. In fact, truth be told, they are almost impossible to tell apart. All the girls have long, poorly bleached hair that is screwed up into some sort of ponytail with wisps and snakes cascading everywhere. They have numerous rings on numerous fingers and a plethora of piercings in all parts of the ear: lobe, cartilage, middle, back, front. Like an urban tribe who've had a fight with a piercing gun; some of them have even graduated on to their eyebrows, noses or lips. The boys are equally as uniform. Their hair is short, they have curtain fringes, red spotted cheeks and long necks, gaping shirt collars and trousers that stop above the ankle.

Mr Gilbertson's door is open when we arrive.

"Hello, hello, hello," he says, getting up from behind his desk, his arm extended in greeting. He is short and round, his pale green shirt is straining to contain him and his brown tie flops to one side of his buttons. His hair is sparse and his forehead is dank with sweat. His dusty office overlooks the playground and is piled high with books, papers and photographs of him and his family, his two children who, by the looks of the uniformed shots, also attended Carlton Academy. There's Mr Gilbertson with various sporting teams dressed in shorts, their hands on their thighs and a ball and a cup placed between them. To the left of his desk is a glass cabinet jam-packed with silver cups and shields of various shapes, sizes and shades of tarnish. And on his desk is a steaming mug of milky Nescafé.

"Please sit down," he says, pushing his thick, black square glasses back up his snub nose before he indicates two chairs on the other side of his desk. "Now," he says, sitting down and rubbing his hands together across his stomach. "What are we going to do with you, Ella?"

He is much more charming and conciliatory with my daughter than I could ever be. Personally, I want to stand up with my hands firmly on my hips and shout at her until her whole face shines with spittle. But Mr Gilbertson seems to be much more worried about her "growth mindset" than he is with her sodding lazy approach to studying. He seems to think that there must be some "root cause", some specific reason that Ella might not been doing her homework and handing it in, other than abject teenage sloth.

"Is everything alright at home?" he asks, looking directly at me, his head cocked with concern. There's a long pause. What am I supposed to say? That I hate my husband? He barely speaks to me? I drink too much? I'm overweight, unhappy, lonely as hell, and I'd sell a kidney to go on holiday?

"I think so," I venture.

"Oh," he leans over his desk, his fat hands pushed upwards and together, pointing towards the ceiling, like a church steeple. "Are there *issues*?"

"Well, um . . ." I am actually not sure what to say. There are no issues other than Ella being a lazy sod who is not engaged in a single lesson and would frankly rather be walking up and down the Kilburn High Road, eating chicken nuggets with her mates while discussing the latest caramel-flavoured vape. Yet I now suddenly find myself in the position where I am trying to defend her. "It's a hard year this year . . . isn't it?" Mr Gilbertson nods and pushes his glasses back up his nose again. "And, well . . . Ella is finding it all a little stressful." He nods again. So stressful, I think, that she spends all day, every day changing the shade of her bloody nail varnish in her room while listening to offensive rap music.

"It is a difficult time," he concurs. "Very difficult. I think maybe we should think about lightening Ella's load a little."

I glance across to see my daughter sitting up, super straight, smiling sweetly. This suddenly feels like some sort of stitch-up that they have planned together. I fought with tooth, nail and an elaborate system of bribes to make Ella study for eight GCSEs, and now I feel them slipping slowly between my fingers.

"I don't think there is any need for that," I say sharply.

"Well . . ." He puffs out his cheeks. "If a job's worth doing, it's worth doing well . . . as the saying goes. And a bird in the hand . . ."

I am about to shout "makes hay while the sun shines" and "a stitch in time . . ." in his fat, conceited face when Ella suddenly pipes up, "Well . . . I could drop French?"

"French? No!" I spin around to face her. "You can't drop French. You need French! Everyone needs French."

"Technically only the French need French," replies Mr Gilbertson. He really isn't helping matters.

"And anyway, you can always use Google Translate?" Ella smiles.

"No," I say simply.

"It is her weakest subject."

"But you're good at French!" I wail.

"Not anymore!" Ella shrugs in such a complacent way, I am just about ready to commit infanticide.

"Absolutely not. We're not touching French. We're keeping the French. How about dance? No one needs to know how to dance unless they want to be a dancer. And you, you're frankly not one of those!" I scoff.

Mr Gilbertson looks horrified. "Ella was *excellent* in the end-of-term show!"

"No, she wasn't! She was bloody appalling. She was at the back, hoofing around, like a hoofer." They both turn to look at me, their eyes and mouths wide. "What?"

"I'll think you'll find your daughter expresses herself very well through the medium of dance."

"Fine!" I say, springing out of my chair, my heart pounding with fury. "This is bloody ridiculous! I'd rather she expressed herself though the medium of French, but I can see this is a conversational *cul-de-sac*! That's French, by the way!" I pick up my handbag, sling it over my shoulder and head for the door. "I'm out of here, and I'll see *you* back at home!"

Ella makes as if to follow me out of the door, but Mr Gilbertson stops her. "Close the door and sit down," I hear him say as I start down the corridor. "Tell me, is everything really alright at home?"

I march down the corridor and through the front door of the school. Unfortunately, the doors are on slow returners so I can't actually make them slam. I stride out of the front gate, gurning with fury, and straight onto the zebra crossing, only to be nearly run over by a white van.

"Oi!" shouts the driver out of his window. "Watch it!" I stop in the middle of the road and flip him both birds. As he slowly rolls past me, he pauses the van and yells. "How are the hot flushes then, love?"

October 3rd

Fuck. Last night was a disaster. I drank too much. Well, actually, to be fair I drank the usual amount (four wines and a vodka and tonic) that I normally do, but for some reason it made me overemotional, very weepy, and I picked a fight with Husband and then promptly broke some semi-precious china (who am I kidding, normal, rubbish china) and burst into tears. I blame him for being so disassociated with family life that he doesn't even know where his son goes to school. I blame Ella for wanting to give up French when she knows that I love it and studied it and still pretend to be able to speak the bloody thing fluently even when ordering lunch in Café Rouge. I blame Sally's husband, Will, for being ill and putting the fear of God into my best friend and turning her world upside down. I blame Rob for divorcing Claire and Claire for having an affair and making us all look at our husbands and think – is this it? And mostly I blame White Van Man for pointing out what miserable old cow I am.

I mean. Really. Where did it all go? The youth? The joy? The firm skin? The fresh face? The spring in my step? The mirth in my laugh? The hours in my sleep? Why does everything now seem so flat and hard and difficult? I know we're supposed to be a long time dead, but I had no idea you could feel just that, while still being bloody alive.

October 4th

My mother has a special ringtone (a trumpet) on my phone; that way I can brace myself before I pick up. Fortunately, she doesn't call me that often. It's apparently a waste of money and she'd rather spend her cash on other more useful things like silk scarves and gin. However, when she does, she is prone, much like my children, to picking up the conversation almost exactly where she left off. And Jacqueline – don't ever call her Jackie as she won't answer, is deaf to Jackie and the J of Jacqueline has some sort of a soft Charles Aznavour J to it, it's French, her name, or so she says – anyway, Jacqueline has the memory of an elephant on Ritalin. I always thought that older people were supposed to grow a little softer around the edges, a little kinder and gentler in their dotage and frankly a little more absent-minded. But not Mrs Rees, and certainly not Jackie. Jackie can remember every fuck-up I have ever made and she ceaselessly reminds me of them every time we have a conversation, which is thankfully not that often.

But here she is, calling me at 8.25 in the morning. I'm in my car, of course, driving Pig to school, having just waved off Ella who didn't even wait to turn the corner before she rootled through her bag for her vape.

"This is Granny," I hiss at Pig, who's sitting on the back seat covering his legs in green dots with a Sharpie pen.

"No one likes her, why is she calling?" he asks.

"Hi Mum!" I reply, shouting into my mobile that's stuck to my dashboard using Blu Tack. It's practically hands-free and about as high-tech as I get.

"I haven't got long." Oh yes, and she's always doing you a favour when she calls. She's just about fitting me in. "So I was talking to your father," she begins. "And he was wondering what you were doing for Christmas?"

Christmas? Christ! What is it with parents? They ambush you when you least expect it; somehow they always know when you're vulnerable, hung-over, shaking with caffeine, stuck in a traffic jam desperate to pee. You'll agree to anything. Anything to get them to stop talking, anything to get them off the phone, and most certainly something you absolutely don't want to do. Ever.

"Christmas?" My voice is so high, I sound like I've been sucking helium.

"Yes, dear." My mother's voice is dripping with something – it's either sarcasm or irritation – it's hard to tell which.

"But it's October?"

"I'm busy and you're, occasionally, busy and plans don't make themselves, now, do they? So while I have you on the phone, do you have any plans for Christmas?"

"Um, well, I was thinking about—"

"Good, that's a no, so Richard and I were thinking of having the whole family for Christmas, we thought it would be nice."

"Nice? What, everyone?"

"Jenny has said she'll come."

"From Australia?"

"I spoke to her yesterday and she's so thrilled she's booked her flight."

I bet she has. It's starting to rain and my wipers squeak and judder across the windscreen. Dear Jenny, with her perfect life and her perfect kids and her nice husband – Reasonable Dan – he always sees the good in everyone and everything, he barely drinks, he has one beer and says that's enough and goes jogging every sodding morning. I'm younger than Jenny, by three whole years. But everyone always presumes she is my baby sister. They live in Byron Bay and Dan commutes to Brisbane every day, where he teaches sports science. I love Jenny, of course I do. But her perfect striped blonde hair and her pert butt cheeks are more than a little annoying. And don't get me started on Coral and Josh, who can not only surf and do cartwheels on the beach, they're charming, with white teeth, and have read all the Harry Potters.

"That's great," I reply, my head slowly lolling forward towards my steering wheel.

"And it'll be so nice for the girls to get together," says Mum. I can hear her smile. "Seeing as they are almost the same age."

"Coral is a little younger."

". . . And Ella is very sophisticated."

She doesn't mean that in a good way. When Jacqueline uses that word to describe my daughter, she really means grubby and a little bit urban. She doesn't approve of where we live, or where we send our children to school. If we can't afford to pay to go to a "nice school", as she puts it, then we should leave town and go somewhere leafy, at least the crowd would be a little less "rough".

"Well, that sounds great," I say, ignoring her last comment.

"And how's little Sam?"

"He's with me in the car, say hi to Granny," I strain my head round to see that he has covered himself in spots and is now working on colouring in two large green patches on his knees. The little shit. He's now going to have to go into school like that. Why? And it's a Sharpie! "Say hello to Granny."

"NO!" he says, looking up and sniffing up a snake of snot. "I hate her."

"Hello, Sammy! Granny here!" Her voice booms out of my tinny phone speaker.

"Say hello," I hiss out of the corner of my mouth.

"NO! I hate her!"

"What did he say?"

"He sends you lots of love, Mum, he's just doing his spellings in the back of the car."

"Oh, such a good boy!" she coos. "Don't be like your sister, she never did work hard, that's why she's so stupid."

"Sorry, Mum, I've got to go." I hang up.

"I hate her," says Sam, scribbling away. "Everyone hates her. She's got no friends and she should go and die in a hole."

"Stop bloody colouring your legs!" I shout as I pull up outside school. "Look at you, and now you've got to go into school like that and everyone's going to think I'm a crap parent!"

There's a gentle tapping on my window.

"Look!" I yell. "I'm moving!" I wind my window down and look up, expecting to see a traffic warden and instead it's Ab Dad, Dave.

"There you are!" he says, sounding rather relieved. "Are you coming for coffee?"

How much box wine did I drink the other day? Did I promise to go out with Dave? I can't remember. All I know is I'm not wearing my contact lenses and I look like a boiled egg. My brown hair is scraped into an elastic band at the back of my head as it needs a wash, my specs are smeared and I haven't brushed my teeth, or at least it feels like that. Frankly, who knows?

"Um," I hesitate. I'd really rather not. But then, there's a loo in the café and I'm desperate for a pee.

"Bye," says Sam, slamming the door.

"Bye!" I yell after him.

"Shall we?" asks Dave, making to open my car door.

"Fine," I say, getting out of the car. "But only a quick one."

I follow him down the street, staring at his rather toned behind in a pair of baggy jeans. He is wearing a loose-fitting grey jumper (possibly cashmere?) and some loafers without any socks. I idly wonder to myself if he's not sporting any underwear.

"Here she is!" he declares as he opens the door to the overpriced café around the corner from the school. All red and white with gingham tablecloths, it's a place I normally avoid, mainly because it's full of mothers I hate and coffee I can't drink and pastries I can't afford.

"Here I am!" I declare back. What a shit. The romantic coffee just became a class meeting. I am beyond delighted. In fact, I have gone full circle from delight to actual fury.

"Great!" declares Power Yank with the shiny white matching teeth and a-hole. "You all know Erica." She

75

smiles to indicate bloody Erica with her swingy ponytail and her elastane-coated thighs.

"Hi," she smiles, exuding minty freshness.

"And David," continues Power Yank.

"Thank you, Madison," he says. So that's her name. "Thank you, team!" he adds, pulling out a chair with so much testosterone I half expect him to straddle it. Except he doesn't, he sits down and neatly crosses his legs.

"Right." Madison smiles. "So . . . we need to have ideas for Entrepreneur's Week for what we, sorry *they*, can make. As, obviously," she smiles again, "we *have* to win."

"Go Year Five!" whoops Erica, and she's not even American.

"Now David," starts Madison. "As the honorary man on this panel, what do you think?"

"Well." David's head waggles with self-importance. "We could make and sell some biscuits?"

"Biscuits!" Madison can barely contain her disdain, so she doesn't bother. "That is *so* Year One. Erica?"

"Stress busters?" Erica's off. "You know, stress balls you squeeze made out of balloons filled with quinoa. I find quinoa is better than rice, plus I have loads of it at my house as I bulk-bought four kilos from Whole Foods, but my husband won't eat it as it gives him indigestion. He's a pulse-iac."

"Are schoolchildren stressed?" I venture.

"Have you not read the reports?!" asks Madison, her baby-blue eyes round with horror. The rest of her face is naturally, or unnaturally, immobile. "Their cortisol levels are through the roof! They've got exams and everything . . . Good idea, Erica! You?" she asks me, pointing a square, white-tipped nail in my face.

"Me?"

"You!" She nods briskly, looking down at her notepad, clicking her pen. "Ideas."

I blink behind my greasy specs, I run my tongue along my furry teeth. "How about something fun?"

"Fun!" Madison sits back in her chair and looks at me as if I have lost my mind.

"Yes, fun."

"But we want to *win*," stresses Erica.

"Stress busters," declares Madison.

"I agree," says David.

I shoot him a look. Tosser! I thought he was my friend and now he appears to be crawling up Madison's highly bleached orifice.

"I can't believe you did that," I say, as we finally leave the café. Having agreed on the division of labour and how many balloons need to be purchased and what time the class are all supposed to be meeting at Erica's place on Sunday.

"Stress balls?" I add.

"Oh God," he replies, running his hands though his thick dark hair. "Anything for a quiet life." He laughs. "Over the years, I have learnt to pick my battles. And that was not one I wanted to enter into."

"I could see that."

"Susie and I divorced a couple of years ago," he continues. "And frankly, that taught me a lot. We are now in a good place, a really good place, but you know, I now know when to let go and when to stand my ground."

"That's very Zen of you."

"I meditate."

"Excellent." I find myself walking a little faster towards my car.

"I have a mindfulness app," he trots along beside me. "I do thirty minutes every day. I sit on a stool in my bathroom."

"You sit on a stool in your bathroom for three and a half hours a week?"

I am now marching towards my car. My heart is pounding.

"Oh, Jesus fucking Christ!" I throw my hands in the air. "Not another parking ticket! That's another sixty quid! Shit! Shit! SHIT!"

"Breathe," says David, as he comes alongside me. He places his hand ever so gently on my shoulder. "Breathe . . . Deeply in two, three, four . . . Deeply out two, three, four . . ."

"Oh, fuck off."

October 7th

Three days later and David and I, plus Madison and a couple of other mums are at Erica's place stuffing balloons full of quinoa and tying the ends in a knot, which is a hell of a lot harder than you'd think. Actually, it's agony, unless I am doing it wrong, which I probably am.

Erica has, somewhat unsurprisingly, one of those soulless, characterless houses that was designed by someone else with the intent of interesting and offending no one; so it is therefore almost entirely white, with a small white yapping dog to match. In the middle of one of those Richard Curtis-type crescents with a communal garden at the back that only six people ever use, Erica appears to have one of those perfect London lives that you only see in films. Her husband works abroad, or at least I have never seen him (perfect), and her children don't appear to make any mess whatsoever (also perfect). In fact, as I stand, shoeless (they are left at the door for fear of filth) with a hole in my socks, looking around the smooth, sleek kitchen with handleless cupboards, foodless shelves and stainless surfaces with not an appliance in sight (save the shiny silver hot/cold/boiling/fizzy or still tap over the sink), the only evidence of Jasper and Caesar's (oh, yes!) existence are some Headmaster's Award certificates stuck on the fridge. Her two sons did answer the door with shiny smiles and a direct look into the eyes, but they have long since disappeared into the benevolent arms of some broken Oxbridge graduate who's sold his soul for 40K a year and the summer on a yacht, bobbing around the Med. They're catching up on subjects that I was utterly unaware were taught at Pig's school – Latin and Mandarin. Caesar has totally immersive Mandarin on Sunday afternoons, apparently. While Jasper is just crazy for coding. Pig, I know, currently has his fist in the pick 'n' mix at Westfield as Husband is taking both him and Ella to the cinema, so he can have a snooze in the dark, while I make the stock for Entrepreneur's Week.

"That's actually impressive," said Husband as he left the house this afternoon.

"What is?"

"The children seemed to have learnt the first rule of entrepreneurship," he smiled on the threshold.

"Which is?"

"Delegation."

So, while my son pops dolly mixtures down his pie hole, I'm the one bent double over a bowl of quinoa, snapping my fingernails off with the aid of twisted multicoloured rubber! Meanwhile, Erica is on quality control.

"I think you need a little more in that one," she says to me, plucking a red ball out from the bowl and weighing it in the palm of her hand. "It seems a little quinoa-light to me."

I would normally think of shoving the quinoa-light bag somewhere painful, but Erica is not totally stupid and she has anaesthetised her workforce with bottles of wine, expensive snacks and some tunes on Spotify. In fact, if the job weren't so fiddly and painful on the fingers, I would go so far as to say that we were actually having fun. Erica looks immaculate in some silk tea dress as she tops up the glasses with chilled white wine and hands round the little smoked salmon rolls, and Dave is standing next to me, wrist-deep in quinoa, wondering how big he needs to make his balls. Even Madison is being quite entertaining, talking about what the other groups are doing and how much better our idea is than theirs.

"Another group is making smoothies!" she says. "I mean, purlease! Can you imagine the health and safety with that! When you give the whole school a stomach ache!"

"Or diarrhoea!" I add, laughing. The other mothers look at me; only Dave joins in.

"The Deadly Dealers are making buckets of slime," she continues, after a hiatus. "Like that's going to win anything."

"How do you know all this?" asks Dave, looking up from his bowl.

"What do you mean?" asks Madison.

"What they are all doing?"

"Oh," she looks as puzzled as she can. "I listen on the stairs." He nods slowly. "And of course, Mr Hancox tutors Saffron on Saturday and he tells me *everything*."

"You have Mr Hancox?" Erica stops in her tracks.

"We've had him for years," says Madison with a wave of her manicure. "Saffron and Fi both have him every weekend."

"What?" Dave stands up. "You employ James's teacher? Mr Hancox? At the weekends?"

"Sure." Madison nods.

"So he works a six-day week? The school during the week, and then for you at the weekend?" He is talking slowly, as it all dawns on him. "Mr Hancox?"

"He only works the morning as we like to go away for the weekend, you know, the country?"

"Right. And Mr Hancox?"

"Oh, he goes home to his wife, I think."

"You think?"

"I have never asked him," she laughs. "But that's how I know what all the other teams are doing! He tells me."

"Do you have him in the summer?" Erica's eyes narrow.

"Who? Mr Hancox? No—" Madison smiles. "Although he did come and stay with us for two weeks in Gstaad."

"With his wife?" asks Dave.

"No, don't be silly!" Madison laughs again. "She went to stay with her mum in Worsestershire."

"Worcestershire," Dave corrects, before taking a giant slug of wine.

Fortunately, the Spotify kicks in with a familiar tune and Erica turns it up and shimmies over to talk to two other mums the other side of the table. I can sense Dave's still irritated by what he's heard. However, I can't tell if it's concern for the clearly exhausted Mr Hancox and his neglected wife, or whether it's because he's missed a trick when it comes to tutoring the tits off his child and getting his son into the next bloody school. It's only after five songs and some twenty-five stress balls later that I realise Erica has disappeared, only for her to come marching down the stairs dressed head to foot in shining, tight black Lycra. Her hair's pulled back off her face and she is carrying a pink rolled mat under arm.

"Thank you *so* much for coming," she says as I look at her, my glass of white wine halfway to my lips. "We have done such a lot." She inspects the table piled high with multicoloured stress balls. "It's really impressive."

"Is she kicking us out?" Dave whispers in my ear.

"Thank you," she continues, turning the lights off in her garden. "If you could go out through the basement door."

She points a finger at the corner of the kitchen but does not turn around. "Over there."

It is only as the other women go to pick up their coats that I realise Erica has not drunk a drop of wine or let a curl of salmon pass her pretty, plumped lips.

"I'm afraid it's time, ladies."

It's like she's clearing a pub after last orders, except instead of turning the lights on, she's turning them off.

"My trainer is waiting for me, and I hate to keep Giovanna waiting."

Sure, I think. I bet that poor woman has wasted hours of her life waiting for Erica and her pink mat to turn up, wherever the wretched cow works.

"Jesus Christ," says Dave as he stumbles out of the basement door and up the steps to the street. "I have never seen anything like that in my life."

"She has a 6pm with Giovanna, what can I say?" I laugh.

"Bitch, is what you can say," says David. "What a bitch!"

"Well . . . her house, I suppose."

"Do you fancy a drink?" he asks, looking at his watch. "It's only 5.40pm. I know a very nice pub round the corner."

"A drink?"

I can't think of the last time I was ever asked out for a drink. In a pub. By a man. Or by anyone, male or female, now I come to think about it. It was definitely in the last century, that's for sure. 1995? My immediate reaction is to refuse. I'm happily married. Well, married certainly. And us married ladies are not supposed to go out for drinks in pubs with recently divorced men. But what's the alternative? Going home, being totally ignored, asked vacantly what's for supper, while my husband remains horizontal on the sofa, snoring and dribbling gently on his own shoulder. There's the blind indifference from Ella, followed by a lengthy fight with Sam as I try to stop him from killing people on his XBox.

"I'd love to."

"Great," replies Dave, rubbing his hands together. "It's just down here."

I follow him down a narrow, cobbled side street to an old, crooked pub that the developers forgot. Even for early on a Sunday evening the place is quite full. There are low brown tables, small maroon padded stools and a slightly tacky, heavily patterned maroon and orange carpet on the floor. There's a real fire on one side of the room and a couple of wing-backed chairs either side of it, both of which are occupied by florid-looking gentlemen with tufts of silver hair. The one on the left is accompanied by a snoozing, elderly, clotted-cream-coloured mongrel clearly in need of a bath.

"What would you like?"

Dave's on his way to the wooden bar, covered in horse brasses and giant glass jars of nuts. I panic a little. Last time I ordered at a bar Cosmopolitans were all the rage and women still wore tights.

"A gin and tonic?" It was all I could think of.

"Nuts or crisps?"

Nuts?

Crisps?

I must have looked blank.

"Both," he says, clearly tiring of my lack of reply.

Five minutes later, he hands me a double gin and a packet of salt and cider vinegar hand-sliced crisps. I can tell it's a double because it actually tastes of gin when I sip it. The glass is warm and the ice melts almost immediately, but the drink tastes delicious. Every sip is laced with a frisson of illicitness and it goes straight to my head. I find myself running my hands through my hair and smiling at everything he is saying. I laugh a little too loudly and finish my drink rather quickly. He buys me another and I nibble at the crisps. We have another round of doubles. I suggest we go outside for a cigarette; he says he hasn't smoked in years, and he tells me I'm very, very naughty and I'm an awful corrupting influence. I laugh again and flick my hair, and we share a Marlboro Gold under the outdoor heater . . .

October 8th

I can't believe I kissed him. I'm not sure how it happened.
I laughed. He was staring at me, then he looked at my lips
and slowly leant forward and I think I moved closer. But
my God, he kissed me properly. At first it was tentative,
gentle and teasing, then he went for it, tongue probing my
mouth. It felt so fantastic I had to drop the fag I was holding to pull him closer. We ended up against the wall, under
the streetlight, my right leg almost wrapped around him,
as his cold hand hoicked up my bra and cupped my breast
under my jumper. I don't know how long we were there, a
few minutes, maybe five, but I don't think I have felt more
alive and vital in the last ten years. Is this what Claire felt
when she ran off with her bloke from work? Well, then, I
can see why she did it. I can see why she took those risks.

I am half tempted to call her as soon as I wake up
at 6am. Husband is still snoring, obviously, but I can't

sleep. I kissed him. I lie staring at the ceiling. I touch my lips; they feel hot and highly sensitive. It's like the slow-burning fire in my soul has finally been stoked and given some oxygen. I close my eyes: I can see his face, taste him, smell the heady mixture of alcohol and cigarettes. I feel sick, my cheeks are flushed, I run my hands across my stomach. His arms were so firm; his back was so broad. If I'd had a few more drinks I might well have had sex right there on the bins. Bin sex. God, that sounds so exciting.

"What are you doing?" Husband sits up in bed and turns the light on while simultaneously releasing a guff of flatulence. "You're rolling around all over the place."

"Nothing!" I say, my cheeks flushing. "I can't sleep."

"Well, get out of bed, because some of us bloody can and there's," he glances over at the clock, "an hour left on the alarm."

I want to phone Sally because I know she'd find the whole thing gripping, and she'd swear a lot and shout in all the right places and exclaim "Shut up!" and tell me to think twice about shagging him, but Will's due in hospital later today to get the results of his biopsy and I'm not that selfish. I could speak to Claire, but somehow her resigned don't-go-there face might put such a dampener on things that I wouldn't even manage to get to the snog before she poured water on the few baby flames that have been lit. So I decide I'm going to call Kate. Kate has a Tinder profile,

Kate's actually had bin sex. Kate carries condoms and has a vibrator in her bedside table. Kate would understand. But no one can get hold of Kate until after 9am. She obviously doesn't have to do the school run, so before 9am she's either doing one of two things: catching up on her exercise routine in the gym, or catching up on her sleep in bed. Sometimes she does call before 8am, but that's when she's doing the walk of shame and she has to be talked down off the cliff edge of regret, or out of the dank swamp that is her hangover.

It's 8.50am and I'm sitting in the car outside school. Sam's in his sports kit repeatedly kicking the back of my seat and I am peering through the fogged-up windscreen of my car, hoping to see him, Dave, walking down the street. My heart is beating faster; my breath is short and I am so craving sex that I could probably do Mr Hancox. I can barely sit in my seat, I'm squirming, so hot to see him, even my gear stick is looking enticing. Dave? Where are you?

"What are we doing?" asks Sam, drumming the back of my seat with his trainers.

"Waiting."

"Why?"

"Because I say so."

"Parents always say that when there's no reason for something." He coughs down the back of my neck. "I'm going in," he says, flinging open the car door.

"Don't you dare!" I crick my neck trying to tell him off.

"Yeah, well, watch me," he says, getting out of the car. "They're giving out free Haribo to everyone who gets in before 9am."

"Stop it!" I shout.

"What?" he says, looking at me rather shocked from underneath his distinctly long fringe. "I'm going to school!" He waves his hands at me in exasperation. "That's what I am supposed to do! Oh, hello James—"

"James!" I leap out of the car. "James! James, James." I look up and down the street. Where's Dave?

"Hi," says a voice. It sounds a little French.

"Hi."

"I'm Suzette."

Suzette! Suzette is tiny and neat with dark, cropped hair, pale skin and a pillow pout that actually looks natural. She's wearing a black polo neck with lots of silver necklaces over the top and a slim-fitting, tight black skirt. She looks about twenty years old.

"Are you James's nanny?" I ask, shaking her tiny little slim hand.

"No, his muzzer." She smiles.

"His?"

"Mothzer," she says again, trying extra hard to do the English *th*.

It wasn't her accent that I didn't understand.

"Oh." I nod.

Fuck. It is like a kick in the stomach. Suzette is petite and dressed in black with lips and a haircut and an accent. I've been handed my No Competition notice right here, on the steps of my son's school.

"I am not usually 'ere," she continues. "But this morning my ex, he is very ill."

"Oh?"

"The hangover, I think," she smiles. "I don't mind." She shrugs as only French people can. "I like to be late for work." She laughs and pouts. "I hate my work." Of course she does, she is so cool.

"Oh, really?" I can barely speak.

"I am a lawyer."

Of course she is.

There's the smile again. Even her front teeth are cutely crooked. Do all French women look like Juliette Binoche?

"Human rights?" I ask with the last breath in my body, imagining her and Amal Clooney crossing their fine ankles in a meeting room, looking immaculate and earnest about saving the Rohingya people.

"Corporation," she replies. "Tax," she adds. "Helping big pharma, you know, basically not pay zer bills."

"Good."

"No, it's not good. It's very bad . . . but, you know . . ." She shrugs again. "So Davide was out with an old friend last night and I am here, while he is still in bed."

"An old friend?" *But we've only just met each other?*

"From university. They studied history together." She takes hold of James's hand. "Now come along James, show me your classroom."

He lied! He didn't say he was making stress balls with some drunk mothers from school! I am now an 'Old Friend from University'. I could not be more delighted. Nervous. Anxious. Worried, obviously. But to hell with it, I am his University Pal!

I wave Pig off with more joy than I have ever managed at 9am. And I get into the car and immediately call Kate.

"Hi!" she answers after one ring and sounds super breezy, if a little breathy.

"Are you jogging?"

"Of course I am. Three times round the park, before work. I love it, I feel great! It's me! It's my new routine."

God, I hate single people. They have a routine. They have time to jog, time to shower, time to go to the hairdresser, have their nails done. They are not lurching from one low-level car crash to another. Forever chasing their tail, hounded by guilt, cooking endless meals and eating the burnt bits because no one else will. I bet they don't make do with the Parson's Nose. Sundays must be bliss. Actual chicken breast. Or I bet they can go out for lunch, drink too much and have a sleep in the afternoon. They are not shouting about homework or watching football up to their armpits in cold, dark mud. They can sleep when they want and for how long they want. God, I miss sleep.

"So how long has *this* routine been going on?"

"I'm on Day Three." So nine times round the park and counting.

Single people can also change their routines at the drop of a credit card. The rest of us can't move stuff around at all. If we've managed to carve out a teeny, tiny window on a Tuesday at 6pm, we are sure as hell not going to change it. It's sacrosanct, hewn in bronze.

"Good."

"I feel great!" she says. I'm not sure whom she's trying to convince. "Better than I have in ages. It also means I can't drink so much – you can't run on a hangover . . ." She laughs. "But I feel so much better than I did when I went to the gym. I hate the gym . . ."

"Good . . ." I pause. "I'm glad you hate the gym."

"It's for idiots." She jogs and huffs and puffs. "Who wants to do squats? Squats are for cunts!"

"I've snogged someone who's not my husband . . ." She carries on jogging, it's taking a while to sink in. "With tongues."

"WHAT!" She stops jogging. It's sunk in. "Who . . .? When . . .? Where . . .? Wait, I'm sitting down . . . Is he hot?"

So I tell her ALL about Dave. Well, not ALL. I don't tell her his name, obviously, but I say that he's someone

I met recently through a friend of a friend, it's almost true, and how we ended up going to a pub and snogging under the heated lamp outside.

"Wow! Actual snogging with tongues," she says, finally, getting up off her bench and loudly stretching. "I can't believe it! *You!*" She laughs, a little too enthusiastically for my liking. "*You!*"

"Yes, me!" It's a little snappy. But then why is it SO surprising that someone might snog me? Am I that hideous?

"Are you going to get a divorce?"

"Don't be ridiculous!" It's my turn to laugh a little too enthusiastically. "Of course I'm not. I've got children. Life is shit enough without having even less money to live on."

"I know, look at poor Claire."

"I know, poor Claire. She's planning on moving up near me. Or so she says."

"She told me." Kate exhales loudly down the phone. "So much cheaper where you are. Much, much cheaper . . ."

October 15th

I can see Sally through the plate glass window as I approach the café. She is sitting staring at the menu. She looks thoughtful, or exhausted, I am not sure which. She's not moving at all. It's unlike her to be looking at the food, she hates food; it bores her and slows her down. Claire is on her way, I know, as she's WhatsApped me her ETA three times in the past ten minutes. Kate can't make it as she's got a work thing in the centre of town, which is just as well, as I don't think she'd be able to keep the snog a secret at this lunch, which is good, as the lunch is not about me, but Sally. She organised it, so it's her lunch, where she gets to be Queen, but actually looking at her through the window, still wearing her coat at the table, her eyes on the menu, I imagine she is going to be quite monosyllabic and not terribly Queenlike at all.

I'm just about to open the café door when a trumpet sound goes off in my bag. It's Mum. I debate whether to drop the call, but I know she'll just carry on calling until I answer. She thinks because a phone is mobile, it should be answered at all times, especially when she is calling. If she wanted to leave a message she'd call the landline, if only I'd give her the number.

"Hello, Mum."

"Right, so . . ." And she's off. Dear Jenny this and Dear Jenny that, in fact Dear Jenny is such a sodding "dear" that she's now staying until New Year. That's over a week. That's ten whole days at Mother's. Poor, Dear Jenny. I am thinking, does she really know what fresh hell she'll be entering? "So I'm thinking you should do the same."

"Sorry?"

"For what, dear? . . . Otherwise Coral and Josh won't have anyone else to play with. And I'd hate for them to be bored. Having come all that way."

"Why would they be bored?"

"Darling, we all know there's nothing to do in the English countryside in winter."

There! Finally! She said it! I can't believe it. I've spent my whole childhood telling her that. Years of complaining that all the adults ever did was sit and talk and drink wine and have lunch and then go for long, boring, rotten, dreary grey walks through the mud and mire then come back, drink some more, eat some more and then do the whole thing all over again the next day.

"It's very boring," she continues, talking into my stunned silence. "Especially after a life of beaches and surfing and caring for the environment and all those wonderful things those children do . . ."

"Yes . . . I'm afraid I have to go now." Before I actually kill you.

"You always have to go," she complains. "I have no idea why you are always so busy."

"Bye!" I can still hear her talking as I hang up. "Claire!" I say as she pulls up in front of me on an electric bike. "That's very woke of you," I add as she climbs off it and locks it with her phone.

"Fuck off," she replies. "Rob's taken the car."

"What? Forever?"

"Of course forever, that happens in a divorce. You get fleeced and shafted up orifices you didn't know you had and in ways you didn't know even existed."

She whips off her red bobble hat, throws a small black rucksack over her shoulder and marches into the café.

"Sally!" she says, pressing her cold cheeks against Sally's tepid face. "How are you? How's everything? How's the—" She holds her by the shoulders and puts her head to one side.

"The operation is tomorrow," says Sally, turning her fork over and over in her hands.

"Tomorrow?" I ask, pulling up a chair.

"Will seems to be fine about it." Sally shakes her head in disbelief. "I'm the one who's most upset." She is spinning her fork at great speed now. "He's being really practical. It's a simple operation, there's a tiny bit of downtime, apparently, when you have to sit on a rubber ring or something like that and then he gets checked again and then . . . and then . . ." Her voice trails off.

"And then it's all fine," I say, patting her knee.

"Plenty of people go on to have more children," says Claire.

"I don't want any more children!" Sally looks more confused than annoyed.

"You know what I mean."

"Yes, I do," nods Sally. "But I don't know . . . I just don't want to think about it. Poor man, and he's being so brave . . ." She looks at us both and then suddenly she can't keep it in any longer and it's like she's coughed up a fur ball of emotion. Her pretty, dark eyes fill with tears that cascade down her cheeks, mascara slithering along behind. Her hands are shaking and she is fighting to breathe between the sobs. "I just don't want him to . . . die . . ." She finally says the word and turns and collapses on the nearest shoulder, which is mine.

"Oh my darling, he won't, I promise you." I squeeze her as tightly as I can. She feels so little, like a child. It's as if all the fight has gone out of her and she can't keep it together any longer. She puts her arms around my neck and sobs.

"He's strong and brave and people just don't die of these things anymore. I promise you. The doctors know what they are doing. I promise he'll be fine."

"He will," adds Claire. "Because he has you by his side."

"And you're strong and a team," I agree.

"And he'll be fine." Claire reaches across and pats Sally's arm.

"He will," I say, hugging her a little tighter. "And so will you."

October 18th

"I think you should get a job," says Husband. He's pacing around our small kitchen, drinking a glass of wine the size of a birdbath. He probably needs it. He's opened some bills, which is always a mistake and the perfect way to guarantee a bad night in.

"I know," I agree.

I'm stirring what I am hoping is going to be a vegetable Thai green curry, although at the moment it is looking decidedly brown. Maybe those old aubergines were not a good idea. Not that it matters greatly; Husband eats anything, sometimes even out of the bin, and Ella and Pig have already eaten their tea/supper – jam, toast, cereal and a couple of Pop-Tarts: all the food groups, and are both wearing earphones, watching different screens. Ella, I presume, is watching *Sex Education* (again), and Pig will most certainly be watching someone else play *Fortnite*. Personally, I can't see the pleasure in watching someone else play a computer game. I mean, why? *Sex Education* I get, it has a narrative and is about sex, what's not to love about that when you're fifteen years old? Even if you have watched all the series three times over. But watching a bloke, in a tracksuit, playing a computer game is a whole other level of time-wasting. It's Olympic-level timewasting.

"You agree?" Husband looks a little shocked. "Oh?"

"I'm dying to do something, I'd love to earn some money. The children are at school long enough now for me to be able to do some proper hours without having to pay someone else to look after them, which is always the problem, being able to earn more than the cost of childcare."

"Good!" He nods.

"And marketing is a transferable skill."

"Well, it is mostly social media now," he says.

"Apart from that," I smile, giving the curry a brisk spin around the pan.

"But it is mostly social media," he repeats.

"Apart from that."

"Apart from that . . . you're employable. Just about . . ."

There's a pause. He exhales, puffing loudly as he picks up the super-thin three-page local newspaper, that's mainly about campaigning against the threat of HS2 on all of us. He takes a sip of his wine.

"There!" he says, slapping the paper down on the counter. "There's one right there!"

"Oh, really?" I lean over, a little excited.

"And it's part-time. And it's marketing. Both the things you want."

"Amazing."

"Bounce seeks a part-time marketing assistant," he reads.

"Bounce?"

"Yeah." He looks up. "You know the trampoline park down the road? It's very close," he adds. "And I bet there's parking."

"I'm here for a job, actually." I smile.

"A job . . ." It is now his turn to look surprised. I am clearly about thirty years too old for the place. "Oh?"

"I'm here to meet, er . . ." I pull a piece of paper from my coat pocket. "Deborah Day."

"Oh, Debbie," he says, indicating again towards the row of empty chairs. "I'll just give her a buzz. If you wait there."

A few minutes later Debbie comes marching down the stairs dressed in skintight navy leggings and the same yellow T-shirt. She is wearing box-bright white trainers, a heavy pair of eyebrows and has a figure that doesn't move a millimetre, despite the fact that I follow her buttocks as she jogs swiftly up the stairs. She clearly works out. Every day. Possibly twice a day. Or all day.

"I'm always in here," she admits. "Every morning I do at least thirty minutes on the trampolines. It's good for the legs."

There's a pause while we both admire her splendidly toned legs.

Her giant office, the size of five of my sitting rooms, overlooks the trampoline park. One whole wall is entirely made of plate glass. The top half even has a window that opens on to the hall below. I glance down. There are about twenty-five different trampolines and foam pits and ramps and bouncy walls; it looks like just the place if you're five years old and full of Red Bull. Through the closed window,

I can hear the beat of soft rock music. There is also an acrid smell of sweat, sugar and feet that hangs in the air.

"I used to be fat," continues Debbie. "But since becoming manager here, I'm addicted." She leans across her desk and cracks open a Diet Coke. "Can I get you anything? Tea? Coffee? Water?"

"No thank you." I eye her Diet Coke.

"Take a seat."

I flop down on the blue L-shaped cube sofa next to her desk. It is so hard, it reverberates up my spine and gives me whiplash.

"So . . ." she says, keeping her firm buttocks parked on the edge of her desk as she runs a long, fluoro-pink nail over my CV. "You can type – computer skills?"

"Yes, I've got those," I reply, without entirely giving away what they are. "I have my own computer. With a keyboard," I add, just to make sure I sound convincing.

"And you're good on the phone?"

"Too good!" I laugh. She doesn't.

"And you've done marketing before?"

"Years." I could add the word 'ago', but it doesn't seem relevant.

"Good, good," she nods, looking down the side of the paper. "And part-time?"

"I have two children, so I need to be around for them."

"Of course. What are their ages?"

"Fifteen and nine."

'Oh! I have an eleven-year-old." She smiles.

I am glad I am sitting down. "Wow! You don't look old enough." I immediately sound like my mother. "How cool!" I sound even more like my mother. "Single parent?" I am my mother.

"No. Happily married, actually." Her thick eyebrows shoot up her forehead. "I met Jay at school. Carlton Academy."

"My daughter's there!"

"No way! So's my son! It wasn't called that then, when I was there. It was Carlton College. I don't know why they think Academy sounds better. Jay was a few years above me. But we've been together ever since. He owns a whole load of gyms in the area. Boxing, that sort of thing. First Box?"

"Oh yes, I know them very well." I am lying, but I think I might be getting away with it.

"Great!" she smiles. "Well, that's settled! You're in!"

"I am?" I couldn't be more shocked.

"Well, you're local and our children are at the same school."

That's the old girl network right there, I think, making a mental note to call my mum and point out that Ella's school isn't quite so shit after all.

"I can't wait," I say. "So, when do you need me to start?"

"Next week would be great." She nods. "I'll get the contract sorted, send it over on email. Your office is right next to mine, with a view over the park."

"Brilliant," I enthuse. I am sure I'll get used to the smell of feet.

"Great," she says again, and walks over to what looks like a large filing cabinet. "What size are you?"

"Me?"

"Yes."

"Um . . . twelve." I'm lying again, mainly to myself.

"You look like a Large to me." she replies, turning around and handing me a pile of neatly packaged yellow and blue clothes.

"What's this?"

"Your uniform."

"Uniform!"

"Yellow T-shirt, blue leggings." She looks down at her own. "We all wear a uniform at Bounce!"

"We do?"

"Oh yes." She nods. "It's good to be on-brand – you work in marketing." She slaps me on the shoulder. "You should know all about that!"

October 18th

Husband thinks it's the funniest thing he's heard this century.

"You! In a uniform!" he hoots. "It sounds sexy! Is it sexy? Do you have to wear a little hat?"

"No." My reply could not be flatter.

"A tie?" He giggles. "Is it like a school uniform because if it is, I want photos . . . Short skirt? Tight shirt? Bending over to pick up your ruler? A uniform!"

And on and on he goes . . . In fact, he finds the whole thing so goddamn hilarious he pours himself a pint of wine and disappears out into our ivy-clogged garden to phone Mike, Matthew and Chris. "Have you heard . . .?" He then repeats the same hilarious story over and over, where the words "Bounce!" and "uniform" cause him to crease up so much he's actually crying as he sits, gripping onto the arms of the white plastic smoking chair.

I am so angry; I actually want to punch him. I don't, of course, I just sit inside, chewing my lips and drinking a bottle of red wine to myself, resolved to refuse to have sex with him if he ever asks. That'll learn him, to take the piss when I am just trying my bloody hardest to get through the day without falling apart. I was quite pleased I'd found a job. I'd been so nervous about getting back into the workplace. I couldn't believe I'd been employed at my first attempt. So what if I have a company rucksack and tracksuit instead of a car?

October 19th

"The question is, should you accept the job?" asks Claire, shuffling her tarot cards.

"What do you mean, should she accept the job?" asks Kate, pouring herself a large glass of wine. She's taken up lunchtime drinking as a way of compensating for her early-morning jogging. "She's hardly inundated with offers. No offence," she adds, causing just that.

"No, no, she's right," I agree, mainly because I have to. "I'm hardly wallowing in opportunity." I take a glug of wine. I'm also drinking at lunchtime, seeing as this is my last week of freedom and I am soon to be employed. Or at least, I think I am.

"What do the cards say?" asks Sally, who isn't drinking because otherwise she'd cry.

Sally apparently scared herself a few nights ago when she had a gin or three and then shouted at Will for being such a bastard and so irritating for being ill and then cried herself to sleep in the spare room. So she's now strictly on water until he gets the all-clear. Whenever that may be.

Claire hands me her deck of tarot cards. "So . . . shuffle the cards and then you ask the deck your question and then you pull a card. Just one. And then you give it to me."

"Only one?" I ask.

"Yup. I do it every morning. Just one. You ask the deck a question and then you act on the response."

"What?" Kate looks confused. "What sort of question?"

"Oh, you know, should I do this or should I do that? Like, should I call up so-and-so and follow up on this proposal or will this deal work? Or shall I meet the girls for lunch or not?"

"What?" Kate sits back on her seat. "You actually ask that?"

"Yeah, sure." Claire is nodding away, like this is totally normal.

"And what if the cards said no, don't join your friends for lunch?" Kate's eyes narrow.

"Then I wouldn't go."

"Fuck me," says Sally. "Do you always do what they tell you?"

"Yup."

Silence gusts across the wooden corner table in Totally Organic, one of those restaurants that persuades you that

eating a Got-No-Beef burger is "like, totally good for you".
It was Kate's choice, of course. Kate's vegan now during
the day, due to global warming. Kate bites her bottom lip
and takes another sip of wine. Sally sighs and drinks her
water. She's clearly too tired for the fight. She's too tired
for most things. And I look at Claire and try and frown.

"Always, always? Like, you never ignore what the cards
say?"

"Well, I am not fully across the meanings of all of them
quite yet," continues Claire. She is either ignoring our
collective incredulity or is genuinely unable to see it or
understand it. "Zoya, the tarot teacher who comes into
the shop on Tuesdays is only halfway through the major
arcana."

"The what?" Kate and I both ask at the same time.

"Arcana," Claire replies flatly. No more explanation is
needed. "Anyway." She smiles briefly at me. She's clearly
irritated. "Time for you to choose."

"Oh, sorry!" I pick up the pack and shuffle and think
what the hell is my question? I'm a little clouded by wine and
also there are a couple of women on the uncomfortably
close table next to us who are listening. "Um . . . Will it all
be OK?"

"Fine," nods Claire, half closing her eyes, bonding with
another level.

"Is that it?" asks Kate.

"I couldn't think of anything else," I snap.

"Really?" She looks at me; her eyes are round, and she has one eyebrow raised. "There's nothing else? A friend. Or anything?"

"No." I glare at her. Now is not the time to mention Dave. Sally is too upset and Claire is clearly having some sort of existential crisis that involves the crystals and pints of patchouli oil. My dirty laundry doesn't need airing right now. And besides, there are a couple of women sitting next to us whose ears are frantically flapping now.

"It doesn't really matter what she asks," says Claire. "The cards know and they never lie."

"See," I say to Kate. "It doesn't matter." I hand over the card.

"The fool," declares Claire. "That's good!"

"It is?"

We all lean in to inspect the card. Our two neighbours snatch a glance.

"The Fool! The Fool! The Fool!" Claire's clearly trying to remember what she learnt in last week's class. "It's joy, it's freedom. It's living your true life without a care. He has money in his hand, the sun on his back and he is off on a journey filled with joy!"

"Oh? It doesn't mean I am a fool?"

"Oh no! Far from it. It means that you should embrace your inner hopes and desires and go for it!" She punches the air a little. It feels awkward. Even the other two on the next-door table suddenly stare into their coffees.

"Honestly, it's a great card." She clears her throat and looks at Kate and Sally. "Anyone else want to shuffle?"

"No thanks," says Sally, her hand in the air. "I'll pass."

"Hashtag me too," replies Kate, picking up her phone.

Perhaps it was The Fool that made me answer the phone to David on the way back home in the car. Perhaps it was The Fool that made me agree to meet him. Or perhaps it was the three glasses of Pinot Grigio at lunchtime on an empty stomach with no sodding carbs as I am trying to look less *Large* in my yellow T-shirt.

October 20th

My heart is beating so fast I think it's only a matter of time before it leaps out of my actual chest and breaks two ribs. What am I doing? What am I doing? *What the hell am I actually doing?!*

It's a Wednesday, the middle of the week, and Dave and I have booked into a hotel to have sex. There. I said it. I am so anxious and nervous and excited and frankly terrified and twitching, I'm sucking down the fags like I'm a lab experiment. There's a small pile of butts outside the car door where I've parked up, like I've been staking out the place, like a private detective. Which I have. For the past half hour.

We've chosen a discreet little hotel in Bayswater, which is far enough away from our usual stomping ground so that no one will even vaguely recognise us, and close enough for the school run. We were being practical when we booked it, despite my bottle of wine. And both James and Sam have chess club this afternoon which means neither of us has to be at the school gate until 5pm. Dave has told his office he has a meeting all afternoon, and I have no one to tell anything to, mainly because no one ever asks me what I am doing or ever enquires after my day anyway. It is clearly simply so bloody dull that no one is interested at all in how it went. The same as the one before. And the one before that. Well, not today. Today I'm going to have sex with someone who isn't my husband. I am going to sleep with someone different for the first time in sixteen years. And I'm petrified.

It's 2.05pm. Dave is late. We've asked for an early check-in at the Bayswater House Hotel and the earliest they'd do was 2pm. I am here. He is not. I'm beginning to panic a little. Perhaps he's not coming? Perhaps he's got cold feet. Perhaps he's gone off the whole idea. Perhaps . . . then I spot him breezily walking along the road, his arms swinging, his suit jacket flapping, his blue tie waving in the wind; he is smiling. He looks entirely without a care in the world and not at all like someone who's about to have afternoon sex with someone else's wife. Then again, I am not sure what *they* look like, having never done this before.

I leap out of my car and wave from the across the road.

"There you are!" He grins from the opposite kerb, rubbing his hands together like he's about to tuck into a Sunday roast. "Shall we?"

We walk into the lobby of what is essentially a small converted town house. The walls are white and the carpet is thick and cream and there's a small, highly polished table in the middle of the room, working a giant floral display the same size as the table. Opposite the front door is the Reception, a shiny wooden desk with a green leather-boarded blotter, two chairs and a bell, which Dave rings. We check in as Mr and Mrs Smith, which we both think is highly amusing. The neat, bald man behind the desk doesn't register an expression. The whole hilarious ruse is somewhat destroyed a minute later when Dave has to hand over his credit card to the receptionist, who returns the card moments later calling him "Mr Cavendish".

"No luggage?" he asks quizzically, glancing at our feet, as he hands over the key to room twelve.

"Um, no," replies Dave. I can feel my cheeks blush. We are rank amateurs.

Dave and I step into the small, mirrored lift to the second floor and as the door slowly shuts we both look straight ahead. I stare at my reflection in the doors, except I can't look myself in the eye. It feels weird. Without doubt this is an act of betrayal and I am feeling highly uncomfortable. The journey up the two floors seems to take an age. Neither of us is talking. The lift doors open at last and we walk the few steps down the navy-blue carpeted corridor to number twelve. Dave opens the door.

"Oh, this is nice," we both say at the same time.

And it is quite nice. There's a high, big double bed in the middle of the room, wooden wardrobes on the right, a couple of bedside tables, pretty lamps, a nice, modestly patterned rug, a small fat floral armchair and a trouser press. Dave swiftly takes his jacket off and pops it on the trouser press. He turns around and immediately starts to kiss me. What! No chat, no nothing. He is tentative to start with and then quickly starts to probe with his tongue, deeply into my mouth while at the same time he's unbuttoning my shirt. I am kissing him and running my hands through his hair and I can feel his erection on my thigh. But I am panicking. It's broad daylight and I am standing up. I *have* got my best bra and pants on (pale pink lace: matching) I made sure of that. They're the ones I bought to go and see an expensive gynaecologist about ten years ago when I had some money and could afford to have a smear test done by a doctor who did all the girls' fannies at *Vogue*. I'd always wondered if he introduced himself that way at parties. A posh fanny doctor, as opposed to a normal, common fanny doc. Anyway, at least I have my best pants on, but I had not banked on standing in the middle of the hotel room with the sun streaming through the window. I'm going to have to breathe in. For quite a while. My shirt hits the floor, rapidly followed by my skirt. My bra and pants are not far behind. They hit the floor without comment. One hundred and fifty pounds' worth of underwear dismissed like a two-for-one in Marks and Spencer. He is running his hands all over me, cupping my breast, stroking my buttocks. I am wriggling and writhing to his touch, moaning a little by way of encouragement; he puts his hands between my legs and then stops.

"Christ!" He takes a step back to have look. "You've got hair!" He is looking down at my crotch with astonishment. "*No one* has hair anymore."

What? No one? Quite literally no one? I have the last bush on the planet? But I took the corners off just last week. I used a home wax kit; what the fuck is he talking about? No one indeed!

"It's amazing!" He steps forward as if to stroke it like some small marsupial. "It's so beautiful." He is now actually stroking it. "And so soft, it's so female. So woman." He is kissing me and running his hand through my clearly massive bush, curling the hair around his fingers. "I think I want to eat it!"

Oh, Christ! Before I can say anything I am standing stark naked, while he is on his hands and knees, his face in my bush and I am staring out of the window, looking at the people working in the office opposite and I haven't even had a glass of wine. In fact, this is probably the first sober sex I have had in sixteen years, possibly more. So while Dave's on his knees, lapping away at my hirsute minge like a cat drinking cream, all I can think of is wine, and please God don't let the woman who's typing on a computer opposite look up from her desk. Then suddenly he's up and he pushes me back onto the bed. Thank God, I'm horizontal at last, I can exhale. At least.

But Dave won't stop talking. "I am in awe of a woman's vagina," he continues, as he strokes my belly. I breathe in again and try to keep everything as firm as I can. I really wish he'd just shut up and pop it in. I'd like to be ravaged. Not examined. It's far too bright outside as it is.

"It is a miracle, isn't it?"

"What?" I really don't want a chat.

"A woman." Jesus Christ, can't he shut up?

"The shape of her." Is he writing the lyrics for a song or something? "The way they curve here and here." He is running his fingers down the sides of my hips, it is erotic I'll grant him that, but it is also deeply ticklish. "Let me look at you . . ."

"Enough of the looking and the talking," I say. I can't really bear it anymore. I grab him by the back of the neck and pull him towards me and shove my hips underneath his. If this is not an invitation to get on with it, I don't know what it is.

He takes the hint and, rising up slightly, he dives right in. Oh? I was, truthfully, expecting a little bit more ceremony than this. But here we go. Well, at least Dave is off. At a pace! It's like being shagged by a small randy terrier with a cock the size of a white wine cork. In, out, in, out, in, out . . . It is so swift and vigorous I begin bouncing up and down on the bed, and the springs are joining in. Dave, sadly, takes this for enthusiasm.

"Oh, go baby! Go baby! Go baby!" he coos in my ear. It's like being on one of the sodding trampolines at BOUNCE! We slip out of sync for a minute as our hip bones clash, and he headbutts me on the chin. "Oh, sorry! Woops!" But he's soon back on it and we bop along for another forty-five seconds until he slows a little and starts to bellow in my ear. "Wow . . . wow . . . wow . . . woooooah!" He then collapses on top of me, like a dead weight, pinning me to the mattress, huffing heavily, his hot breath whistling in my ear. Then there's a pause, a hiatus in the huffing, and then the puffing turns to sniffles, which turn into snuffles. I think he's crying.

"Oh my God!" he announces, suddenly pushing himself up on the bed, propping himself up on his elbow. "That was so good, so, so good. Look at me! I mean, look at me!" he laughs a little, wiping away a tear. "I always cry after great sex, it's like yoga, a release, all that tension, I mean, man! That was great, so, so great, amazingly great, just great, great . . ." He's beginning to sound like Donald Trump. "You're great!" He rolls me over slightly and slaps my arse. "Great."

I glance across at the bedside table. The small alarm clock is showing the time: 14.22. There's another two hours and thirty-eight minutes till pick-up. What on earth are we going to do now?

October 22nd

What the hell did I do?

I'm cloaked in guilt and a pale yellow ill-fitting T-shirt that is straining over my breasts and fanning tightly under the armpits. I am not sure which is worse. The guilt or the trussed-up chicken T-shirt? Both make me feel suffocated and uncomfortable, itchy and scratchy and sick and utterly, utterly miserable. I thought affairs were supposed to be liberating and exciting and make you shed pounds and decades at the same time?

So why do I feel so terrible?

Was it the sex? I mean, it was hauntingly bad. I have lost count of the amount of times in the last forty-eight hours I've caught myself staring into my coffee and suddenly gasping for air at the utter humiliation of him petting my bush and squatting on the hotel room floor in broad daylight, his head firmly between my thighs while I watched

"Stacey in Accounts" go through her emails. We did it twice, mainly so I could expunge the first experience, and we still had two hours to go before the end of chess club. But the second attempt was equally as uninspiring as the first. It climaxed in a sort of frantic eighty-three thrusts-per-minute sprint to the finish, a sobbing bellow in my ear and a slither of weeping snot shooting down the side of my neck, followed by a good twenty minutes about why he got divorced from the seemingly utterly perfect Suzette. She didn't talk to him enough, apparently. She never really asked if he was OK. She didn't need him. He likes to feel needed. And she was always disappearing off to Paris. She clearly had a lover. Somewhere. But Dave had insisted on a No Contest divorce, because he was just that kind of guy.

He's also the kind of guy who spends ten minutes looking for my bra, which had somehow miraculously disappeared in the throes of said exciting passion. He'd been keen to give up sooner, but all I could think was that it was £65.00 of pale pink lace and I was damned if I was going to leave it behind. But in the end we did. Or I did. So I ended up standing outside chess club waiting for Sam to emerge with my tits around my waist and my nipples like two sturdy acorns protruding through my white shirt.

"Hi!" says Madison, her gleaming smile glinting in the sun and her hair swinging away like My Little Pony. "How are you?" She stares at my nipples. "Where have you been?" she asks, appearing to be questioning them directly.

"I've had a super-dull afternoon," I say, folding my arms, and immediately regretting the decision as my born-free bosom cascades over the top. "You?"

Fortunately, Madison has had an utterly fascinating afternoon of industrial-strength retail therapy, which culminated in her buying herself a super-jazzy, expensive gold bracelet that she jangles in front of my eyes for a good few minutes, which is something of a relief as its brightness and sheer volume and weight in gold most certainly detracts from the donkey boobs and the conker nipples and indeed the somewhat clammy, pink-cheeked arrival of Dave.

But Madison rarely misses a trick.

"Dave," she says, looking him up and down. "Your hair's wet."

"Yeah," he agrees, running his hand through it and giving it a shake. "I have just been home to shower."

"You have?" I blurt.

"Sport?" asks Madison.

"You could say that," he replies. "Oh look, here's James!"

Sport? What am I now? A round of golf? A jog in the park? A kick-about with the lads? So now, of course, as well as the guilt, there's the indignation. Is it possible to be both needy and furious? Embarrassed and wanting to see him again? I'm really far too old for this, aren't I? I haven't been on a date since New Labour was in power and almost no one can remember that far back. The person I need to speak to is Kate. Kate's been on Tinder. She knows all about casual, filthy, car-park sex and is surely au fait with Four Star polite afternoon sex as well. But it's my first day at Bounce! and my boss Deborah Day won't stop popping into my office to see if I'm OK.

"Anything you need," she says, her discombobulated head poking around the door. "Just shout."

"Yes, yes, thank you," I nod, tapping a pile of paper on my desk, exuding efficiency, even if I am not quite sure where it goes. "I will."

"I mean, anything," she persists. "I'm right here." She points down at her huge, bright, white wedged trainers, or at least the spot in front of them.

"So I see."

"So, anything?"

"Yup."

She smiles. "Right here." She points again.

In the end, I can't bear it any longer and slip off to the egg-yolk yellow communal toilets and, ignoring the smell of spilt Fruit Shoot and stale urine, I plonk my arse down on the black toilet seat and call Kate. Actually, I accidentally press FaceTime.

"Shit," says Kate as she picks up. "Are you OK?" She squints. "You look like you're in hospital. Is that a gown? The yellow thing?"

"No," I whisper.

"Why are you whispering?"

"I'm at work."

"Is that your office?" She peers at the screen. I can see right up her nose. "Let me have a look."

"It's the toilets."

"Urgh!" She recoils suddenly, as if she can smell what I can, although I can't now, not anymore anyway. "What are you doing in there? You're not crying at work already?"

"I need to talk to you."

"Oh," she replies, not appearing particularly interested.

"I FUCKED him!" I say it extra loud, just to get her attention.

"No, no vanilla syrup," she says, her teeth gritted, her smile a little rictus. "Well, that's very interesting, Derek . . . , but I'm in Starbucks, picking up my latte. Leave it with me, caller." Two minutes later, she is in a park, on a bench, or at least that's what it looks like.

"Derek?"

"Well, that was bloody fucking embarrassing, thank you! The whole of the bloody Starbucks looked at me, including the hot barista I've been flirting with for months."

"I bet it wasn't as bad as the sex," I reply.

Her eyes narrow as she looks at the screen. "So you slept with him?"

"Yup."

"Why on earth . . .?"

What a question. Why on earth indeed . . .?

"Because my husband doesn't love me anymore? Or did he even in the first place? He ignores me. I am so bloody invisible that I may as well not exist. He laughs at me trying to get a job. Everything I do is shit. Useless. Everything about me is a joke. My children ignore me. Come to that, everyone bloody ignores me." I sigh, loudly. "I have no feelings, apparently. I'm the punch bag. I'm everyone's punch bag. No one ever asks me how my fucking day was. I'm irrelevant. *Totally* irrelevant. I don't exist. Even my own mother finds me boring." My voice is getting louder and louder, as the self-pity grows. "The whole world finds me boring. *I* find me boring. I'm so boring, no one even makes clothes for women like me anymore. It's either cropped tops from ASOS or pistachio slacks from Debenhams; no wonder they've gone bust. I hate everyone, everything . . . the only thing I like is wine. But even the wine isn't strong enough anymore. So I fucked Dave. I fucked him to feel alive. To feel normal. To feel liked. To feel needed. Adored. Actually bloody touched, for once. And away, he liked my full bush . . ."

"You've got a full bush?" exclaims Kate, aghast. "Have you entirely given up?"

At that point, the toilet in the next-door cubicle flushes. My mouth slowly opens. I hold my breath. Shit.

"Hello? Hello? HELLO?" persists Kate, tapping the phone. "I think you've frozen? Hello . . .? You've frozen. I'll call you right back."

October 23rd

It's been a week since Will's had his left testicle removed, and I haven't seen Sally at all. I feel guilty. Guilty that I haven't been round. Guilty that my best friend should be on her own at such an awful time. And guilty that I am such a terrible friend. Why am I always feeling guilty?

And don't get me started on Dave . . .

Yesterday, I sent him a sort of blasé "we must do that again" sort of message on WhatsApp and he's seen it, I know he has. It's turned blue, with the two ticks and everything, and he hasn't replied. I keep checking if he's online, what time he was last seen. Every ten minutes. It's infuriating, it's frustrating. I'm being ghosted by a man who weeps after he orgasms; it doesn't get more tragic than that.

It's Kate's fault. She told me to send it. She called me back in the office, and above the noise of screaming children doing star jumps and the repetitive beats of Europe's

"The Final Countdown", she told me to text him, be cool, not be the arse who doesn't respond. After all, I don't want tension at the school gate, or worse, during Entrepreneur's Week when we are flogging the stress balls at three for a fiver (which I think a little overpriced, personally, but Erica said that it was the only way we, sorry, *they* would win). So I did. Text. And now nothing. I bet he doesn't feel guilty. Does he even feel?

"Hi."

Sally answers the door wearily with large grey bags under her eyes and a face the colour of builder's putty. She is wearing a huge navy jumper and tiny tight black leggings and looks like a little child.

"How are you?" I ask, handing over a bag of mixed pastries I bought at the overpriced red-checked café by the school.

"We're fine," she replies. "Come in."

Sally's normally immaculate sitting room and kitchen bar area is a tip. It looks like she's been burgled and they stayed behind to have a bit of a party while they were at it.

"Excuse the mess," she lamely waves around the room. "I just don't have the energy to pick up all the Lego and the socks or do the washing-up."

The sink is piled high with milk-splattered cereal bowls encrusted with Rice Krispies and Ben is lying on the sofa, half asleep, his mouth sticky with jam, still dressed in his pyjamas.

"How's Will?" I ask, picking up a small red sweatshirt and sitting at the breakfast bar.

"He's in pain." She bites her top lip. "A lot of pain . . . You can go upstairs and see him if you like. He shouldn't be asleep, I've just given him some breakfast."

"Don't worry, I've come to see you, really."

"Oh. Right. I'm not sure I'm very good company. I haven't really slept."

"When was the last time you had a shower? Washed your hair?"

"Oh." Sally is genuinely stumped. She picks up a lank bit of dark hair and lets it fall. "Um, I can't remember."

"Listen, why don't you go and have a shower. Take as long as you want, I'll look after Ben. I love Ben. We're friends, Ben and I. Why don't you just go upstairs? Take your time." I give her a little shove in the direction of the stairs.

"If you're sure?"

"Absolutely."

By the time Sally comes down the stairs, washed and brushed and looking like an entirely different species, I have cleaned the kitchen, washed up, unloaded the dishwasher, laundered the child, changed him, picked up the Lego and de-jammed his face. I've even had time to polish my own halo while I boil the kettle and make a vat of very strong coffee.

"Oh, thank you so much," she mumbles over and over, standing on the stairs. "That's so much better than flowers or chocolates or bloody bottles of wine that people keep on sending. You're a good friend."

"Coffee?" I am sounding breezy.

"Don't mind if I do," she smiles. "Oh, look at BenBen." Ben grins toothlessly from the sofa. "You look so clean and sweet and delicious. Thank you, darling." She sighs. "God, it's been a tough few days."

"I bet."

"They think they have got it all out though, the cancer, that is."

"That's good news."

"I know." She takes a sip of her coffee. "I just wish Will would be a little less demanding."

"Really?"

"Jesus." She rolls her eyes. "I can't tell you how many times I have run up and down those stairs. It's like being in a bloody boot camp. It's my fault I gave him a bloody bell. Can I get this? Can I get that? Could I possibly add a little agave syrup to his coffee, he doesn't like the taste of sugar anymore. It might be the drugs, you see, it might be the painkillers that make him so needy . . . Christ!" She throws her hands in the air. "I wish he'd just fuck off! I love him so much, but I am the world's worst waitress."

"Fup off!" comes an echo from the sofa.

"Oh great," says Sally, glancing across at Ben. "Now the bloody baby's learnt to swear."

"Fup off!" repeats Ben and smiles.

I smile. She'll be OK. Sally. It's when she *isn't* swearing that the world should worry.

"So how are *you*?" she asks, taking another sip of her coffee. "All OK? How's Ella?"

"Vaping, expressing herself through the medium of dance, dropping French. She's tried to pierce her tragus using a kit she bought off Amazon."

"Her what?" Sally grimaces.

"Tragus."

"Where the hell is that?" She crosses her legs carefully.

"Somewhere on the ear. Lobes are so last century, when there are conches and helixes and traguses or tragi, who knows. Blood all over the carpet, obviously. And a lot of shouting. Oh, and she's managed to tattoo a stick man on her wrist."

"A tattoo?"

"Oh yes. A stick and poke tattoo, apparently. They've all got something scribbled somewhere these days, like a handy notepad by the phone."

"No one's got landlines anymore." She sighs.

"But Will's going to be fine?"

"He should be back at work in a few days or so. Or at least, that's what the doctors are saying. I can't see it myself though." She nods. "There'll be check-ups and all that stuff . . . but . . . you know . . . no chemo . . ."

"Really?"

"Mainly because he caught it so early because of that medical thing. Apparently, when you are middle-aged like Will is, not me, obviously, I'm waaay younger, but when you are Will's age you are supposed to have everything checked. Bollocks, arse, heart, that sort of thing. So . . ."

"Totally fine?"

A little tinkling bell rings upstairs. Sally inhales deeply and gets slowly to her feet and walks towards the stairs.

"Room service." She smiles stiffly. "Yes, he will be. The real question is, will I?"

October 25th

Ever since her trip to the communal toilets, Deborah Day has been avoiding me and avoiding making eye contact, which, when you consider there are only two people over the age of thirty-five who work in the Bounce! building – her and me – it is making the whole "new job thing" quite a lot more stressful. Also, I keep having to ask her stuff. Ordinarily, when I knock on her door, I suspect she might have been able to hide or appear extremely busy in a meeting or something, but since almost the entire building is made of glass with glass walls, glass doors with a direct view on the trampoline park below, it is quite difficult for her to disappear.

I gingerly tap on her door for the third time this morning. She needs to approve the fliers that are being slipped inside the free *Children and Parenting* magazine that gets handed around the NW6, NW10 areas. This was one of my first marketing ideas, which she happily approved of, before she heard me confess to an extramarital affair while sitting in the bogs. Or maybe it was my admitting to having a bigger bush than Moses saw engulfed in flames on Mount Sinai that makes her no longer able to meet my eye. Terrible topiary or adultery: which is worse?

"Hi Deborah," I say tentatively, pushing slightly at the door. "Do you mind if I come in?"

"Um . . ." She places a neon nail on her lip as she tries to think of something. Her eyes dart left and right as she attempts to conjure a lie from somewhere. But Deborah is naturally nice so is struggling a little. If that had been Ella, some elaborate well-formed lie would have been concocted rapidly from the ether, like when she'd sworn blind that she hadn't stolen my skirt and ripped it up the back and put it back in the cupboard, despite there being photographic evidence of the skirt at a party on Snapchat. Or was it Insta? "Sure," says Deborah. "Why don't you pull up a chair?"

By chair she means a large blue felt cube of which there are three in the office. Unwieldy, heavy and highly uncomfortable, they were designed by someone who'd never been to a meeting in their entire lives, or a bloke. I shove the sample of fliers under my chin and drag the cube towards her.

'So," she says inhaling through her back teeth and looking straight down at the fliers. "Talk me through what you have done."

"Well, I have a photo of, er, Steven from Reception in his uniform and his arms are outstretched towards the Bounce! building and he's smiling and saying 'welcome'." I find myself doing the quotation marks in the air. "And on the back, there are loads of photos of the trampolines and the prices and sock hire and all that . . . um, that sort of stuff."

"Right . . ." She looks at the sheet of paper and flip-flops to one side and then the next. "And you chose Steve, because?"

"Well, he's young and he has a nice smile." He hasn't, obviously. But he was the only one on Reception at the time when the photographer arrived. On the wrong day. I'd hoped to use one of the two other less aesthetically challenged girls who also work on Reception but they were not around.

"I'm not sure Steve really says Bounce! Do you?"

Poor Steve doesn't say very much at all. And what he does say he garbles at breakneck speed into the top of his T-shirt as he stares at his feet in total embarrassment. I had to promise him fifty quid in order to get him to smile for the camera.

"He's young," I try.

"And got no kids," says Deborah, nodding and staring at my handiwork, flipping it back and forth in the hope that it might look different.

"Well . . ." I can't argue with that.

"In fact, if I look at him, he looks a bit like he bothers children."

"What?"

"That facial hair."

"What facial hair?" Steve has barely enough testosterone to feather a moustache.

"You can't be too careful." She sniffs and then looks me straight in the eyes for the first time in days. "You should do it."

"ME!" Panic floods my body so rapidly that every single nose pore springs open with a sudden rush of sweat. My armpits are damp with terror. My cheeks turn the colour of a first-class postage stamp.

"Yeah." She nods, loving her own idea more and more. "You . . ." And then she starts to freewheel her concept, rolling her hands out in front of her. "In the uniform." My buttocks clench. "Leaping up in the air." My pelvic floor screams. "'Looking fun'." It's her turn to do the aerial quotation marks. "On one of the trampolines." Fuck. "You have one of those nice, approachable faces. Mumsy . . . even. It'll be great."

"But we don't have a photographer," I say, knowing exactly what her response will be.

"I have my mobile phone." She grabs it off her desk and waves it about. "And the quality is amazing." Exactly that.

"Sure," I reply. For there is nothing else I can say.

I spend the next forty-five minutes leaping in the air, pulling my pelvic floor up so tightly my ovaries snooker my tonsils, trying to "look fun", while not actually peeing my rather small pants. Had I known, I might have worn the huge elasticated pair I save for weddings and funerals and a sports bra to keep my rack from taking my eyes out. But no. The humiliation is total. I am forced to leap with my thumps up, my fists pumping the air, my legs akimbo. All in all I work up quite a sweat "being fun" while being watched by a group of seven-year-olds having a Princess Party.

I then go back to my desk and wait for the inevitable to happen. The large JPEG mock-up takes twenty minutes to arrive in my inbox. It's me. Fist in the air. Mouth open. Sweat stain in the armpit. Legs (looking shockingly much fatter than I had thought in those leggings) akimbo. With my face mercifully partially obscured by my left breast that appears to be higher than the right, so only my right eye and open mouth are visible. "Bounce!" declares the flier. "Fun for everyone. Including Mums!" Wow.

"I've ordered seven thousand," says Deborah's email that accompanies the JPEG. "In the larger size. Why go small, when we can go BIG!!!!!! Whatcha think?" What do I think? I think I want to die. Kill her. Kill myself. Probably in that order. "That's great!!!!" I reply. "It looks brilliant!! Go marketing. Go you!! Go!!!!" I send it.

I think I might need a drink. Immediately.

I look at my phone. My options are limited to say the least. Sally is sad. Kate is at work. Claire is up to her armpit hair in lotus-shaped candles. I could go straight home, I suppose, and trip over the scattered shoes in the hall and wait around while no one asks me about my day. I could cook the same old terrible supper and drink a bottle of wine entirely to myself by 9.05pm and go to bed and pass out with my mouth open, catching flies by ten, too knackered to stay up for The News. Come to think of it, I can't remember the last time I actually made it to The News. I mean, the whole News. A year? Three years? Ten?

Dave it is.

He picks up immediately and he suggests we go to the same pub where we snogged like teenagers under the hot lamps. He doesn't say it like that, of course, but it seems that, when having an affair, subtext is all. Just the very idea of going back to the scene of the crime is exciting.

It's early but seasonably dark, which is a relief. So ordering a double gin at 5pm doesn't seem so bad.

"Sorry about not calling you," he says as he chinks my glass. "It's just been one of those weeks when I haven't been able to find a good twenty minutes for a proper conversation. At all. I have kept meaning to, though . . . And I'm not a great texter."

"Aren't you? I hadn't noticed." My lying voice is a good/irritating two octaves higher.

"Good." He nods. "I didn't think you were one of those needy women who has to be told how brilliant they are at everything or how beautiful and funny they are. You don't need that crap! You're not that sort of girl."

"No!" I guffaw, bouncing up and down on my bar stool. "Aren't they awful!"

"You're one of those women who just gets on with things." He smiles. "You're capable."

I was once called "sturdy" by a priapic man in a five-star hotel suite in Brighton who I actually quite liked, and I marched out of the room thinking that must have been the least sexy thing a man can ever call a woman. But now, sitting here, "capable" takes it.

"Capable?"

"Yeah." He leans forward with his half-drunk, dishwasher-warm pub glass ready to chink mine again. "Here's to capable girls like you and having sex again in the very near future."

"Here's to capable-near-future sex." I smile.

Any port in a storm.

October 27th

Turns out that our "capable-near-future sex" was grabbed in the back of his Lexus around the corner from the pub at about 8.30pm that night. Or was it 8pm? I'm not sure as "recollections may vary" as they say, because I don't remember a huge amount of the build-up, or indeed, the execution. I just remember four gins and the back of my head repeatedly banging on the door handle of the rear passenger seat, while I had a calf, somewhat gymnastically, wrapped about the driver's head rest. Dave, naturally, collapsed on top of me, in an explosion of orgasm and tears, and cried into my left double-D cup, while I quietly stared at the white textured ceiling, thinking: *this really and truly can't be it?*

I made it home just past 9pm to find that I still had to cook Pig some supper. Dad apparently had some urgent meeting with the sofa and was incapable of doing anything other than lying horizontally, while watching some extremely violent cop drama with subtitles. So I stumbled around the kitchen and ended up at the hob making scrambled eggs.

It was a mistake to begin with. Who knew that the hob was at the perfect height? All I had to do was rub myself gently against it while stirring the eggs. It didn't take long. Seven or eight times, I moved up against the dial. Gas mark six, seven, eight, nine, ten . . . I even managed to stifle my final, grateful gasp. If only Dave knew he'd been outperformed by a Bosch Series 2 from Currys.

*   *   *

"Are you sure you are on the right drugs?" asks Kate, two days later, as we both chase a thankless-looking fish fillet around our plates in some overpriced, chilly, panelled restaurant in Marylebone.

"What do you mean?"

"I think you might have a little too much testosterone in your system."

"Testosterone?"

"Well, I don't know of anyone else who's wanked off on their hob in their own kitchen."

Truth is, I had been to "see someone" about my hormones. After White Van Man had disabused me of my thinking I was still hot to trot, I'd trotted off to see my GP, who'd prescribed some pumps and pills and potions. I'd shoved a few of them on here and there and had frankly forgotten which was which. I'm not very menopausal, really, anyway. I don't constantly flap my hands in front of my face complaining about the temperature, and I can easily remember where I parked my car. I'm only forty-six, for Christ's sake. There are plenty of eggs in this old basket!

"Shush!" I say, glancing quickly around the room.

It's mainly full of middle-aged men with beach balls under their expensive shirts, tucking into plates of steak and pots of chips. It really is true that with the advent of Botox, Pilates and Spanx, the middle-aged woman improves with age; they look like their teenage selves, but better. Whereas blokes over fifty age like dogs: one year is the equivalent to seven and, eventually, all of them appear to be pregnant.

"It happened to one of the girls in the office," says Kate, sipping her water. "She overdid the testosterone tube and could think of nothing else other than shagging the postman. She thought if she collared him quickly, they'd be done in a few minutes and he could carry on delivering his redundant fashion catalogues and credit card bills down the street."

"And she had too much testosterone?"

"Oh yes." Kate nods again. "It turns you into a beast. Think man, and then some. Either that, or your body has finally woken up now it's getting some action."

"Not much action," I say, stabbing a slice of avocado.

"More than it's had in a decade," continues Kate. "And that's including childbirth."

She's waving her fork at me. It's one of Kate's favourite tropes that married people never have sex, whereas the singles are rutting like rutting deer at the height of the rut. Clearly, if she says it enough times, it'll make up for always being given the child's room in the attic with the single bed and the rows of psychotic dolls whenever she gets invited away for the weekend.

"Anyway," she continues. "How's it going, and are you getting a divorce?"

"I don't think two shags is grounds for divorce," I say.

"How many did Claire have? I bet it wasn't many more than that."

"Are you sure?"

"It can't have been more than five, I'm sure I could count them on one hand. But it's the lying more than the cheating, isn't it? It's not the crime, it's the cover-up that gets you in the end."

"I suppose it is," I reply. "Only no one ever asks me anything in my house. So my conscience is clear. No need for a cover-up."

Kate laughs a little. "I suppose there is an upside to being totally ignored." She picks up a piece of frisée lettuce on her fork. "Tell me you've sorted out your bush?"

"Well . . ."

The truth is, I haven't. I haven't had the time, and frankly Dave seemed to like the idea of a new pet. Although I have to say, the other night in the back of the car, I seem to remember, vaguely, he was a little less enthusiastic.

"Really?" Kate looks like she might be sick. "Honestly, what's wrong with you? Think snooker ball." I look puzzled. "Smooth and silky and soft and not a hair."

"Not one?"

"Not one."

"Not even . . ." I glance over my shoulder.

"On your shoulders!" Kate is beyond horrified. She's dropped both her knife and fork and is covering her mouth with her pretty manicured hands.

"No – arse crack!" I say, far too loudly for such a smart restaurant. "There," I look over my shoulder again.

"You have hair up your arse?" Kate flops back into the leatherette banquette seating.

"A little bit," I venture.

"You have quite put me off my lunch." She pushes her £15.75 pence salad into the middle of the table. "Do you have any fags?"

We stand outside on the street for a while watching the well-heeled walk up and down Marylebone High Street shopping away their afternoon, filling in time between beauty appointments. Kate suddenly realises the time: she's late for a meeting, and she grinds her fag butt into the ground, leaving me with the bill.

"See you tomorrow for dinner at yours," says Kate as she kisses my cheek to leave.

"Can't wait," we both pretend.

October 28th

Does anyone really like a dinner party? I can't help but think how bloody miserable they are, as I am laying the table. Why am I having one? It was Husband's bloody idea. Everyone coming would much rather stay at home eating some cheese off their lap, while watching *Silent Witness,* not having to talk to anyone. Hosting a dinner is like a war of attrition. The closer it gets to 3pm, the more everyone looks at their phone, secretly hoping that someone else is going to cancel. The mere whiff of a lack of babysitter. The hope that someone's child is unwell. Surely the only real reason to have children in the first place is so you don't have to go out to a dinner party? I stare at my phone. I could cancel. It's my dinner. But . . . I could say I have a "work crisis". Some of the springs have snapped on a trampoline? I have given myself food poisoning? My hoisin duck wrap was off? My own children are ill? But by

6pm, despite my constant staring at my phone, sadly no one has cancelled. The dinner is on. Clearly, even Claire's tarot have given her permission to go! And I feel suddenly exhausted by the whole prospect.

I have to cook for a start, and when you reach my age you can't serve rubbish. It has to be palatable, and preferably vaguely recognisable as something Jamie, Nigella or Yotam (as nobody calls him) might actually serve "at home". The days of undercooked chicken and a bag of Maltesers are over. And there's a hell of a lot more chopping to be done. I'm making some chicken and tomato baked thing from Jamie's *5 Ingredients* book, although I have forgotten the olives, so it's technically four, but who's counting? Olives are overrated anyway. And they break your teeth.

The first to arrive is Sally. She is half an hour early and I'm still in my leggings from work, although thankfully not in the tight, tit-binding T.

"Thank fuck for that," she announces, shoving a bottle of chilly wine at my chest as she walks through the door. "I'm sorry I'm early." She peels off her slightly damp mac and rams it right next to the cold bottle. "I just had to get out of there, I'm desperate for a drink."

Pig is supposed to be on "coat duty" but he's too busy watching flat-earth conspiracy theories on YouTube and turning his fingers yellow eating Wotsits, and Ella is out "studying" with her friend Abby from Carlton Academy. So it's me on coats 'n' door as Husband is "opening wine", which apparently takes hours and is hugely complicated and most certainly a male job of rank and distinction that involves a lot of important research – photographing the labels and checking their suitability/expense on some wine app.

"Good," says Sally, as she marches into our small, hot, sweaty kitchen, her hand open and ready. "You've opened the wine."

"Red or white?" asks Husband, already nursing a glass of red the size of a children's paddling pool.

"Which one is stronger?"

"Well, the vodka," he replies, waving a large bottle of Smirnoff Red.

"I'll have that with lime and soda."

"Skinny Bitch," nods Husband.

"I most certainly am," replies Sally, sitting down at the table with an *ouff*. "It's the worry and the nerves and the three bloody children."

"I'll make it strong, then."

Husband bends over his drinks tray meticulously, mixing like he's about to cure cancer, or if not, at least the effects of it on an anxious, overwrought spouse.

"Sorry Will's not here," says Sally, slouching on the table. "He's catching up on stuff he's missed at work, which appears to be a lot. Poor man. You would have thought they'd give him some time off, he's only just standing, but when you're your own boss, I suppose you have to keep the show on the road. Cheers!" She takes an enormous slug of her drink. "But I mean, fuck it, he could come out to dinner, couldn't he?"

"Oh, don't worry," replies Husband. "It means I have you all to myself tonight!" He chuckles. I look across at him. What is he doing?

"It's a girls' night, plus him," I add.

"Oh," replies Sally, taking another big sip of her vodka. "This should be fun."

Poor Sally, I think she was hoping for a rather more exciting night out. After all, she's barely seen anyone in weeks and she's wearing a very expensive pair of heels that she can hardly walk in, and she's blow-dried her hair. She's also dressed entirely in white like some sort of spa therapist, which is her go-to when she's going out. I'm sure it's a reaction to three boys hurling spaghetti all day, for as soon as she's ditched them, she dons the most 'dangerous' colour possible.

"How is Will?" asks Husband, sitting down and immediately crossing his legs and putting one hand over his crotch.

"He's fine," nods Sally, knocking another glug back. "He's a bollock down, obviously, but apart from that he's fine. Weirdly fine." Her large brown eyes narrow, and glance slightly to the side. "Do you think he's in denial?"

"How's he supposed to react?" Husband takes a sip of his wine. He needs both hands for the glass, but his left returns rapidly to his crotch. He is clearly terrified that his bits are withering on the vine by their mere proximity to Sally.

"Cry, maybe?" suggests Sally. "Talk about it? He was in bed for a few days while I waited on him, hand, foot and one bollock and then he rose like Lazarus and went back to work. Meanwhile, I'm crying and wringing my hands and making sure not to say the C-word in front of the children and trying to keep everything normal and it's like water off a duck's back to him. I caught him whistling the other day, putting his tie on in the mirror. Fucking whistling! Who does he think he is? Fucking Dick Van Dyke?" She drains her glass and waves in the general direction of Husband.

"That's definitely denial," says Claire, standing in the kitchen, taking off a giant black and white tasselled scarf last seen on a member of the Mujahidin. "Sam let me in," she says, placing a bottle of kombucha on the table. "I terrified the pants off him tapping on the window. God knows what he's watching."

"Mum?" asks Sam, following in after Claire, still attached to his iPad, dragging cords and earphones in his wake. "Can I have a Coke?"

"No."

"Why not? You're drinking."

"So?"

"It's not fair if you're drinking and I'm not allowed to."

"Oh, fine," I say, waving in the direction of the fridge and finishing my glass of wine. "Take one and finish whatever you're watching and take yourself off to bed."

"Sure," he says, still staring at his screen while simultaneously opening the fridge door. "I've only got twenty minutes left anyway."

"Good." I've lost interest. Sally and Claire are already ensconced at the table and I'm missing out.

"Hey mate!" says Husband, shooting Sam from across the room with his index finger like they're great ol' pals from the gym. "Whatcha watching?"

"Whaaat?" Sam removes an earphone.

"Whatcha watching?"

"*The Blair Witch Project.*" Sam cracks open a Coke with a hiss and leaves the room.

"It's a classic case of denial," says Claire, opening her own bottle and pouring herself a drink. "Have you tried this?" she asks, holding up the glass of golden liquid for us to inspect. "Very good for the gut." She taps her own, just in case we are unaware as to where exactly it is located. "It's all about gut health these days."

"Is it alcoholic?" queries Sally.

"No."

"Oh." Sally shakes her head, a little revolted.

"So, it is denial?" I ask.

"Oh yes." Claire is nodding, her very long earrings swinging in agreement. "Oh, do you like them?" she says, following my gaze. I don't. "Mystique." She plays with her lobe a little. "One of the perks of the job. Twenty per cent staff discount."

"Great," both Sally and I say at the same time.

"Useful," I add.

"Oh, it is," confirms Claire. "Come Christmas you'll all be getting something from the shop. Talking of Christmas, what are you guys doing?"

"We're going . . . away," announces Sally. She tries incredibly hard not to sound smug, but still the sentiment sneaks out. It was the pause before the word "away," that sealed it.

"Oh nice," replies Husband, straddling his chair. "Somewhere warm?" he asks.

"Anywhere but here," I hear myself saying out loud.

"Maldives," she replies.

Frankly, I would have preferred it if she'd farted or thrown up all over the table. Jealousy is an awful thing. It mugs you from behind when you least expect it. Breathe. It takes a moment, but I manage it.

"How wonderful," I say. "You've had a terrible time, you deserve it." There. I did it.

"Yes," agrees Claire, leaning over and patting the back of Sally's hand by way of overcompensation. "You definitely deserve it." Claire's smile is a little tight, but she manages it too. "How about you?" she says to me.

"Oh, Christ!" I roll my eyes. "I'm going to Jacqueline's with my older sister and her 'practically perfect in every way' children, where I shall be tortured on a daily basis for being an overweight failure with idiot children and no career to speak of. Upon which I shall drown myself in mulled wine and hope to make it to bed before I hit my head on the door frame and fall unconscious."

"Sounds about right," agrees Husband, taking a restorative sip of wine. "You?"

"I'm on my own," declares Claire. "Rob's got Jade, he's stormed the moral high ground, fenced it off and is working it for all it's worth. It's the first divorced Christmas and, as the 'perp', my punishment is to be on my own."

"Awwww." Now it's Sally's turn to pat Claire's hand and then everyone slowly turns and looks at me. There's a silence.

"Umm," I begin. Husband coughs and simulates rapidly cutting his throat with his index finger, his head bowed behind the ball-sack-saving chair back. I look at him and his swift slicing movements and, for some reason, it spurs me to do the exact opposite. "Then you must come to us. My mum would be delighted!"

"Are you sure?" asks Claire, looking sweetly relieved, her earrings now swinging with delight.

"Absolutely. I can't think of anything better. You must come. And stay as long as you want. Don't you think, darling?"

Just then the doorbell rings and there's an almighty scream from the sitting room.

"I'll get it," says Husband, taking a huge glug from his glass, only too delighted to leave the room.

"God, sorry," says Kate as she staggers a little into the kitchen. "I'm late and I've already drunk the wine I was supposed to drink . . . bring." She raises her hands in the air. "And I have terrified the shit out of your son!"

"It's his fault for watching *The Blair Witch Project*," I say, getting up to kiss her. She stinks of booze. "Where have you been?"

"You'll never guess." She smirks a little, looking at all four of us looking at her.

"Er, no, we won't." My husband shrugs. "Haven't a clue."

"So," says Kate, sitting down and filling her wine glass up to the top. "I had this new client turn up at the office today, he came to discuss the brief with me and at the end he said, do you fancy a glass of wine? And there's nowhere nice to drink round near our office and then I remembered I had a bottle of organic red wine in the car. It was for you." She grins at me. "But I knew you wouldn't mind."

"Not at all."

"If was for a good cause."

"Absolutely." I nod.

"So, is he nice?" asks Claire.

"He's great, funny, good-looking, single," smiles Kate, taking a swig from my glass. "I think he might be a keeper. And I'm not saying that because I'm pissed."

"No," agrees Claire.

"Although a pint of wine does tend to make any bloke more attractive," muses Sally, chasing an ice cube around her glass with her finger.

The dinner continues on in this vein. We sit, slightly cramped, at the round, wobbly pine table Husband and I bought fifteen years ago when we were high on hope and still laughed at each other's jokes. I serve some edible, if not very interesting, chicken, without olives, but with rice, while Sally and Kate play "marry, shag, bin", slowly working their way through the Tory Cabinet. Claire, after ditching the kombucha for tequila, joins in but upgrades the quality of shag by adding in historical figures as they were, but not now, as that would necessitate exhumation. Which is a relief. Sally has a massive crush on Warren Beatty and Claire is equally keen on Oliver Reed (each to their own), so I'm thankful we were going fantasy fuck rather than reality.

I clear the table without incident and suggest a course of cheese, which is greeted with collective negativity. Only Husband fills his plate with a wheel of brie, a fistful of biscuits and an A4 slice of cheddar.

"Do you know what I really want," says Kate, waving her hand at me. "A Magnum."

She must be drunk. Kate never eats sweets or chocolate; she'd rather have fifteen fags than pollute herself with a pudding. I open the freezer and deliver a box of Mini Magnums to the table and before I turn back around to close the door, the box has been demolished and Kate, Sally and Claire are all tucking into Mini Classics, waving the sticks at each other.

I am about to sit down when the front door slams shut and there's something amounting to another scream in the corridor.

"Jesus Christ!" Ella comes storming into the kitchen, brandishing what looks like a magazine and a fistful of papers in her hand. "What is this?" She deposits the magazine and the papers on the table. "How *could* you?" She stares at me.

"Have you been drinking?" I ask. Her winged eyeliner is smudged and she's got lipstick on her braces.

"HOW COULD YOU!" Her stare is dramatic. Her body is tense.

"How could I what?"

"This!" She jabs the table with her short, nail-bitten index finger.

"What?"

The whole table is silent, mostly appalled at the appearance of Ella with her buttock-skimmer skirt, her cropped top and her boobs so underwired that she could possibly lick her own cleavage. She was supposed to be "studying" with Abby from Carlton Academy, not going out clubbing! Then, slowly but surely, we all look down at the table, and at the flier, surrounded by Magnum wrappers and glasses of wine.

"What," whispers Claire, "is that . . .?"

Yes. It's me. I can see it's me. I am only hoping that the rest of the table can't quite get to grips with the image. Or equate the two of us together. But, yes, it's me. I have a fist in the air, a tit over one eye, a sweat patch, a camel toe and thighs that could smother a small child. Perfect.

"Is it . . .?" Husband slowly turns to look at me and frowns so much his little tiny eyes disappear.

"Oh . . ." says Kate, flatly.

"Crikey," adds Claire.

"Holy fuck!" says Sally, her hand moving quite slowly towards her wide-open mouth.

Holy fuck indeed.

October 31st

Short of crawling through every side street in the Kilburn area on my hands and knees, peering through letterboxes or picking up the piles of fliers that appear to have been scattered all over the pavements of NW6 like fallen autumn leaves, my only course of action post-flier-gate is to brazen it out. Ella's response is to not speak to me for the next two days, which suits me fine as I am not terribly enamoured with her at the moment either. Her clubbing outfit was nothing short of "pole dancer on her night off" and she's obviously been going out on the town with Abby three or four times a week; no wonder I've been doing her homework and she's given up French. Pig couldn't care less and can't understand what the fuss/tension is about; just so long as he's kept in *Fortnite* skins he's happy, along with the occasional can of full-fat Coke. It's only Husband who keeps spontaneously bursting out with laughter at the image that has clearly been etched onto his frontal lobe. One can only assume this is during moments of abject boredom, which appear to be every twenty minutes.

Pig's school is fortunately a flier-free zone – no one from his school lives in our part of town, and if they did, they would never admit to it, let alone acknowledge a free flier. None of them read anyway. That's not to say that they aren't all members of book clubs, for they are. But they rarely read the books, and they spend most of the evening drinking copious amounts of wine and bitching about other people's Instagram.

"So? What are you coming as tonight?" asks Madison, standing next to me in the queue. She smiles, it's blinding, even in the dull grey morning light. I must have looked baffled for she continues. "You're dressing up, right?"

"Me?"

"For Halloween? You've got to get dressed up for Halloween."

"Isn't it just for the children?"

"Halloween is wasted on children. All that candy, it's disgusting. Last year Rick and I went to THE most amazing party, and I was in this cute little basque, with stockings and a thong and this little cat mask." She makes a cat shape over her already quite feline face. "And we had *such* fun." She leans over and whispers in my ear, her fat shiny lips popping against my lobe. "We had THE best sex that night. Rick was at it like a dawg. In-sat-iable."

It's 8.25am, it's drizzling, and I have barely met Rick but the idea of him being a "dawg" . . . is a little unpleasant, to say the least. My only real recollection of Rick is him taking out two toddlers who had the misfortune to be standing at the end of his lane at the finish line for the father's race. He was so keen to win he saw the loss of two mobile phones and his Tesla keys on the track, plus two under-fives, as worthwhile collateral for the glory of a red rosette.

"He's such a dawg!" she repeats with a little laugh, mainly to herself. "Oh! Hey, Erica!"

"Hey!" Erica grins back as she makes her way over through the increasingly territorial crowd. "All ready for tonight?"

"Hell, yeah!" Madison offers up her hand and Erica high-fives it, even though she isn't American. "What are you coming as?"

"Oh, just a witch," replies Erica.

"Home clothes then," I reply, trying to join in. They both turn and look at me.

"So how many are coming to yours?" continues Erica, ignoring me.

I'm not really listening as she ticks off the guests on her well-manicured hands.

"And you're coming," she informs me. "With Sam, and your daughter . . ." She clicks her fingers in front of my nose.

"Ella?"

"Ella," she nods. "The whole gang."

"I'll have to come after work."

"Work?" Madison looks at me a little quizzically.

"I work at Bounce. In marketing," I add quickly.

"Bounce?" The frown eludes her.

"An exercise facility," I explain.

"That trampoline place up north somewhere?" I nod. "Oh . . . I dropped Saffron and Fi off there yesterday for a party. They had this weird poster outside of some middle-aged woman with her fist in the air." I smile, hoping against hope. "You should really upgrade that." Her square-tipped finger points in my face. "Yeah," she confirms at her own suggestion. "It can't be good for business." They open the school doors and there's a sudden, violent surge not dissimilar to the Harrods' sale. "See you at six," she cries as she's carried off, by a sea of blow-dries and the gentle waft of Givenchy.

Over at Bounce! Deborah is delighting in the fact that her marketing strategy has resulted in seven women approaching the park to see if they have exercise classes for the over-fifties. Clearly my target audience.

"You see," she says, grinning, standing in Reception and hydrating herself, having just done a quick twenty minutes on the main trampoline. "I told you it would work! This place is empty most of the day with the kids at school, so we need mums to fill in the daytime slots after the early-morning toddlers have gone home. So I'm book-ing in classes." She sucks determinedly at the teat of her water bottle and pulls out a sheet of paper from her satchel and flapping it out in front of her, she reads. "Mums and Tums. Mums and Bums. Mums, Bums and Tums and, um, Total Mums."

"Uber Mums?" I suggest.

"What? The taxi? No."

"Um, what's the difference in the classes?"

"None," she replies. "But I think we're onto a winner. Shall I book you in? You may as well, you're stuck here all day anyway."

"Let me think about it," I say, walking towards the stairs, suddenly conscious of my tums, bums, tons and total lack of fitness.

I sigh slightly when I reach the top. I don't see Husband or Rob or Will for that matter worrying if their arse looks big in their trousers, or if the five-month-old they all seem to be gestating shows through their T-shirts or strains over the top of their swimming trunks, or bothers them while chugging back their beers, or prevents them from ordering another round of pork scratchings. Why do women spend half their lives hating themselves? And the other half look-ing back at photos thinking they didn't look *that* bad after all? A life of anxiety and regret. No wonder I drink too much.

At my desk, with the smell of feet and coffee in the air (the café on the other side of Debbie's office is already full of wall-eyed mothers pretending to watch their preschool toddlers in the foam park below, while sending Snapchats to their friends), I sit down and go through my emails. It's not a hugely long list, and mainly consists of spam from various websites I have visited while at work. There's one from Sally making sure that I am going to Madison's Halloween party. "Promise," she insists. "What are you wearing? Do you have a costume? I can't be arsed," she types. "I really can't. Although I could put on a polo shirt and some slacks and come as a 'Karen'?" I look down at what I am wearing and realise I'm almost there.

At about 6pm, after a day of fruitlessly calling up various local magazines and trying to place adverts in their next issue, as I leave Bounce! I walk past the noticeboard. Deborah's been busy – there are numerous Mums and Tums posters pinned up for different times of the day, complete with a Bic biro sellotaped to a string and embedded into a lump of Blu Tack. I see my clenched fist has been used as some sort of middle-aged lady call to arms; I also see that one person has signed up to all the classes and, on closer inspection, that person appears to be me. I contemplate scrubbing my name out, but I don't. Maybe it's a sign?

Madison's fragrant home has been pimped to beyond its already really rather glamorous and expensive life. What is more usually one of those huge wedding-cake-type houses, with front gates that buzz open and flowers in window boxes that get updated every season, has been turned into a Hammer Horror spectacular with webs on the windows and skeletons hanging from the roof, a giant smoking cauldron on the porch and an enormous tarantula in the off-street parking space. It's impressive. She must have spent days doing it. Or someone did. A whole team probably. Mr Hancox would certainly give her a ten out of ten for effort, if only he was allowed out of Erica's basement.

"Welcome, welcome," she says answering the door, dressed like a French maid with an axe through her head and stitches around her neck. "So lovely to see you!" Madison is on autopilot, or drunk, or high on Haribo, because she never normally speaks to me like that.

"Wooooo!" says Sam, through a couple of holes in his white sheet. He puts his hands in the air. "Trick or treat!"

"There you go!" says Madison, giving him a little pat on the back. "And what have you come as?" she asks Ella, who is standing next to me, exuding nothing but fury at the idea of attending any party that Pig might be invited to.

"Your worst nightmare," she replies, with a metal smile that glows green by the light of the smoking cauldron.

"And what's that?"

"A teenage girl," declares Ella, and walks straight past her and into the hall.

"Sorry." I shrug.

"Come on in," smiles Madison and takes a large swig of her punch.

Downstairs, and her kitchen island is groaning under the weight of Halloween-themed food. There are piles of sweets – eyeballs, fangs, witches' hats. There are giant snot-green jellies, ghost-shaped meringues, pumpkin-shaped crisps and sticky ribs made to look like the Devil's fingers, as well as masses of slices of pizza. The room is packed with screaming children dressed in highly curated costumes, mostly borrowed from a theatrical store. Sam appears to be the only one in something home-made. Most of the mothers are wearing a little nod to Halloween, cute devil's horns, some sexy cat's ears, nothing that detracts too much from their overall fragrance. Still, there are a few who have really embraced the theme. Madison – the Murdered French Maid. Erica – as Harley Quinn, sporting white bunches and hot pants and some very fetching cowboy boots. She looks fabulous; clearly Giovanna's training sessions have been worth it. There's also a bloke dressed as a shower unit, complete with dagger and floating plastic curtain.

"Excuse me," I say. "What have you come as?"

"The shower scene in *Pyscho*," he replies. "It's me!" He opens the curtains.

"Jesus, Dave!" I take a sip of my very sweet fruit punch. "You've made an effort."

"Not really," he says. "I recycle the same old thing every year."

"There you are!" sighs Sally, taking a sip of her punch and wincing. "Gross," she adds, putting it down on the table. "Hi," she says, sticking her hand out. "Sally."

"Oh." I can feel a sudden rush of blood to my cheeks, my heart is pounding. My two worlds are colliding and one of them is dressed like a shower and the other is wearing Devil's horns, carrying a small plastic trident. 'This is . . ."

"James's dad," says Dave, shaking her hand. "He's in the same year as Sam."

"Nice outfit, James's dad," replies Sally. "I'm the door-mat to Nathan, Alfie, Ben and fucking Will, although he's not in anyone's year." Her voice is high and her cheeks are almost as flushed as mine. "Can I have a word?" she says to me.

"People! People!" Madison is standing on a chair and clapping in her own kitchen. "It's time!" There's a cheer and some of the children raise their single-use plastic pumpkin-shaped buckets in the air. "It's time to hit those streets." She points to her lower-ground side door. "It's time to ter-rify the neighbours . . . load up with candy. It's fun time! It's Halloween!!!" The cheers get louder and louder. "It's time to TRICK or TREAT!!!"

The applause is rapturous! Dave is whistling loudly from inside his shower curtain. God, I hate fun. There is noth-ing more unappealing than things that are supposed to be fun. I look around the room. Ella is leaning lividly against the wall, scuffing the wallpaper with the sole of her boot. Pig has a meringue gently exploding in his fist. James is waiting patiently next to his father, dressed in a *Scream* mask, admiring his long-nailed gloves. This is hell. I am desperate to go home.

"I've just tested positive for chlamydia." Sally whispers in my ear.

"What?" I shout over the shouting.

"Chlamydia!" yells Sally.

Dave's head suddenly pokes out from behind his shower curtain.

November 7th

The last week has been more hellish than the hell that was Madison's Halloween party.

Firstly, Sam, James, Saffron and Caesar LOST Entrepreneur's Week, despite Erica's husband (who used to work at Saatchi & Saatchi) coming up with the name for the stress balls – Don't Stress – and him creating a logo and a poster and printing them all up at work, as well as making matching T-shirts for the boys. They lost. Erica threatened to appeal. She booked an appointment with the headmaster. But Madison told her: "In the words of *Frozen* – Let it go!" So there was a lot of coffee drunk in the red gingham café, with me forced to be in attendance, bemoaning the victory of the Not So Innocents and their smoothies that unfortunately didn't give the whole year diarrhoea and therefore won the competition.

"They just bloody mashed up bloody fruit," complained Erica, a small cotton handkerchief in her hand. "How the fuck is that 'entrepreneurial'?"

"Yeah," nodded Madison, equally bereft, unable to cope with the first-ever loss of her entire life. "Where's the skill in that?"

Dave somehow contrived to not be there. He is working on a project, apparently.

Secondly, Sally is on her knees. Somehow, in some way, and for some bloody reason, one-ball-sac Will has managed to give his wife chlamydia. He keeps swearing he hasn't had sex with someone else, that he caught it off a towel in the gym or maybe he picked it up in hospital. But Kate keeps telling Sally that's not possible. That you only get bacterial infections like chlamydia from sex or sharing sex toys. The latter makes us all a little nauseous as we sit in the brown Misery Café, discussing the matter at 9am on a Saturday morning.

Claire has insisted on the venue as she has to open the shop at ten and it's just around the corner from Mystique. Sally doesn't care where she goes, just so long as she can leave the house, and I am pretty much of the same opinion. And Kate, well, Kate can do what she's told as she has nothing else but "free will" for the rest of the week.

"I'm telling you," says Kate. "And I don't mean to be mean," she adds. "But you can't get chlamydia from a towel. Can you, Claire?"

"Don't ask me," replies Claire.

"You're medical."

"I'm not, I'm a counsellor and I trained in the last century, so there's a lot I have forgotten."

"But you did science?"

"He swears blind he hasn't." Sally plays vigorously with the sugar packet. "I am not sure what to believe. I mean . . . he's never looked at anyone else in his life."

"Well, that's for sure," I agree.

"True," nods Kate.

"If it's anything, then it's probably a one-off,' advises Claire. "A survival thing. I haven't died, but am I still a man? That sort of idea. Proving he's still male, and got it, as it were."

"Got it?" Sally curls her nose in disgust.

"How about 'I haven't died so I really want to love and appreciate my wife'?" asks Kate, sounding surprisingly romantic, for someone who spends most of her free time swiping left or right. "Don't go out shagging. Or sharing sex toys."

"Honestly," says Sally. "Stop it with the sex toys. Just the image of Will with fluffy handcuffs is enough to make me ill."

"It'll be more than handcuffs, believe you me," adds Kate. "You can only really get lice off handcuffs."

Thirdly, Ella's been suspended. The lack of preps, the lack of attendance, the paucity of attitude have all got too much for Carlton Academy, and they called me in the middle of the day at Bounce! and asked me to come and collect her from school. I suggested that she walked home by way of punishment, but I was told it was against health and safety rules for her to be kicked out of school in the middle of the day. I wanted to say she has a fake ID saying she's eighteen years old if there was any problem with the police. Instead, I had to leave work, which wasn't that much of an ordeal, and collect her during my lunch hour.

"This is SO inconsiderate," I yelled across the gear stick. "I've had enough of this. Why can't you just bloody do some studying!"

"Because I bloody hate school," she yelled back, her head wobbling, her streaked blusher shining orange in the sun.

"Don't swear!"

"Bloody's not a swear word."

"Yes it is."

"And anyway, why not? You bloody swear all the bloody time!"

"No I fucking don't!" There is something about Ella that makes me lose all sense of proportion or rationale. I can't help it. I can't control myself. I would never have spoken to my Mother Dearest like this.

"Well . . . I am leaving school after GCSEs and there's nothing you can do about it!"

"Oh yeah?" My head was rattling like a cobra's tail. "Well . . . then . . . I'll . . . I'll throw you out of the house!"

"That's brilliant parenting!" She leant back in her seat with contentment. "Then I'll be homeless and become a prostitute and get a drug habit."

"If that's what you want to do, be my guest!"

"Then you'll be sorry."

"I won't."

"You've always loved Sam more than me."

"No, I haven't."

"He's your favourite."

"No, he isn't."

"You've always hated me."

We sat in silence in the static traffic. Both hating each other. It's amazing how long a minute is when you're stuck behind a bin lorry feeling furious. I sighed. She sighed.

"Listen," I said. "Why don't you buckle down and just get these exams out of the way and then, you know, you can do the stuff you really want to do?"

"Like what?"

"I don't know. Art? You like that."

"And dance."

"And that . . . *Can* you do A Level dance?"

"I don't know, I'll find out."

"I promise you, life does get better after GCSEs. You'll be amazed what it's like when the path is clear and there is some sun on the horizon." She turned and smiled at me. "Do you know you've got a massive spot on your chin?" I asked.

"I'm well aware of that," she replied. "Why the fuck did you point it out?"

"I'm sorry, I don't know. And don't swear."

"Well, you have a fucking massive moustache. It's like hanging out with an Afghan hound." She got out of the car and slammed the door.

I flipped down the sunshade and slid back the mirror and leant forward to inspect my top lip. She was right. I appear to have a hamster living right under my nose.

November 12th

Husband has gone away for work, which is a massive relief. It means the level of methane in our bedroom is back down to WHO levels, toothpaste doesn't decorate the bathroom sink, there's zero snoring and I can drink a bottle of wine to myself and chomp a whole tube of Sour Cream Pringles without having to share, while watching cosy crime thrillers, dressed in my orange terry dressing gown. In short, bliss. I have to pretend I am missing him, obviously, as I expand on the sofa awaiting the phone call at about 7pm where we both run through the day, and I say something interesting about the children. I have just popped five Pringles in my mouth at once as the phone goes.

"Hi there," I mumble.

"Now right," comes a familiar voice, picking up exactly where she left off. "I gather from your father . . ."

"Mother! How did you get the landline number?" I sit bolt upright and splutter, little processed potato flakes scattering all over the sofa.

"You rang your father on it the other day," says Jacqueline. "And also, he tells me you want to invite a friend for Christmas."

"Mmm."

"Are you eating?" Jacqueline despises food and the weakness in those who use it. She seems to have survived thus far in life on a diet of dust and gin. She always claims that she was named after Jacqueline Kennedy because she was so glamorous, although the fact that she was built like a swizzle stick and injected her arse with amphetamines every morning to keep thin was something she also embraced. The "no woman can ever be too rich or too thin" ethos of the charming Wallis Simpson was also one of her little mantras we heard when growing up.

"Crisps."

"I didn't ask what you were eating. I asked *if* you were eating. Could you please refrain from chewing in my ear? It's disgusting. It's like being in a farmyard with the masticating cows and sheep. Anyway, it's not even supper time."

Jacqueline is also a stickler for timing. Meals, such as they are, are served at specific hours of the day. Breakfast at 8.30am. Lunch at 1pm sharp. Drinks (most importantly) at 6pm and supper is at 8pm. I remember one Christmas when Ella was about seven months old and we'd waited all day for presents and booze, and finally at about 5.45pm I was so exhausted I went upstairs to bath Ella and put her to bed, only to return downstairs less than half an hour later to find all the champagne had been drunk and a small pile of gifts (mine) piled up on a chair. They had started, and indeed finished, without me.

"What took you so long?" my mother declared, as she drained her glass and the last of the bubbles. "You know we start at 6pm."

"I'm on my own tonight," I say.

"How is your life?" she asks.

"Going well, actually."

"Well? That's nice . . ." There's a pause. She sounds wrong-footed. "For a change."

"Ella's . . ."

"So, Richard says you want to invite a girlfriend for Christmas?"

"Yes."

"I have to say it's most irregular. A girlfriend . . . girlfriend? Has *The Change* turned you into a lesbian?"

"The Change? A lesbian? No?" There's quite a lot to unpick in her question. "No!"

"That's good. Although I have to say, Richard was getting quite overexcited about it all. Do you remember what he was like with those girls on *Strictly*? It's terribly cool to be a lesbian these days. Isn't it? You could be cool, darling!" She pauses again and I am waiting for it. "At last. But you're not."

There it is.

"Wouldn't that be amazing? To be cool, at last," I agree.

"Jenny has lots of lesbian friends. Loads of them!" Here we go. "What are they called now?"

"LGBTQI+?"

"No, Barbara and Delphi."

"That's two."

"I know!"

"She has two lesbian friends."

"Well, it's more than you. *And* they're a couple. But that's Australia for you, very liberal." She laughs her liberal laugh, and I can see her liberal face from here, tight, with a rictus grin and overcompensating liberal eyes. "Anyway," she inhales. "Back to your little friend . . ."

"Claire."

"Yes, Claire, tell her she is welcome, poor girl. On her own for Christmas . . . Was it a messy divorce?" She can't help herself. "I mean, all divorces are messy, aren't they? But was hers? Was it very bad? Where are her poor little children?"

"She only has one."

"Only one. Oh . . ." I can hear her brain ticking away, trying to make this a salient point, a reason, a something, possibly for the divorce. "And she, or he, or they (liberal laugh) is not spending Christmas with her . . . interesting. So the child is alone, with its father?"

"Her daughter. This year. Yes."

"Her *daughter*. Gosh . . . How's your other little single friend, Kate, does she want to come for Christmas, in for a penny, as they say?"

"She usually spends Christmas abroad, or with her own parents."

"Kate has parents?"

"Anyway, Mum, I must go. Sam is being suspiciously quiet and I have to feed him."

"Cooking something nice?"

"Deliveroo."

"How disgusting," she replies and hangs up the phone.

I pop three more Pringles in my mouth and climb off the sofa, looking for Pig. Upstairs, I open his bedroom door and poke my head round the corner and can't see him. That's weird. I knock on Ella's door. She can't hear me obviously as she is doing her homework with her headphones on. I knock again. Nothing. I open her door and find her indeed wearing her headphones, but she's not doing her homework, she's painting her nails.

"Ella!" I tap her on the shoulder.

She turns swiftly around. "Whaaat?"

"I thought you were doing your homework?"

"I have," she replies. "It was easy."

"Oh great," I smile. "Have you seen Sam?"

"He's looking up porn in his bedroom." My blood runs cold. My heart stops. My mouth falls open. "Oh, don't worry," she continues, picking at the pink varnish on her nails. "Everyone has a look, once."

"But he's *ten*."

"Ten, twelve, fifteen . . . they're all at it."

"How do you know that's what he's doing?"

"He asked me how to spell it."

"Maybe if you can't spell the word porn, then you're probably too young to watch it!" I am horrified. With her. With him. With the whole bloody horrible world that they are growing up in, where everything and everyone is sexualised. Where *Love Island* is fine and under boobs and arse cracks are permanently on display and everyone wants to fill their lips and freeze their faces. And what you do, say, think and achieve means nothing unless you look like a superannuated Barbie doll on hyaluronic acid. "I can't believe you." I collapse onto her bed and I feel my eyes stinging with tears. "That's so irresponsible. Do you know once he's seen it there's no going back to the age of innocence? That's it! Childhood over. Boom! How could you!"

"Relax, Mum," she says. "I told him it's spelt p-a-w-n. He's been looking at crap watches for hours. He's delighted."

I knock on his door. "Sam?"

"What?" I hear the rustling of a duvet and the frantic shutting of a laptop.

"What are you doing?"

"Nothing."

I walk in and he's sitting bolt upright in bed, his cheeks flushed, smiling sweetly like butter wouldn't melt.

"Ella tells me you've been – surfing the net?"

"No."

"That you've been looking stuff up?" I sit down on his bed. I'm contemplating doing "the chat". The chat that you're supposed to have with all teenage boys about how to treat girls and respect and consent. It really isn't my job to do this. It is surely Husband's? Oh God. Deep breath. Why is it always me?

"So you know girls . . .?" I start.

Pig looks at me and rolls his baby-blue eyes. "You're not going to give me the chat about a cup of tea, are you?"

"What?"

"A cup of tea."

"What's a cup of tea got to do with the price of fish?"

"God." He exhales in abject frustration, like he's soooo over this. "So . . . if a girl asks for a cup of tea and you give it to her there and then, that's fine. But if she asks for a cup of tea and then falls asleep on the sofa while you're making the cup of tea, you can't wake her up and force her to drink the cup of tea. Also, if she asked for a cup of tea on Monday, it doesn't mean that she'll want another cup of tea on Friday. And if she's drunk a cup of tea once, it doesn't mean she *ever* wants it again. No matter how many times you offer her a cup of tea, no thank you means no thank you."

"Right." I'm quite confused. I think I might have drunk more wine than I thought.

"Just because you've given a girl a cup of tea once, it doesn't mean she ever wants to drink it again. She might want coffee," he adds.

"Coffee?"

"*Tea*." He nods and winks and taps the side of his nose.

"Oh *tea*!" It's the most bizarre euphemism I have ever heard. I wonder idly if Dave and I should go out to tea? "So have you been looking at tea on the internet?"

"No!" he says, looking horrified. "That's *disgusting*. But I have found some very nice watches. Do you want to look?"

"Sure," I say, feeling palpably relieved to have dodged The Chat for another night. "Budge up." I climb into bed with him. He's just had a shower, he's in fresh pyjamas and he smells so clean no one could possibly be cross with him.

"Have you seen that?" He shows me a revolting gold and diamond watch that looks too heavy to lift, let alone get it close enough to your face to tell the time. "That's the sort of watch Juice WRLD used to have."

"Juice Box?" I ask, just to annoy him.

"I hate you, Mum! You're SO annoying."

"I know," I say and kiss him on the forehead.

November 17th

"Oh, it's you," says Mrs Rees, as she opens a small crack in her front door, before stepping back to reveal an electric-pink floral tabard.

"Don't I normally come every other Tuesday?" I ask.

"You didn't last time."

She's walking with her back to me, through her crowded, umbrella-packed hall and into her sitting room, where Winston, the cat, is sitting on the white leather sofa, immobile, inflated, looking very much like a stuffed cushion, watching *EastEnders*.

"I WhatsApped," I say. "To say I couldn't."

"Did you?"

"And you read it." I scramble around in my handbag, riffling between the curled receipts, bent and broken fags and a half-opened packet of Wrigley's Extra. "It says so on my phone. Look, there's a double blue tick, you read it. I did say I couldn't come."

"I don't remember reading it," she says with a wave of her clawed hand, still manicured to pink-tipped perfection. "I always think you lot are so rude. What happened to making a phone call, calling people up, having a chat, rather than messing people around at the last minute, without a care in the world? What's wrong with you all? A meeting is a meeting. An appointment is an appointment. It's not something that you think you might do, unless you get a better offer somewhere else. You can't just send a text five minutes before you're supposed to meet. It's rude. It's disrespectful. I mean, I might have made you a cake."

"Oh, I am so sorry, Mrs Rees, I really am. Something came up at work. I had to do a photo shoot. I'm sorry. Did you make me a cake?"

"No." She sits down on her white sofa and slightly opening her legs, she leans forward to pick up her cup of tea, takes a noisy sip and puts it back down. "And I've seen your photo shoot for that place you work at—"

"Right?"

"Fucking awful." She sniffs. "What are you doing? Leaping in the air like that? A woman of your age. It's embarrassing. What do your children think? I bet Ella's embarrassed, poor kid, her mother making a fool of herself like that. Who do you think you are? Nadia Comăneci?"

"Who?"

She simply shakes her head again and picks up her cup and hands it to me. "Make us another brew, will you?"

It's not a question.

I walk into her kitchen. Little has changed since the 1960s. She has a free-standing gas stove, a couple of beige Formica-fronted units and a row of white ceramic jars with their contents labelled in black capital letters on the front. Her sink is square and made of white porcelain – it's old and chipped – but I bet they'd flog it for three grand in Daylesford. She has pale green floral Formica square tiles on the floor, a few curling at the edges, and a small red, round, wooden-legged table in the corner of the room with two chairs. One is pulled out. The other is firmly lodged in the corner. It hasn't been used in over a decade.

While I wait for the kettle to come to boil on the stove, she shouts at me from the other room.

"Winston went missing last week," she begins.

"Oh yes!" I shout back. "I presume you found him." I laugh.

"Well, yes, as he is sat here, I imagine I did."

"Of course."

"First off I thought he'd been catnapped, you know that? For money? There's a lot of it going on. Especially around here. People nicking other people's pets and then charging them to get them back. You've seen the posters."

"I have."

"I was ever so worried. Walking up and down the road, calling out his name. Hours and hours, I was. And then, when I didn't get a ransom note, I thought, maybe he's been run over."

"Oh no."

"So, I called the vet's to see if anyone had handed in a dead cat."

"Is that what you're supposed to do?" The kettle's boiled and I shove a couple of teabags into her brown china pot.

"How the hell should I know? Anyway, the vet's not heard anything and turns out Winston's not dead."

"No," I say, pouring her a cup of tea and adding the milk and sugar, before handing it to her and sitting back down on the sofa, next to Winston.

"No, much worse than that."

"Worse?" I glance at the cat, it looks OK.

"Yes, he's being fed by the family next door and he's moved into their house. The bastards. They bought him his own bed and everything."

"What?"

"That's much worse than being dead," she continues. "Dead, I could've coped with. Dead is a tragedy. But that. Disloyal little shit. All it takes is a pouch of Kitekat trout 'n' jelly and he's bloody anyone's. Twelve years, I've had that cat!" She looks sternly down at Winston, and the cat slowly closes its eyes with smug contentment. "No wonder he's so bloody fat. He's had two suppers a night for months. I've had to buy the bloody Kitekat now. It's expensive, let me tell you. I mean, what else was I supposed to do, otherwise he's going to pop over the wall at a moment's notice . . . How's your friend and her divorce?"

"Oh," I pause and take a sip of my tea. "She seems OK. She's on her own for Christmas, so I've invited her to stay with me."

"That's nice of you, dear," she says with uncharacteristic warmth. "I've been on my own for Christmas for the last twelve years." She shifts in her seat. "It's only a day. That's what I tell myself. Just one day. But you'd think it's the most important thing in the whole world. Commercialised bollocks, if you ask me. When I was a child, we barely celebrated the thing. I remember having to go to church at midnight and we'd wake up early for our stockings which were granddad's socks stuffed with fruit and nuts and a chocolate bar if we were lucky, and that was it. We'd eat some sort of meat on Christmas Eve. But the turkey thing's American. We'd have a goose, if we were very lucky, and some potatoes, but we wouldn't buy the goose until very late on Christmas Day when they dropped their prices. We didn't have a fridge. No one had. Eggnog. Plum pudding. Bed. That was it. Now it goes on for months. Months and bloody months of it. It's alright for everyone else, but for us lot, stuck at home on our own, with nothing but the telly, it's bloody boring, let me tell you."

"Aren't you tempted to go and see your children?"

"Well, Nick's in South Africa and I am not going anywhere near there. Awful place. What he sees in that continent I have no idea." She curls her top lip. "And Janice has married Pavel and I can't understand a word he says. Nah," she says. "I'd rather sit here on my own and have a sherry and watch the Queen."

It's on the tip of my tongue. The idea of bringing Mrs Rees to spend the festive season with Jacqueline and Richard would be too much fun by half. I suspect they might even end up agreeing on a good many things. How spoilt and awful this generation of children are; how lazy and awful my generation is; and how much better things were during the war, when there was integrity and backbone and lips were stiff and, in my mother's case, simply no one was overweight.

"You could always come and stay with us for Christmas?" I suggest, quite shocking myself. My mother would actually kill me.

"You?" Mrs Rees looks me up and down as if she has never seen me before. "With your family?"

"Yes?"

"I'm alright, thanks," she sniffs. "I like my sherry and the Queen, thank you very much."

"Oh, OK," I reply, feeling my cheeks flare with embarrassment.

There's a pause. We both stare at the telly. Fortunately, the Queen Vic's buzzing in *EastEnders* and there's plenty of chat.

"Do you want a ciggie?" she asks, reaching into the front pocket of her tabard and offering up a Lambert & Butler.

"Thanks." I take one.

"So," she lights up and inhales. "What's going on with you?"

"Me?"

"Yup." She exhales. "You."

I'm a little stumped. No one's asked me this question since before I had children.

Post-partum, women seem to cease to exist. Even when you're having a baby, you're simply referred to as "Mum". "How's Mum today?" "Can we take Mum's blood pressure?" "Does Mum mind if we give her a seven-foot episiotomy?" And then once the children are born, you are even more invisible. They (the children) see you, of course they do, but only as part of the service industry. Food, warmth, hugs, love, clothes, money, etc. But no one else does. The high street will flog you stuff, but only to help you look after the children. They guilt-trip you into spending huge, unnecessary amounts of cash. But they cease to cater for you as a person, unless you want some elasticated easy-on slacks that are machine-washable and don't need ironing, as you're too busy with everyone else to warrant spending actual time on yourself. You're also never photographed alone again. Not that you want to be because you're wearing elasticated slacks. But frankly, no one is interested anyway, you are merely a prop for the main event. Them.

"Well, Ella is not doing well at school and Sam's obsessed with gaming . . ."

"I didn't ask about them, I asked about you."

"Oh," I say. I smoke my Lambert, just to buy a few seconds. "I'm OK," I shrug. "Tired, fed up, could do with a holiday, the usual."

"I'm sure it's hard work keeping it all together. And you've got an older mum as well." She nods. Jacqueline would love to hear that! "You're the squeezed middle. I hear about them all the time on the telly."

"If only I had a middle," I laugh.

"You're not bad-looking," she says. "Don't do yourself down all the time. If you made a bit more of an effort, did your hair, had your nails done, you might look quite nice. You never know until you try. It's easy to lose your way when you're your age, you know. I know, I did. People didn't talk about things back then, which might be a good thing. You all talk too much these days. But I remember feeling terrible and miserable and sad. I do. My children had left home, and it was just me and Stan and the telly. I was just overwhelmed with disappointment. It happens to us all. *Life*. It's how you deal with it that counts. Sort your hair out, for a start." She pats the back of her immaculate, steely-grey curls. "I go once a week. It makes me feel better. And get those nails done." She looks down at my hands, appalled. "Not for anyone else. Who cares about anyone else and what they think? Just for you."

"Isn't this conversation supposed to be the other way around?" I ask, fidgeting in my seat. "Aren't I supposed to be helping you?"

"But you are, dear." She smiles. "You're making me feel useful and that's all any of us old bags really want. To feel useful."

November 30th

Kate calls me back within seconds of me leaving her a message. She's still trying to get eye contact with the hot barista who works around the corner from her office.

"All I want is a bloody chocolate powder fucking heart on my latte," she whispers down her phone. "Is it too much to ask?"

"On a latte, yes. No one puts chocolate on a latte."

"You know what I mean. Anyway, your message was intriguing. A full makeover? You're finally getting rid of the My Little Pony look and the moustache."

"Moustache?"

"Oh, sorry."

"Why didn't you tell me?"

"The same reason why no one ever tells you that you have spinach in your teeth. What am I supposed to say? 'By the way, babe, you've got a 'tache, it's big and ginger and sitting on your face like a cat'."

"Ella told me I had one the other day."

"What can I say? Out of the mouths of babes . . . etc. So what do you want, the full snooker ball, with hair and nails?"

"The works!"

"No one says that anymore."

"Right, is there one place that does it all?"

"No. You've got to make lots of different appointments. Have you got a pen and paper?"

"Yup."

"Right . . ."

Kate sits at her desk and opens her phone and hands over all her secret telephone numbers to all the smartest places in town.

"If they say that they don't have anything till after Christmas, tell them you're my friend and ask to talk to Anton."

"Right."

"Don't take any shit, as they are used to women who are complete bitches and so hangry they can't see straight. Most of them haven't eaten since the last century and are so bonkers they are liable to walk out of a moving car. So don't be nice. Tip big and you'll be fine. Oh, and say you want a choppy bob."

"Really?"

"They're *the* haircut of the moment."

"Is it?"

"Very now."

"And anyway, you need to get rid those split ends."

It takes the world's most expensive hairdresser all of thirty seconds to cut my hair off. Without so much as a by your leave, he slices through the back of my hair and takes off seven years' growth and about five years off me and chucks it nonchalantly in the bin. Then there's another forty-five minutes of delicate snipping and tweaking and twisting and fluffing. I am almost in a trance by the end of it, as he completes his tantric moves and slowly withdraws to admire his own creation.

"There!" He puts his hand under his chin and rests it on my shoulder. "Sooo much better."

He's not wrong. I feel jaunty and flirty and broke. He's not cheap, obviously, he's a friend of Kate's, and since she has no leaching offspring she has found other, more amusing ways of spending her money. I just close my eyes and hope the card makes it through the machine without the alarm bells going off and a gang of men in black coming to take me away in a van. "Tip big." Kate's words are reverberating. "How big?" Twenty quid turns out to be the going rate for the girl who washed my hair and sixty to the maestro himself. Christ! I could have gone on holiday for that!

Next up was full body depilation. Which is just as painful as it sounds. Moustache, toes, bush, over the knees, up the crack. I am so covered in wax I feel like a toffee apple. I leave the place on fire, literally, well not literally, but my skin feels like it's tingling and pulsing with pain, and my pants are sticking up my arse. They've clearly left some wax where the sun don't shine, and it's very uncomfortable indeed.

Two doors down and it's eyebrows and nails. Mani, pedi, brows – can be bought as a combination. So, the lot. They dye and shape the brows and take a razor blade to my feet, such is the level of neglect.

By 6pm it's all over and I look like I've just stepped out of a salon, which I have – several. And I feel great. Really, I do. It's like a dry husk has been removed, the hair coat of lassitude has been thrown off and I feel worth at least £635 – which is what the whole thing has cost me. "Beauty hurts," my mother used to say. Mainly your wallet, as it turns out.

I return home triumphant, zingy, swingy. I'm almost expecting the popping of champagne corks, a brass band, bunting, a parade and raucous applause as I enter our three-down, four-up house. Instead, I come home to the cheesy stench of Domino's pizza and the brash shouting of Saturday-night TV.

"Oh," says Husband, looking up from his iPad for a split second. "You look different. What have you done?"

"Different. *Good*?" I smile.

"What have you done to your eyebrows?" says Sam, walking into the kitchen with earphones on. "They look gross. Have you drawn them on?"

"Different. Good?" I ask again.

"Different. Good," he repeats. He doesn't look up. He carries on rubbing his finger all over his iPad.

"Well, I think you look great, Mum," says Ella, walking into the kitchen and opening the fridge. "The choppy bob is very now," she says, looking me up and down. "Especially for the middle-aged mum."

December 4th

It's Will's forty-something-or-other birthday and we are all standing around Sally's kitchen unit trying to get a drink.

It's a little bit early to be celebrating Christmas, also frankly it is actually someone else's birthday, but most of the guests have already gone for it. There are more sequins on show than a ballroom dancing display in Blackpool. Sequin dresses, sequin trousers, sequin jumpers. Apparently, nothing says the festive season more than a whole load of shiny plastic sewn onto a pullover. The run-up to Christmas really is the time when "Taste" takes the month off, and its mate "Jesus Christ will you look at that" takes over. And no one embraces Christmas more than Sally.

She's out of the blocks before you can say "Bonfire Night". For no sooner has she put the pumpkins away and packed up the fake spiders' webs than she's cracked open the box of baubles and reindeer in the loft. The first thing that's up is an enormous flashing green wreath with red bow effect that she sourced at Argos. It has various manic modes of throbbing, undulating and pulsating, all of which piss off her neighbours, which I presume is precisely the point. Next out of the box is an inflatable Santa who bobs and billows around in her diminutive front garden. The only problem with the voluminous Santa is that he is regularly stolen and beaten up by the posh urban youth in her area, who think there's nothing more "totes hilare" than smacking Santa in the chops and pretending to steal from his sack. He's been hauled down the street a few times only for the joke to wear a little thin by the time they reach the Portobello Road, when Santa is as flat as a pancake and resembles nothing more than a red rubber paddling pool. He's well known enough now in the area for the fruit and veg guy who sets up on the corner to pick him up and deposit him back on Sally's doorstep before the children have even woken up, which as Sally will tell you, is bloody early.

Her other favourite bit of festive cheer is the *Now That's What I Call Christmas* album that blasts through the speakers in her kitchen. From the moment you cross the threshold you're bombarded with Bing, Bowie and Bublé. It's enough to force blood through the eardrums. Sally loves Christmas so much that, in another world, she would surely have been happy to sport green hot pants in Harrods, while being goosed by middle-aged men as she directed their spoilt, fat children towards the grotto.

Either that, or she'd own one of those miserable parks in Middlesex where the polystyrene snow's blown away only to reveal a muddy field and the fact that the reindeer are sheep wearing plastic antlers.

"This is fun," says Claire, necking a Moscow Mule and shouting above the music. She steps from side to side in her gold wedge heels and nods her head in time to the beat.

"Is it?" I ask, trying to work out if she's being serious.

"It's better than a late-night stock check, that's for sure."

"Rob's here."

"Christ."

"I know. Sally did ask, and he's Will's friend. That's divorce for you, isn't it? Sides. No sides. Having to get on. Keep the show on the road. Avoid each other. Be civil. When inside you are dying. You look great, by the way." She smiles over the rim of her glass. Her head is still nodding. "New hair. I like the eyebrows. Best thing I've ever done." I stare at hers. "Tattoos," she says, running an index finger over one of her brows. "I've had them permanently drawn on. Makes all the difference."

"Go you!" I say.

"Oh yes!" She drains her glass. "Go me! I'm stone cold bloody broke. I owe the taxman a fortune, I have no money to pay my VAT, but I've got fucking good eyebrows!"

I look at her; she is biting the inside of her mouth and looks like she's on the verge of tears. George Michael's *Last Christmas* is crooning away above our heads. It's not helpful. A song for the broken-hearted. Claire puffs through pursed lips. This is not the place for a breakdown.

"To fucking good eyebrows!" I say quickly.

"To fucking good eyebrows," she repeats.

We clink glasses.

"Who the fuck is Will talking to?" asks Kate. "Good hair, by the way. Excellent hair. Worth every hundred quid, I'd say." She turns away from me and looks the length of the kitchen island, which is crowded with glasses in various states of fullness and hundreds of bowls of crisps, pretzels, nuts and mini mince pies. "The brunette with the tits?"

Up the other end of Sally's unit (not a euphemism), right next to the incongruously scarlet Smeg fridge, Will is deep in conversation with a magnificent-looking brunette with tits, encased in a tight black bandage dress, wearing expensive-looking drop diamond earrings and a marvellous blow-dry. She is pushed and tweaked and cantilevered in such a way that it's hard to work out if the tits are all her own work or that of a surgeon with a very discreet side door just off Harley Street.

"Crikey!" says Claire, ladling out another beefy serving of mule into her glass. "I think that's his business partner, Valentina."

"What, Val!" says Kate, with a giggle.

"Don't call her that," replies Claire, her tattooed eyebrows raised. "She only answers to Valentina. Or at least that's what Sally says. She looks terrifying."

"Terrifying," I agree.

"She looks like a bloke," says Kate.

"Noooo," says Claire, squinting a little through the sequins, the booze and the darkness. "Not a bloke, just terrifying."

"Don't be stupid, let's go and chat to her. It'll be a laugh! Come on!" Kate marches over, dragging us in her wake.

"Hi, I'm Kate," says Kate, shoving her hand out, very much between Will and Valentina.

"Oh, hi guys!" says Will, taking a swift step back, his hands slightly in the air, like he's been playing with fire. "Hold that thought," he says to Val, his finger raised.

"I will." She parts her plump lips. Her décolletage rises up and down, her diamonds twinkle in the dimmed LED kitchen lights, she smells of Chanel No 5 and I already hate her. "Oh, Will?" He stops immediately in his tracks. His face expectant. "Could you serve me a little glass of very chilled champagne?" Her French-polished thumb and forefinger come softly together to indicate quite how small a serving she wants. It's teeny-weeny-tiny, just like her waist. It's apparently so small it's hardly worth pouring into a glass. I am half tempted to yell, "Bring me the rest of the bottle, Will!" But, truthfully, I'm not brave enough. "So, you're all Sally's friends?" she says, with a shake of her blow-dry and a rattle of her diamonds.

"Yeah," says Kate, and nods, standing with her legs apart like she's been on a How to Succeed in Business weekend near Luton. "We've all known her for years . . . loads of years."

"Actually, I fucked her elder brother," I add, for good measure.

They look at me. "You must know her really well then," concludes Valentina, smiling widely and appreciatively and beautifully at Will as he hands her a tiny measure of champagne in a beautiful crystal goblet.

I look down at my plastic beaker full of warm ginger beer. "I was at their wedding," I add, pointedly. "How long have you known Will? When did you start working for him?"

"I don't work for Will." She looks me in the eye, like a snake about to pounce. She's a man's woman, that's for sure. Not one of the girls. I don't see her dancing to "Single Ladies", pissed as a fart on tequila. "We're partners."

"It's unusual to find a woman in finance," chips in Kate.

"It is?" I almost hear a hiss as Valentina's head spins to lock eyes with Kate. "I don't find it so. I think women and finance are a perfect match: our brains are capable of thinking around a problem, our thought process is not linear and in this new world, that's a good thing. Those who can't think laterally have, and will, be replaced by algorithms. Like half those poor boys in the City." She doesn't so much as take a sip of her drink, rather she merely dampens her plump, shiny lips with her champagne. "The only thing we are not so good at is making dispassionate decisions. And all decisions should be dispassionate. As soon as you let your emotions get involved, your judgement is clouded and your thought process is incorrect."

I simply nod and drink. "Bollocks," says Claire. "If you take that to its logical conclusion, there's no such thing as self-sacrifice, and the humanity of the human race is built on love and self-sacrifice."

"That might make you a nice 'mum'," says Valentina. The word sticks to her lip gloss making her spit out the last consonant. "But you're never going to be CEO of a FTSE 100 company with that sort of opinion."

"How very eighties of you," says Kate, picking up her glass. "Come on, Claire, I'm going to get myself another drink."

Valentina looks a little flustered. No one wants to be accused of being forty years out of date, especially when she is clearly pretending to herself and her surgeon that she wasn't even born in that era.

"What does she do?" asks Valentina, her eyes boring into Kate's strapless, toned back.

"Advertising," I say.

"Of course she does," says Valentina. "I can tell by her shoes."

I look down at Kate's feet. She is wearing expensive-looking shoes with even more expensive red soles. I'm not sure why they indicate she works in advertising. But . . . I glance swiftly down at Valentina's; they are covered in hard silver square studs and are extremely high. I have to say my initial professional guess would be prostitute, not high-finance executive, but then what do I know?

"So-o-o, where are you from?" I ask, taking another slurp of my drink.

She looks at me with her impenetrable eyes. She is poised and rigid with Melania-like steely, glacial perfection. A small part of me withers. I am about to be labelled as a racist. Why did I ask the question? There is a pause, a lull; why am I always the idiot who has to vomit into the conversational void? Why can't I stand still at a party, smiling, being inoffensive, mute, not saying anything at all? It's so bloody English to keep the conversation going, to fear the silence, even if it is being filled somewhat by the dulcet tones of George Michael.

"Why do you ask?"

"No reason," I think I might be whispering, awaiting the end.

"Moldova," she says eventually, in such a nonchalant way I think I might kiss her.

"Oh, how fascinating. What an amazing place to come from. You must be so proud. So interesting. What with all those beautiful . . . um . . . churches and things . . ." I am gushing, I know, but I'm going to keep going until I am stopped or cancelled. Will returns as I am talking. "We're just discussing, um, Moldova . . ." I smile.

"Why?"

"Because that's where Valentina is from!" I am beaming, like I have just discovered how to turn water into wine, or something even better.

"Oh yeah," he nods. "She hates the place, couldn't get out of there fast enough, full of hookers and gangsters, isn't that what you say?" He laughs. She laughs and touches his forearm, giving it a long, languid stroke. He grins and stares at her hand, unable to move.

"Will," she purrs. "Don't tell all my secrets!" She lifts her glass and dampens her lips again with champagne.

"Oh look, there's Sally!" I point down to the other end of the kitchen unit.

"Yes, there she is," confirms Valentina, with a curl of her champagne-moistened lips.

Sally is hooting with laughter, wearing a red sequin dress that clings to her curves, all of them, and she is sporting a pair of Christmas trees on a hairband that bob and dart and duck and dive on the top of her head. I'm sure the festive boppers with a green fluffy marabou headband finish might have been a brilliant idea at 6pm this evening as she was having a little glass and talking to her children, but now they look a whole lot less witty. She looks like a kindergarten teacher who's been at the punch.

"Hi," I say, finally making it down her end of the unit.

"Hi." She grins at me. "This is fun, isn't it?"

"Great," I lie. "I see you've gone early with Christmas."

"Well, you know me." She grins again, shaking her head by way of demonstration. "I see you've been talking to 'She Who Must Be Obeyed'."

"She's quite a piece of work."

"You can say that again. Has she told you she studied at Oxford and INSEAD yet?"

"INSEAD?"

"Some bloody business school that makes grown men play with themselves as soon as they hear it muttered through those superannuated lips of hers."

"No, just that she's from Moldova. Full of hookers and gangsters, so she says."

"She'd know," says Sally.

"She's not much of a laugh though, is she?"

"No."

"She wouldn't wear Christmas tree boppers."

"That's for sure."

"Will doesn't fancy her, does he?"

"Countess Dracula! Don't be ridiculous. She'd have him for breakfast!" She smiles again. "I've got to go and get the cake."

Slade are now playing in the kitchen, and I am just about to lose the will to live. I can see Husband leaning with his back against the sink, deep in conversation with Rob, who is studiously avoiding eye contact with Claire, who is pretending to have as much fun as is humanly possible in a crowded kitchen, drinking warm drinks while listening to terrible music. They are both ignoring each other, while also knowing exactly where the other person is in the room. It's like a dance. Quite a sad dance, where the drunken over-ebullience of one partner elicits nothing but patronising pity in the other.

"Hi, I'm Scott."

Tall, dark Scott clearly goes to the gym; he's got a floppy, thick fringe that he must spend most of his life running his hands through.

"Do you mind if I grab a drink?" he asks. "I've been waiting for the toilet for hours, and I'm parched!" He laughs, he throws his nose towards the ceiling, his nostrils are frosted like a margarita glass. He's clearly made good use of the facilities. "I work with Will," he starts, as he serves himself a glass of Moscow Mule. He takes a swig. "That's rank." He puts it straight back down on the table. "Anything else here?"

"There's vodka," I suggest, pointing towards the bottle of Absolut on the side.

"Do you fancy a shot?" he asks.

"Why not?"

"I'm Scott," he says again.

"I know."

"How!" He seems astonished.

"And you work with Will."

He sniffs deeply. "You're amazing!"

"You just told me."

"Oh? Have I? Apologies, it's been a looooooong lunch and I've just had a fat one in the toilets." He taps the side of his nose. A little shake of white powder falls down the front onto his French-blue shirt. He doesn't appear to notice. "Do you want some?" He fumbles in his suit pocket.

"No thanks."

"Sure?" he gestures around the room. "It's nearly Christmas. And . . ." He leans in like this might be the clincher. "It's organic."

"Organic coke?"

"Ssh-shhh." His eyes dart around the room. "Or they'll *all* want some. Seriously," he adds, his chin raised, his frosted nostrils pointing again towards the ceiling. "It's really good shit. Trust me. It's this friend of mine's son, who's not really a dealer, who deals it. He's a gardener who does coke on the side. He's mainly into flowers. But they deliver to your door in a little box. You know, like Amazon. It's really cool. It's organic and, you know, actually, quite good for you."

Cocaine dealers are apparently like chiropractors, no one has a bad one.

"HAPPY BIRTHDAY TO YOU!" Sally starts the singing and soon the rest of the room joins in. Some thirty to forty of us, all trying to give it some gusto. After all, Will's had a terrible year. He's a testicle down. But Will's a survivor! And we all appreciate that.

"HAPPY BIRTHDAY TO YOU!" The cake is a giant Eton Mess covered in a fountain of candles and glitter.

Sally has made it herself. And you can tell. She approaches Will, who is still standing next to Valentina.

"HAPPY BIRTHDAY DEAR WIIIIILL." Sally puts the cake down in front of him and he smiles and kisses her on the cheek.

"HAPPY BIRTHDAY TO YOU!" Everyone applauds and Will wields a huge knife and screams as he plunges it into the strawberries, meringues and cream. The clapping and the whooping continue and then someone shouts. "WISH! WISH! WISH . . . MAKE A WISH!"

And suddenly, Sally is standing right next me. The kitchen is full of heat and people and noise. She leans over.

"I think I might be pregnant," she whispers, straight down my ear.

December 5th

On the grand scale of hangovers this one has to be verging on a ten. A ten out of bloody ten. My mouth is dry, my eyes are stinging, I smell like a pub carpet, I feel like a pub carpet and there's a drill going off in the side of my head. Even the grey light of dawn is offensive.

Sally's revelation was like a slap to the face. I should have felt happy for her. I know I should. A baby is, of course, a joy, no matter how rocky, or maybe not remotely rocky, the state of their marriage is. But I didn't feel happy for her. I felt the opposite. I was engulfed by a wave of uncontrollable rage and fury. I think, if the truth be told, I'm jealous. Who am I kidding? I know I was jealous. With every fibre of my being. I actually wanted to shout at her. I didn't. But the thought passed through my mind. I'm over the hill and languishing in a barren desert of hopeless, endless disappointment, and she is not. I can't have any more children, and she can. I'm not sure why I feel such abject, deep-seated misery. It's not like I want any more children, ever. My hands are full enough with Ella and Sam, but it's the idea of never being able to touch something, smell something, love something so warm and soft and delicious ever again. That ship has sailed, and Sally has all that joy ahead of her. The nappies and the late nights and the early mornings and the endless feeding all disappear into a fug of nothing in the end. And all you can remember is their dear little chubby hand slipping into yours as you walk along the road.

I drank a lot to drown my sorrows. I stalked that poor old fool Scott around the party until I managed to sample some of his organic wares and frosted my own nostrils until I'd bored enough people for Kate to suggest to Husband that he should take me home. I then forced him to have sex with me, pretending to myself I might be able to conceive if we actually did it for once. His enthusiasm was a little limited, I seem to remember, despite me bouncing up and down all over the place. After about five minutes of him going at it like a Jack Russell, he collapsed on his back and began to snore. Loudly. He didn't even notice I'd had a full Brazilian.

I lie in bed, staring at the ceiling, attempting to have a word with myself. I can't turn into one of those embittered women who always say and want the worst for people. I can't spend my life full of regret and fury. That's no way to live, and I'll end up with the little pinched cat's arse mouth that I deserve. Like my mother. I can't end up being like my mother. That's hell indeed. Maybe I should take a leaf out of Dave's book and take up meditation. But the idea of spending three and a half hours a week sitting in the downstairs lav, gently inhaling the drains, is enough to turn anyone insane. Yoga? Claire swears blind that yoga helps maintain her inner and outward calm. A pause between action and reaction. Only, she consults the tarot to ask if she should go shopping for milk in the morning, so I am not entirely sure she's a reliable witness. I must do something. Sally's going to be pregnant for nine whole months – I can't be livid for that long. It's a secret for the moment, and she's not even quite sure. But when she is, I'll have to be able to look her in the eye and feel glad for her.

Maybe Dave could get me pregnant? We haven't had a "cup of tea" for a few weeks. Perhaps I should give him a call? I know he's not the answer, or even the question, but someone's got to appreciate this £49.50-plus-tip Brazilian before everything starts growing back.

December 10th

It takes Dave a couple of days to get back to me. I bump into him a few times on the school run but it's hard to organise assignations at the school gate with the likes of Erica and Madison hanging around. Especially as they both seem to hang on his every word and he, frankly, seems to enjoy their attention a little too much!

"Morning, Erica!" he says, clicking his back teeth and shooting her across the pavement with his index finger. "Lovely day for it!"

"Hey you!" she replies, sticking him with her square-tipped French polish, like she's joined Madison in the cast of *Friends*. "How you doin'?"

"Great," he nods. "You?"

"Good," she replies, and she's not even American.

Dave also, oddly, seems to have a lot of time for "Coffee Club" as they insist on calling it, which is bizarre as no one drinks coffee and it's not a club. They all have some hideous, self-improving herbal infusion, to which they add honey or agave and then stir for hours with their teaspoons only to ask for extra hot water, on the side, so they can drink it, which, of course, they don't. I've made it to "Coffee Club" a couple of times when I am not going to work at Bounce!, as the idea of sitting in my slightly inflammable uniform while they discuss the pain of travelling long-haul at half-term is not something I relish. But Dave's been there, every time I've gone. And he's looking suspiciously at ease with it all. He knows the names of all the children, plus their siblings, and all the schools they are trying to get into. Apart from half-term-long-haul hell, the other perennial is "schools". They can talk for bloody hours about schools. HOURS! Who's going where? If they were tutored? Who did the tutoring? How much was the tutoring? Did they over-tutor? The dangers of over-tutoring. Did the bloody child (who no one actually knows) in fact, really, honestly deserve that place at all, having been tutored to the max? Or are they just thick and spoilt and rich? And will said thick, spoilt, rich child end up crashing and burning out, wallowing in a cesspit of self-harm, depression and mental health issues and, finally, obviously, eventually becoming addicted to heroin. Should they tutor? And who would you recommend?

"I've got this amaaaaazing guy," says Madison. "He comes to the house and he also plays tennis with Saffron and Fi and takes them swimming and teaches them chess."

"Sort of like a father?" I suggest.

"Oh, an amazing father-figure," she agrees.

"I also have a guy," adds Erica.

"Apart from Mr Hancox?" nods Dave.

"Yes," Erica laughs a little at her own efficiency, brushing it away with a gentle swipe of her hand. "He's amazing . . ."

Tutors, it seems, are like cocaine dealers and chiropractors: simply no one has a bad one.

Dave and I agree over various texts that we should meet for "afternoon tea" at the same hotel where we first initiated our affair, which I suppose is exactly what I'm having. Although it doesn't feel like one. I always thought affairs were uncontrollably romantic, where lovers unbearably pined for each other, shuffling through the day like laudanum addicts, stealing furtive kisses behind blousy rose bushes, or ripping their clothes off amongst the heather on the moor, only to have someone like Ralph Fiennes carefully sew up their frock again with a needle and thread, like he did in *The English Patient*. Somehow a quickie overlooking the M40 doesn't quite have the same allure.

We book into a different room this time, as I really don't want to catch the eye of the girl in the office opposite. Fortunately, it's a little darker at this time of year, so Dave closes the thick floral curtains.

"Shall we take it slow?" he suggests, running his hands through my hair as he unbuttons the silk shirt I have put on especially for the occasion. "We have all afternoon."

Not technically, I think; my car's on a meter and I was planning on doing a bit of Christmas shopping before pick-up. "Let's see how it goes," I say, giving him my most penetrative kiss. He tastes of spearmint with a back note of cheese and onion crisps. I'm pretty sure Ralph Fiennes doesn't taste so banal. Dave has my shirt on the floor and he's cupping my left breast, going straight for the clasp at the back; so much for taking it "slow". He whips his belt off and stamps out of his jeans, leaving them in a pool on the floor. My skirt and pants come down in one swift move and his hand is between my legs as he starts pushing himself against me. I stagger backwards and fall into the armchair.

"Open your legs," he commands, squatting between my knees. "What's happened to the hair?" He sits back on his heels, a little disappointed. "I like the hair."

"You do?" I close my legs.

"Well, it's comforting," he says. "Like fucking your mother."

"What!" I leap out of the chair.

"No! No! NO! That came out wrong, I don't want to fuck my mother. I have never wanted to fuck my mother. It's womanly, it's really womanly, that's what I meant to say. Here." He pushes me back into the chair. "Come on, I'm sorry. Let me take you to heaven and beyond."

He's sounding a little like Buzz Lightyear and an image of Sam comes to mind. "Please," he says, running his fingers up and down my thighs. "I've been dreaming about this all day."

So, I lie back in the chair and spread my legs and try not to think of Sam, where to find parsnips, and what I might buy my sister in Space NK. He's down there for hours with his tongue probing in and out, his fingers joining in, his face, his nose, his chin are right between my thighs, while I make suitably appreciative noises and ruffle his hair. Finally, he gets some traction and I start moaning and rubbing myself against his face, I open my legs further and push him right in there. I am not sure if the poor man can breathe, but I am right on the verge, one more thrust – I grab his hair.

"Jesus Christ!" I moan, my back arching, my legs shaking as I reach a shivering, quivering climax. His face slowly rises from between my thighs. He looks exhausted.

"Happy?" He smiles, very pleased with himself.

"Dave," I nod. "That was fabulous!" It was.

"Excellent," he says, pulling me out of the chair and guiding me towards the bed. "My turn."

Fortunately for all concerned, Dave's turn doesn't take long. His idea of "slow" is another thirty seconds more of thrusting, which ends up with him yelping a little in my ear before he starts to cry, again.

"You see," he says, wiping away a tear. "It's sex and it's you that does this to me. It's the release, the emotional release, the release of tension after my divorce, or maybe it's just the endorphins. Do you think it's the endorphins?"

"I'm not sure."

"I cry after I have been jogging sometimes too," he muses, flicking imaginary dust off his own thighs. "And yoga. It's probably that. Like a good work out?"

"Yes," I nod. "Just like a good work out. Oh, my goodness," I say, looking at his watch. "I have to go." I have fifteen minutes left on the meter.

"Go?" He sits up. "I thought we might go again?"

"I'm sorry, I've got stuff I have to do, it's so close to Christmas and all that . . . stuff."

"Of course, you ladies are so busy this time of year. Erica has all her presents already. And they're wrapped."

"Go Erica," I say, as I scrabble around on the floor for my pants.

A few minutes later Dave and I are in Reception. I hang around as he's paying the bill. I was going to suggest we went halves but there's something so incredibly unseemly about that. Perhaps paying for a shag in a four-star hotel in Paddington is the patriarchy's last stand?

"Thank you very much," says Dave, as he punches his number into the machine. "It was a very pleasant afternoon." Afternoon? It was just under an hour. "Wasn't it, dear?" He turns to smile at me, and I realise in the cold light of day, with the curtains open, that Dave's face is bright red. Scarlet even. It's rubbed raw around the chin and at the end of his nose. What on earth has happened to him?

He walks me back to my car and after studiously checking the street for known-knows, he kisses me and says goodbye. It's not until I start my car that I realise Dave has a virulent case of Brazillian stubble rash.

December 15th

Turns out orgasms are good for shopping. I spent the rest of that afternoon trying on clothes I didn't need, and buying presents I couldn't afford, in a whirl of blissful "fuck-it-ry". Jenny is going to have the best present she's ever had in her life, and Jacqueline is destined for a full Charlotte Tilbury makeover.

I went full-on cashmere. Everyone likes a nice jumper at Christmas, and I even bought Ella her Buffalos that she so desperately wants. I am going to be the most popular person around the tree this Christmas. Perhaps a little less so in January on the third Monday of the month when all the bills come home to roost. But that's next year, and I'm living for now!

I'm swinging my shopping bags, pretending I'm starring in my own film – I'm my Main Character as Ella says – and I'm breezy and fun and about thirty at most, when I bump slap bang into Sally. She looks terrible, quite apart from the three children she is corralling. She has one in a pushchair, the other riding shotgun and the third strapped to the front, quietly suffocating between her increasingly large breasts.

"Hi," she huffs. Her face is grey. "You look like you've had a fun afternoon?"

"Just some shopping." I hold up the bags. "Christmas."

"Yup, that's soon."

"It is." I nod. "Are you OK?"

Her face crumples for a second and then she immediately regains control. "Not really." She grins. "But you know, one has to keep going."

"I'd ask you for a drink, but what with the crèche you're transporting . . ."

"I wouldn't be able to drink that drink, anyway." She grins again. It's rictus.

"Oh, congratulations!" I say.

"Fuck off."

"Oh, come on Sal . . ."

"Don't you Sal me. Will's furious and says we can't afford it and he doesn't want any more, and we have our hands full as it is, and we'll have to move house and I'm sick as a fucking dog. Hurling up all over the place. Anything makes me chunder, the smell of fish, fat, BO is the worst. I puked so badly outside the school yesterday I had to tell everyone I had a hangover."

"Normally . . ."

"I know what happens normally, but I don't want to tell any of those smug bitches that . . . that I'm . . . well, you know what . . . because they'll talk behind my back about me, and my marriage and my thousands of children, and I simply can't fucking cope with that at the moment." Her voice cracks.

"So you'd prefer them to think that you're an alcoholic?"

"A drunk? Yes, I bloody would."

"Right."

"And I bet it's another bloody boy, that's all I need, another bloody boy."

"Mum?" A small hand tugs at her coat.

"WHAAAT!" she yells, her head swivelling all over the place as she tries to find which child tugged at her arm and then she suddenly bursts into tears.

"Here," I say, putting my shopping down and throwing my arms around her. "It's fine. Nothing is ever as bad as it seems. I promise you. And I have seen bad. You will be fine. No one ever regrets travelling, swimming and a baby. Isn't that the saying?"

Sally laughs and cries and looks at me though her tears. "You just made that up!"

"It's a very well-known saying. I'm offended now. Mortally!" She smiles. "Where are you going? Can I help?"

I walk Sally home. Slowly. I'd forgotten how immobile having three children under the age of six actually makes you. Not that I have ever been that encumbered, but being outnumbered to such an extent is exhausting. And there is usually one that's crying, one that's hungry or one that needs to go to the loo. No wonder poor Sally can barely think. She hasn't time to draw breath.

"If you could just put the telly on," she says to me as she opens the front door. "And I'll put this one to bed." She huffs as she unclips number two from the pushchair, while number three is strapped to her front, number one marches straight into the house and drops his blazer and rucksack right by the front door. I follow her into her sitting room, kitchen/diner area and the chaos and mess is overwhelming, worse than the other day. She must have seen the shocked expression on my face as I stand surrounded by Lego and half-broken cars. "Will's away in Switzerland," she says. "Hence the mess."

"I did wonder."

"He's in Lucerne doing some team-bonding weekend with the charming Valentina and his team . . . they're bonding."

"Sounds . . . nice."

"He swears it's not. He swears it's awful. Valentina's complaining about the service. But the idea of someone making me some lunch with a glass of wine would be excellent. They're swimming in the lake," she adds.

"That's going to be cold."

"I think that's the point."

"Very Wim Hof."

"Very," says Sally.

"Don't forget Wim eviscerated himself by giving himself an enema using the jet of a municipal fountain in Amsterdam. That didn't end well!"

"Did he?"

"Let's hope Will doesn't attempt something like that after a schnapps."

"Although . . ." grins Sally, as she walks up the stairs.

December 20th

Only five days to go until wretched, bloody Christmas and I am already over it. I can't drink any more, I can't eat any more and I have no more money to spend on shiny useless crap to put in my children's stockings from a Santa Claus they constantly tell me doesn't exist. The whole thing is a sham and charade of festive hell and to make it worse I have my "Office Party" tonight.

The last time I went to an office, everyone drank flaming Sambucas and pretzels were exciting new snacks from the US. I also had boobs good enough to photocopy and there was a handy fax machine right next door where you could send said boob pics all over the world. Which my friend Alice and I did, once. Full of Sambuca and pretzels, we photocopied our breasts and faxed them to a whole load of customers with the message "Happy Titmus" from All at X&Y& Co. We were so drunk we forgot all about it as soon as we staggered out of the building, giggling into the street. We went back in the New Year to find that we had both been fired.

I am not sure what Debbie has planned, beyond the "Secret Santa" that we've all been instructed to buy (a tenner max) and the compulsory wearing of a Christmas jumper, which doesn't bode well. I'm not a fan of a festive jumper, acrylic and itchy; they purport to be witty, and are invariably not. Although Sam's headmaster did don an extremely unfortunate (Snowman) jumper a few years back with a great big carrot for a nose that flailed around in front of him like a giant priapic phallus. Not only did it appear to have a life of its own, but it also proceeded to poke every child in the eye, or worse, mouth, as he leant forward to speak to them. Needless to say, festive fun jumpers have been optional at the school ever since.

"So, you've got an office party?" asks Husband for the third time, somewhat incredulous and a little smug as he sits on the sofa, picking his feet. "What time do you think you'll be back?"

"I don't think I'll last very long."

"Well, they're all quite a lot younger, aren't they?"

"They are."

I tug slightly at the small tight green (Elf) jumper (complete with knitted golden buttons and detachable belt) that I'm wearing and immediately regret the decision to go. I should have made my excuses. No one would notice if I didn't show. My skirt's too short as well. God knows what I think I'm doing. I am suddenly overwhelmed with anxiety. Why am I always doing things I don't want to do? I spend my whole life dragging myself to places that I don't want to be at. Is that the lot of the middle-aged woman? Or maybe it's just that I have forgotten how to have fun? What is fun, anyway? Whatever it is, I know I bloody hate it.

"I'm going," I say, thinking I'll order my taxi outside.

"Have fun!" he laughs from the sofa, snapping his big toenail off. "I won't wait up!"

Outside on the doorstep, I light up a cigarette and inhale deeply. "Fuck off!" I say, in a little sing-song voice to myself. I exhale and then fumble around in my coat for my phone.

"I see Santa's got himself a new little helper," comes a voice from over the fence.

"Sorry?" I glance over the mass of poorly cut ivy and the giant blue recycling bin.

"A little helper," he nods, looking me up and down. "I'm digging the skirt," he adds, flicking his fag butt expertly into the road. "Dex," he says, pulling at his loose jeans that hang below his Calvin Klein knicker elastic. He lifts his baggy white T-shirt and strokes his own flat, hair-trimmed stomach. "Just moved in," he sniffs. "Ground floor." He sticks his hand out. I shake it. It's warm and soft and has quite possibly come straight from his underwear. "You should come over."

"I'm forty-six."

"Cool," he replies, pushing open his front door. The hall light shines on his face. He is young, good-looking and looks like he's fond of surfing and smoking copious amounts of marijuana. "See you around," he adds with a grin. His parents must have spent a fortune at the orthodontist.

"Bye," I hear myself saying as his front door slams. Ella will be very impressed.

Deborah and the crew have made a massive effort to make her office look like it was the sort of place you wanted to spend any time in. They've dimmed the lights, moved around the blue cubed furniture and put glitter streamers on the walls. In one corner of the room, there's a bar, with boxes of wine and a giant bowl of orange-coloured punch and rows and rows of red plastic cups. How many people are they expecting? There are only about ten of us who work here.

"Hi," says Deborah as I walk in and stand, slightly stumped, at the bar. "Have you met my husband, Jay?"

First of all I notice that Deborah has ignored her own "festive jumper" memo and has come as "Sexy Santa" – all cleavage and rara skirt with a cinched waist and fluffy white fur trim. She's wearing fishnets and red stilettos and she looks fabulous! The hours spent bouncing up and down and drinking cans of Diet Coke have really worked out for her. She has legs and arms and a waist and everything. I am a little taken aback.

"Wow!" I say. "You look amazing."

"You've only ever seen me in uniform." She smiles.

"She scrubs up well, doesn't she?" confirms Jay, who is standing right next to her. In a white, tight-fitting, open-necked, short-sleeved shirt that appears to have shrunk in the wash and lost most of its buttons at the same time.

"I'm Jay," says Jay. His biceps are so shiny and rippling, they look like two fake-tanned seals that have escaped an aquarium. In fact, everything about Jay shines and ripples. His chest is smooth and oiled, his thick dark hair is smooth and oiled and his black jeans are so tight it's a wonder he can sit down. "Can I get you a drink? There's red, white and punch."

"What's in the punch?"

"Alcohol?" he shrugs. "Lots of it."

"I'll have the punch."

"Babe?" he asks Deborah.

She looks at her plastic cup. "Oh, go on, then."

"It's Christmas!" he replies.

"It's Christmas!" she says right back.

Turns out Christmas! is the reason to do many things. Christmas! is the reason Deborah shows off her flips and tumbles and somersaults in front of all of her staff, wearing little more than small black pants and suspenders. Christmas! is the reason Jay takes his shirt off and proceeds to arm-wrestle every contender in the room and, of course, beat them all with his massive Popeye arms. And, as the last contestant is dispatched, Christmas! makes him beat his bare chest like a gorilla in celebration. Christmas! is the reason for the terrible dancing in Debbie's office and the indiscriminate use of paper hats and awful party-blowers. Christmas! is the reason for Steve on Reception managing to kiss Kelly, with a lavish use of his tongue, in public, even though he is frankly nowhere near her league. Meanwhile, Christmas! manages to decorate two of the downstairs toilets in orange vomit. It also makes two of Steve's mates have a long, lengthy snooze on Debbie's blue box cushions and it is also responsible for me ending up smoking joints on Dex's sofa.

It was all going so well. I'd drunk the punch and danced a little to the various festive tracks. I'd cheered on Debbie's Olympic performance in the trampoline park and clapped Jay's strength in the arm-wrestling. I'd avoided skidding in the vomit in the lavs and getting eye contact with Steve as his tongue whirled around inside Kelly's mouth like some superannuated washing machine. I even made my excuses in good time: 10.30pm is a good time to leave a Christmas party with terrible lighting and a strong alcoholic cock-tail that could have any sort of combination of ingredients including vodka, gin, Cointreau, Bacardi, tequila – or all of the aforementioned. I only stumbled slightly out of the taxi when I arrived at home, however I did drop my Secret Santa gift and I was struggling to find my keys in amongst my general handbag detritus, when he says:

"Excuse me, but I think you may have dropped these." He stands at the end of my very short garden path with a red lace thong in his hand. The diamanté Santa face on the front, and indeed only triangle, glitters in the streetlight. Debbie's joke suddenly looks a lot raunchier than I am sure she intended.

"Oh," I slur a little. "Thanks. Very kind of you."

"Someone's going to have a happy Christmas." He smiles.

"They're a joke," I say. "From my boss."

"Your boss! Wow! He nods. "He's a brave man."

"She's a woman."

"Even better." He grins. They must have paid thousands for that smile.

"Ha ha ha," I laugh back and pluck the pants out of his hand.

"Do you fancy coming in for a drink?" he asks.

"You're twelve!"

"Twenty-six," he corrects. "And anyway, I wasn't asking like that. I was being nice. Like a neighbour. It's Christmas!" He shrugs.

"Indeed it is," I reply, walking towards him. "Lead the way!"

Twenty minutes later, I'm sitting on what appears to be a mattress on the floor, covered in an old curtain, with some cushions on it, masquerading as a sofa. I'm smoking a suspiciously neatly rolled joint, going through Dex's extensive vinyl collection, singing along very loudly to some vintage David Bowie, telling him to turn the music up.

"I love this one!" I shout above the music.

"Yeah!" he nods, handing me back the joint.

I would/could have stayed until the early hours, but someone rang his doorbell at about 11.45pm.

"Excuse me," comes a very familiar voice. "Can you turn the music down? There are kids asleep next door."

"Sure," replies Dex, his palms up like he's surrendering in a shoot-out. "Sorry, man."

"I know it's Christmas . . . man." Husband's using his special Cab Driver's Voice that he reserves for plumbers, builders, painters, decorators and now apparently the under-thirties. "But you know . . . the wife will kill me . . ."

"Of course," agrees Dex. He pauses. "They do that."

"Yeah. She's uptight like that, and doesn't like noise."

Husband appears to be standing on the doorstep waiting, hoping, to be asked in. I can feel my heart pounding. I'm sitting on a mattress sofa dressed in an elf costume holding a spliff; this is going to take some explaining.

"Cool," says Dex and closes the door.

December 24th

The trick is to arrive as close to "drinks time" on Christmas Eve as is humanly possible. The idea of sitting on the sofa, inhaling the sweet flatulence of Chow and Mein, my mother's Pekinese dogs, while balancing a cup of weak tea and a doorstop-thick slice of arid, roof-of-the-mouth-clagging Christmas cake is enough to make even the most stoic of saints cry. So, Husband and I have learnt over the years that a 5.15pm arrival is perfect, and by the time you've unpacked and handed over some bottles of warm champagne, everyone is rubbing their hands together, asking if it's time for drinks. Which it is, as it's bloody Christmas! And the only way to get through the whole miserable, fraught, exhausting affair is to be completely and utterly drunk.

The only people who don't appear to know this are Jenny and Reasonable Dan and their pitch-perfect, Harry-Potter-reading offspring, Coral and Josh, who are all playing

Monopoly together, as a family, and not fighting at all, when we arrive sweating traffic, fury and bile.

"Mate!" says Dan, putting down Old Kent Road and Vine Street. "How are you?!" He gets up off the floor in one swift, soundless, athletic motion, his hand out, ready to shake Husband's hand. "Come here." He shakes hands and pulls Husband towards him, slapping him heartily on the back. "Long time no see!" His voice rises at the end of the sentence like he's completely surprised. "Looking great mate, looking great!" It could be a question, but it's not.

"Darling!" says Jenny, flicking her fine blonde hair with her fine long fingers. "Gosh, I've missed you!"

Despite nearly two decades in Australia, marrying a Sydney boy and having two children at Byron Bay High (motto: "The Future is Ours"), Jenny still sounds like she hails from the Home Counties. Occasionally she'll come out with the wrong acronym like BYO when she means PBAB, or refer to the bottle-o when she means an off-licence, "the lend", when she means borrow, and "learnings" when she means . . . um, I'm not quite sure. But other than that, you'd never know that she'd spent the best part of her adult life surfing, barbecuing and running the length of a sandy beach every morning, while the rest of us run the gamut of dog shit, traffic wardens and piss-poor coffee while inhaling exhaust fumes on the Kilburn High Road. No wonder she looks ten years younger than me, when she is in fact three years older.

"Hi, Jen! You look fabulous!" She does. There is no point in not stating the obvious. She is slim, wearing tight black jeans and a black silk shirt which hangs loosely around her flat stomach.

"Hello, Aunty," says Coral, her long, blonde, dead-straight hair swinging around her waist as she stands up and smiles. Her teeth are so white there's a hint of blue at the tips.

"Happy Christmas, Aunty," adds Josh. He's grown hugely since I last saw him. He's twelve years old but appears to have abs and biceps and actual proper muscles.

"Someone's been to the gym," I laugh.

"Who's that then?" asks Dan, glancing up and down the line from Husband to Ella, to me and then Pig.

"I mean Josh!" I laugh extra loudly.

"Don't be mad," says Jenny. "Josh doesn't work out!"

"No," agrees Dan. "He's just addicted to Aussie Rules football."

"What football?" asks Husband.

"Aussie Rules," corrects Dan.

"Where they wear the tight shorts and tight T-shirts," adds Jen.

"Sounds gross," opines Ella from the corner of the room. Her sneer lingers on her lips as she stares down her short nose. She too is dressed entirely in black but looks like a cross between Billie Eilish and a recycling bin. Her winged eyeliner is painted on so thickly it is hard to work out if her eyes are open or if she is, in fact, fast asleep.

"Hi Ella," exclaims Coral. "So nice to see you!" You have to admire the girl for trying, but she's a terrible liar. Her wide, overly sincere smile in no way reaches her eyes. "And you, Sam."

"Hi," says Sam, shyly, before giving a little wave from the hip as he leans against my leg.

"Isn't it *lovely* to have the whole family here!" declares Jacqueline, as she swings into the sitting room through the green baize door. She is wearing a frilled apron over her dark flowered corduroy dress and she's carrying a tray of crisps, prawn vol-au-vents and a small bowl of Twiglets. At her navy-blue-shod feet swirl Chow and Mein. I am always amazed that she never trips over them, and they never yelp as she skewers them with a heel. 'Don't you agree, darling? Richard."

"What?" asks my father, from his chair opposite the telly. He's been too busy looking through the *Radio Times* with his magnifying glass, circling "shows of interest" to pay much attention to the arriving hordes.

"Come along, Richard," Jacqueline continues. "It's drinks time and that is your job, I can't do everything around here.'

"Righty-ho," he says, getting out of his chair. "Bubbles?"

"Where's your little friend?" asks Jacqueline, putting down her tray and pushing away the dogs, who are first to show any interest. "What's her name?"

"Claire. She's on her way."

"Oh?" Jacqueline looks at her thin gold watch. "Doesn't she know we have drinks at 6pm?"

"I think she's got to drop off some presents for her godchildren on the way."

"Godchildren? On Christmas Eve? How terribly disorganised."

"She's been working."

"Working?" Jacqueline snarls in the same way as Ella. That's where she gets it from.

"She works in a shop, so Christmas is a very busy time of year."

"In a shop?"

"Yes."

"She works in a shop?"

"Bubbles?" asks Dad.

"Do you have anything stronger?" I reply.

We all sit around the low coffee table in front of the fire in the sitting room, nursing our drinks and working our way through the reheated frozen snacks that Jacqueline has splashed out on from Marks and Spencer. Husband and I are both working on a three-for-one policy – for every drink that Dan and Jen have, we knock back three of our own. Ella has been offered a glass of champagne and has drunk it in two; Coral was also offered a glass but refused it in favour of fizzy water. Josh is drinking a San Pellegrino and Pig is on his third Coke. Jen is talking to Jacqueline about the garden and Dan is chatting politics, which is frankly not the best thing to do if you don't hail from this hellhole and you live a glorious life elsewhere. But that's never stopped anyone, least of all any expats, who somehow seem to enjoy watching the motherland slowly slide down the pan, as it reinforces what an excellent choice they made to get the hell out in the first place.

"Well, the real problem about your government is Brexit," starts Dan.

"Hold up!" says Husband. "It's not all down to Brexit. You can't blame Brexit for everything . . ."

I drain my glass and secretly hope for Claire to hurry up. The other thing about arguing with expats, or non-locals, about politics, is that you start defending the indefensible and saying things that aren't as mad or as bad as they seem.

"It was the will of the people," says Husband. "And you can't argue with that." Here we go, my Remain Husband is now championing Leave.

"But they were given the wrong information," replies Dan, still nursing his first glass of champagne.

"You can't say that," declares Husband, filling his own glass again. "That's deeply patronising."

"I agree," chips in Dad. "I knew exactly what I was doing."

"But with all due respect, Richard," says Dan, immediately indicating that there is none. "How you voted doesn't really affect you. You've benefited from the biggest property boom ever, and you own your own house, and you have a pension that's worth actual money and you've had the best life and now your generation have pulled up the drawbridge and left the youngsters to fend for themselves."

"Yes," nods Husband, suddenly switching sides.

"Less of the past tense, Dan, if you don't mind," says Richard.

"But you have," continues Dan. "You've retired with proper money, and you take your holidays and drive your jag . . ."

"And pollute the climate," spits Ella from the corner.

"And pollute the climate," adds Dan with a nod towards the corner. "And it doesn't really affect you as . . ."

". . . I'm about to die soon?" suggests Richard.

"Well . . ." Dan pauses. "No disrespect."

"Anyone for a Twiglet?" asks Jacqueline.

"Thanks, Mum," says Jen, leaning over and plucking one stick from the bowl. "That's another thing I've really missed. Marmite. Vegemite doesn't quite cut the mustard."

"Is that your little friend's car I can hear on the drive?" asks Jacqueline, cupping her ear.

Fortunately, Claire arrives at the perfect moment, just before Husband starts accusing my Brexit-voting father of ruining his future and the future of our children, and fondly remembers that he once spent a summer working as a waiter in Paris, and a ski season dressed as a Croque Monsieur advertising the local café in Chamonix, which turned out to be the most marvellous three months of his entire life and now, of course, the best our children can hope for is stacking deckchairs under the pier in Skegness.

"Isn't this house gorgeous," says Claire. "And what a beautiful family you have, Jacqueline . . . you must be so proud . . . and Richard, how handsome you look in your cashmere jumper and tie . . . I love a man in a tie . . . and look at these gorgeous cousins and the dogs . . . oh the dogs . . . my grandmother used to have Pekinese . . . Chow? And Mein? That's so funny . . . a glass of champagne? How delicious, Richard you are really spoiling me . . . Oh, and the tree? What a fabulous tree . . . did you do that all on your own, Jacqueline? How beautiful! What exquisite taste you have. Were you an interior designer? No? Oh? You should have been . . ."

It's a tour de force. Christmas is always better when you have guests. Claire works the room to such dazzling effect that everyone forgets any idea of tetchiness and drinks their champagne and pops the slightly dry vol-au-vents in their mouths and smiles and toasts 'Christmas!' Jacqueline doesn't even mind that Claire calls her "Jackie", twice, which is normally a deal-breaker.

By the time we sit down to dinner and Jacqueline is serving the smoked salmon mousse starter with thinly sliced toast, everyone seems to be having a lovely time, including Ella, who's on her third glass of champagne and completely forgotten that she's a vegan with a terrible wheat allergy and that champagne is a capitalist affectation and symbolic of the patriarchy.

"This is great, Gran," she says, munching away.

"Oh good, darling," replies Jacqueline. "It really is so lovely to have you all here. Isn't it, darling?" She looks down the lengthy table, through the candlelight and at her husband at the other end. "Isn't it, Richard?"

"Absolutely, dear," he replies. "Happy Christmas!"

"Happy Christmas!"

Everyone raises their glasses. Husband, Claire and I knock them back in one.

By 10pm, Dad's asleep on the sofa, and Jen, Dan and the kids have all gone to bed as it's a "big day tomorrow". Husband, Ella and Sam are all on their various screens, TikTokking, Snapchatting and catching up on "Important Stuff", while Claire, Jacqueline and I are slowly working our way through a bottle of Baileys, or Christmas Milk, as Husband insists on calling it.

We started sipping it gently on the rocks but have now decided it doesn't taste too bad tepid and straight from the bottle.

"I honestly think you'd like yoga," says Claire, taking another slug of her drink.

"Really?" My mother is looking perplexed. "Me? But I'm seventy-two!"

"Never too late to start. Don't you think?" Claire looks at me.

"What, Mum?"

"Yup." She hiccups slightly. "She's got the body for it."

"I've always had a good figure, a really good figure," proclaims Jacqueline. "We're that generation. We don't let ourselves go. We don't go to the gym!" She laughs, her nose curling enough for her nasal hair to pop out and shine in the candlelight. "We garden. What's the point of wasting all that money? When all you need to do is rake up some leaves or chop some wood or do a little weeding? That's all it takes." She takes a sip of her drink. "But if you think I should try yoga, I'm sure I could give it a go."

"You're right about everything," nods Claire. "Who needs a gym when you can garden? You're so right. Isn't she right?"

What? Me again? "Mum's often right," I find myself saying for the first time in forty-six years.

"I've been a size ten my entire life," Mum carries on. "My entire life. Look!" She stands up and turns slowly around as we sit and smile and admire her svelteness. "I can still wear my wedding dress."

"Amazing," concludes Claire. "You never told me your mother was so amazing," she says to me.

"Didn't I?"

I am sounding a little hysterical. I am feeling a little hysterical. This is not really going to plan. Claire is my friend, my ally, the one person on my side during this festive shit-show and now she seems to be, if not sleeping with the enemy, bloody buttering it up.

"She's amazing!" says Claire. "Honestly . . . it's extraordinary, you're nothing like each other."

"Right," says Husband, with a stretch and a swoosh from his computer which I half expect to be followed by a quick burst of postprandial flatulence. "It's time . . . come on, kids, it's nearly 11pm, big day tomorrow. Big day."

"What? Eating, drinking and opening presents?" asks Ella.

"That sort of thing," he agrees. "You lot coming?" he asks.

"Sure," I say. "Come on, children." There's a collective moan from the sofa. "Claire?"

"I think I might have one more nightcap with your mum."

"Bit more Christmas Milk?" suggests Husband.

"What a wonderful idea," replies Jacqueline, pushing her glass towards Claire. "Not a big one. Just up to the brim!"

They both laugh uproariously as I make my way towards the stairs.

December 25th

Despite the fact that he has long since given up believing in Father Christmas, after Ella called him a "paedo who preyed on children in their sleep and encouraged them to sit on his lap for presents which is basic low-level grooming", Sam is still up at 6.30am to rifle through his stocking. Which, factoring in that I lay, trying to sleep, rigid, listening to my best friend and my mother necking Baileys while laughing at each other's brilliant jokes, or worse, whispering heavily through the sitting room ceiling, plus the constant heavy snoring emanating from the pillow next to me, means I have had about two and a half hours sleep and look like a rabbit with a bad case of myxomatosis.

"Happy Christmas," mutters Dad as I shuffle into the kitchen at 7.30am. It's still dark outside and the dogs are curled up in their beds. "I'm under orders to get the turkey out of the fridge," he explains. "Otherwise it will never cook through . . . apparently." He huffs and puffs, bending slowly forward in his baggy striped pyjamas and forest- green terry dressing gown. His efforts are illuminated by the light of the fridge, as he slowly brings out a huge baking tray, covered in a yellow-checked cloth that appears to contain a medium-sized child. "Christ," he says as he places it slowly onto the long, well-worn, pine kitchen table. "We're going to be eating this for weeks, look at the size of the thing! And all the other gubbins that goes with it." He sighs, gesturing towards the fridge that is overflowing with sausages and bacon, parsnips, chestnuts and red cabbage. The shelves are stacked high with gubbins.

Oddly, for someone who finds food per se so unpleasant and a piled-high plate utterly vulgar, Jacqueline is Queen of Christmas. Perhaps it's the never-ending deluge of cookery programmes that she bombards herself with in the run-up to Christmas, where she learns to drizzle maple syrup on parsnips or cook ham in cans of Coke. Or possibly it's her binge after a year of dust-nibbling abstinence. Or mostly the faint possibility that Jacqueline might be "bad" at something, is what makes her so good at Christmas.

For Jacqueline is brilliant at everything. Absolutely brilliant, but at the same time she really hates to blow her own trumpet. Or so she says. Husband and I, in the days when we did share jokes and would smirk at each other across the well-worn, pine kitchen table, used to play a game where we would try and find one subject, any subject, that Jacqueline was NOT an expert on. Crosswords, growing dahlias, bread sauce, nuclear fusion, Biden's foreign policy, producing television programmes, baseball, basil, Giotto, Japan – we tried anything and everything we could think of, but she always had an opinion, and she had no qualms about sharing it, at length, and most especially with/at the person in the room whose specialised subject it was. And she would not stand on ceremony. Husband made the mistake, once, of having a friend to stay for the weekend who'd written a play. Jacqueline had not only seen it, but hated it, and then proceeded to tell the author of said play why it was so terrible and how it could be improved. And, as the poor, broken soul drove off into the sunset never to cross our threshold again, my mother patted herself on the back for a job well done, adding, "Some people really do need to hear the truth sometimes."

So Jacqueline goes all out for Christmas, most especially as Jenny and Reasonable Dan are here, plus their fragrant children, otherwise, "how else would they know how it's done?" Christmas is English. So is Father Christmas. Obviously. And Coral and Josh need to know about pigs in blankets as it is part of their heritage. And Jacqueline is Queen of Heritage. Heritage and Christmas. But most especially Heritage.

"Has she stuffed the bird, do you think?" asks my father, lifting up the tea towel and gingerly inspecting the turkey's nether regions.

"Isn't it chestnut at the neck and pork and sage up the rear?" I ask.

"Usually," he agrees. "And goose fat in the potatoes."

"Yup," I yawn.

"Late night?"

"Not especially."

"Your mother was tight as a tick when she staggered into bed." He turns around to flick on the kettle. "I haven't seen her that pissed in years. She staggered in. Two am, I think. She was up with your friend, what's her name, Carol?"

"Claire."

"That's right, nice girl," he sniffs. "Shame she's a spinster."

"Divorced."

"It's very hard to keep up these days. Tea? Or do you want to go straight to the hard stuff?"

"Tea," I nod, scraping a chair out from under the table.

"Before you sit down," he says, unhooking two chipped old mugs from above the kettle. "Can you let those fucking dogs out?"

Dad and I sip our tea in silence. He is looking older than he was last year and he is certainly a little more deaf and a little more entrenched in his ways. He likes things done exactly the same way as he has always done. His tea is in the same mug every morning, his breakfast of one boiled egg and a slice of wholemeal toast hasn't changed in over fifty years, his whisky and his water are always served in the same cut glass. And woe betide anyone who tries to sit in his chair. My mother doesn't have a chair. But my father does. It's right in front of the television, in the prime spot and, like any other silverback, he'll turf anyone out if they've so much as planted half a butt cheek in his seat.

"Morning! Morning!"

Jacqueline breezes into the kitchen. She's dressed in a smart navy skirt and a Guernsey jumper, she's wearing make-up, bright pink lipstick on her determined, focused mouth and pretending she is not hung-over at all. The only evidence of a whole bottle of Baileys is the slight dulling of her normally gimlet-sharp blue eyes. This morning, they are looking a little hazy and hooded, as if she'd much rather we all pissed off and she could go back to bed.

"Have you taken the bird out, Richard?" she barks. My father jumps a little in his seat.

"Yes, dear!"

"And where are the dogs?"

"Outside. Dear."

"Good." She turns and looks at me. "You need some jobs to do, sitting there. Why don't you start on the potatoes?" It's not a question. "Where are the others?"

"My two have done their stockings and are slowly working their way through the bag of chocolate money, lying in bed, and my other half is still asleep."

"Jenny and Dan have gone on a run," adds my father.

"Just so long as they don't come back and huff in my face," says Jacqueline. "What is it about people who go for a jog that they always have to come back and tell you about it? How far they have run and how quickly they have done it, while standing, all pink and sweaty and breathing next to you? No one cares. No one is interested. Jog on."

Wow, my mother's hangover must be terrible, as that is the first mean word she has said about Jenny and Reasonable Dan in their entire fifteen-year marriage.

"I suppose everyone wants bloody breakfast as well," she says, opening the fridge and staring at the mountain of gubbins. I can almost hear her stomach turn from the table. She closes the door again. "I think croissants from the freezer."

As the croissants defrost and crisp up in the oven, the kitchen slowly fills. Husband comes down (fully clothed, he once made the mistake of wearing his pyjamas on Christmas Day and he's never been allowed to forget it); he's followed by both my children who are half-dressed, jumpers over nightwear, mainly because Grandma's kitchen is so bloody cold. For my mother, heating is like food, it should be used sparingly and too much of it is most certainly vulgar. Coral and Josh are, of course, fully dressed in seasonal attire but nothing too obviously festive. And, as the croissants come out of the oven, Jenny and Dan come bursting through the door in a blast of fresh air and morning dew.

"10K," announces Dan, looking at his watch. "10K in fifty-three minutes and twenty-three seconds. Not bad," he nods. "Not bad. Bearing in mind the wines you had last night, Jen." He walks up to Jacqueline and stands with his hands on his hips, his legs apart, breathing heavily. "Not bad, don't you think, Jacqueline?"

"No," she replies, moving away.

"That's seven hundred and forty-three calories." He shoves the Apple watch in her face. "That's a whole Christmas dinner!"

"Lunch," she replies.

"Well, it's a whole one. Look," he says, showing me his calorie count. The smell of sweat and testosterone is overpowering. "What do you think?"

"Well done," I venture.

"What did you do, Jen?"

"Six hundred and fifty calories and fifty-nine minutes."

"My mate Adam's done Couch to 10K," chips in husband.

"But he mainly does couch," mumbles Ella.

"Couch." My mother shivers.

"No, he doesn't," counters Husband. "He can do it in thirty minutes."

"Thirty?" queries Dan.

"Thirty? That's Olympic standard," adds Jen. "Are you sure?"

"Absolutely," nods Husband, never knowingly known to back down from an argument. "He's pretty good." He shoves a croissant in his pie hole to indicate that's the end of the chat.

"He must be." Dan picks up his trainer-clad foot in his right hand and bends his knee back, stretching his quads, or his lats, or some such muscle. His left hand clutches the stove to balance.

"He should be the next Usain Bolt," says Jacqueline, brusquely. "Now could you get out of the kitchen."

"Actually, Bolt's a sprinter," says Dan.

"Come on, Dan," says Jenny, ever able to read the room.

By 12pm I have peeled two kilos of potatoes, prepared a kilo of parsnips (covered them in butter and maple syrup as instructed by Jacqueline, via Nigella) and taken the jackets off two bags of sprouts and crossed them at the bottom. I've drunk two glasses of sherry, had three secret fags out the back and I have yet to brush my teeth and wash my face.

"There she is!" trills Jacqueline as Claire finally, eventually, arrives in the kitchen.

"Oh Jacqueline, Happy Christmas," she says. They kiss. "I don't think I have ever slept so well in my entire life. It's so quiet in the countryside, isn't it? Maybe it's the air. But I feel like I am a princess this morning. Amazing bed. Amazing sleep. Amazing. Also so amazing not to have children at Christmas, amazing . . ."

If she says amazing one more time, I might actually . . . I stab a goose-fat covered potato instead.

"And I've had the most delicious bath."

Who manages a bloody bath on Christmas morning?

"Oh good, there was hot water." She's never said that. "You smell amazing." Or that. Jacqueline walks over and inhales Claire.

"Oh, I *must* give you some, we sell it in the shop, it's all natural herbs and essential oils. You'd love it. I gave you some the other day." She nods over at me. "Wouldn't she love it? Your mum?"

"Jacqueline's strictly a Badedas type," I say, shoving my unbrushed hair behind my ear.

"No, I'm not! I simply *love* essential oils," she declares, giving me her best withering look.

"I wish I'd known, I'd have given you some for Christmas."

"I don't need anything for Christmas," Jacqueline smiles selflessly.

Claire smiles back and crosses her legs at the table. She's wearing a pair of black, high-heeled boots and a long, flowery dress that somehow manages not to look frumpy. Her hair is brushed, her face has definitely been washed, and she's managed to put on some make-up. She is making me feel filthy just by standing next to her.

"Breakfast?" offers Jacqueline; her manner is verging on the obsequious. She seems to have developed some sort of desperate girl crush overnight, which wouldn't matter only Claire is MY friend and it's extremely irritating to become the third wheel to your mother and your mate in the space of a bottle of Baileys.

"Just a little coffee for me," says Claire. "I've got to save up for lunch."

"Of course," agrees Jacqueline. That's a girl after her own heart. "Why ruin it all with a croissant!" She glances across at me.

"Is there any more sherry?" I ask, looking at my empty glass.

"Surely there's something I can do to help?" asks Claire, half getting out of her chair.

"No, no, no!" insists Jacqueline. "You sit down, you're the guest, and you've been working so hard all week, in that shop of yours. Tell me, what else do you sell?"

Jacqueline gives Claire her cup of coffee and sits down, elbow on the table, popping her chin in the palm of her hand, as she listens to Claire list the magnificently exciting array of products they stock at Mystique. She refrains from telling my mother that she doesn't actually own the shop, but proceeds to explain about how the "green" and "ethically sourced" market works.

"I love retail," I hear my mother say as I walk out of the kitchen, to change out of my pyjamas and put on some decent clothes. "I had a great friend who worked at Peter Jones. It's 'Never Knowingly Undersold', did you know that? And what's that famous quote by John Betjeman that come a nuclear war you'd find him in the haberdashery department of Peter Jones as nothing bad ever happens there. Anyway . . . my friend . . ."

I sneak up the stairs and slowly open the door to my bedroom.

It's always been my bedroom. Even as a teenager. When we moved here, when Dad was fired and we needed to find somewhere smaller and in the countryside. It's been upgraded a little since, but if you look carefully at the ceiling, there are still a few glow-in-the-dark stars that still shine briefly, before dying a quiet death at about 8pm. Jenny and Dan are staying in the guest room. She's the oldest child, so she still, after all these years, gets first dibs on accommodation. It's a pecking order that never changes and even extends to our husbands. It's subliminal, but at the dining table, even without thinking, Reasonable Dan will sit further up the table towards the seat of power, which is closer to Richard, than my husband. It's not discussed. That's where they gravitate. Dan gets a better bedroom than my husband as he is married to Jenny and not me. Claire gets Jenny's old room, which is now the posh guest room, and I have not been upgraded at all. Ever. As a result, I am sharing the bathroom with all the snivelling children on the top attic floor, while Jenny et al get to pitter-patter around, wrapped in a towel, between their smart bedrooms and their en suites on the floor below.

"Hi," I say, as I walk into the oddly shaped eaves room above Jenny and Claire. Decorated in floor-to-ceiling pink and white Laura Ashley wallpaper, it is a veritable swansong to the 1980s, where the wallpaper matched the bedding, and the bedding matched the bedside tablecloth, and everything is piped and fringed and complete with lovely little tassels on every corner of all fifteen cushions on the bed. Husband nods from said bed. He's fully dressed, wearing his socks and lying spread out like a spatchcock chicken; he doesn't take his eyes off his screen. "What are you reading?"

"Stuff," he grunts, followed by a swoosh of an email. "Just catching up on some important things."

"But it's Christmas Day?"

"Some people are still working."

"Those without families?" I suggest.

"Mainly those with," he corrects. "How's everything downstairs?"

"Claire and Mum seem to have fallen in love."

"I saw that," he sniffs. "If I'd known it only took a bottle of Baileys to defrost the old trout, I'd have basted her in a barrel of it years ago."

"Who knew she was such a pushover."

"Extraordinary." He stretches on the bed and yawns and picks up his iPad again.

"I think maybe you should go down and show willing," I suggest.

"Willing to what?"

"Help?"

"There are so many other bloody people down there, can't they do it?" He yawns again; a cloud of stale air floats across the bed. "I'm tired."

"You're always tired."

"What's that supposed to mean?"

"Just that, you're always tired, you always have an excuse, you never do anything, you never do anything with the children."

"I am always doing shit with the children!"

"When did you last do anything with them?"

"I'm endlessly doing shit with them."

"Like what?"

"I don't know," he sighs. "I took Sam to a football match the other day."

"That was two years ago."

"Why don't you fuck off?" That's his *de facto* retort to anything he has no response for. "All you do is complain." That's his second. "You're a nag." His third.

"At least Dan plays Monopoly with his children!"

"Don't bring bloody-jogging-perfect-Mr-Nice-Guy-dull-as-ditch-water Dan into anything!" He's sitting up now, his legs have swung over the side of the bed, and he's shoving his socked feet into some shoes. "That man's a pussy-whipped twat!"

"Why is any man who is nice to his wife always pussy-whipped? Can't a man just be nice to his wife and NOT be pussy-whipped?"

"No! The man's an arse. And anyway, our children hate Monopoly."

"That's only because you never play it with them!"

"Fuck off!" He marches out of the bedroom and slams the door.

"Fuck you!" I whisper to no one as I slowly collapse on the bed.

I lie and stare at the peeling stars on the ceiling and wonder what Dave is up to. He's with his parents, I know that. I bet they are dressed in lovely fluffy jumpers all drinking eggnog (whatever the hell that is) in front of the fire and not shouting and telling each other to fuck off loudly before lunch. And we haven't even done presents yet.

The handing out of presents at my parents' house is always a little tense. As children we were made to wait until 6pm, dragging out the whole excruciating day, as we'd roll around, bored as anything on the sofa, watching the clock and waiting, waiting until we could tear open our presents and then shovel down our supper and bugger off to bed. But now, since Reasonable Dan has had a word with my mother, the whole ceremony has been shifted to before lunch. "For the sake of the children."

So at 12.30pm sharp, we all gather in the sitting room, "for the sake of the children", with our various glasses of refreshment and the ceremony begins. My father is ringmaster, and everyone sits in their spot and awaits to be served. It would work a treat if we all had the same amount of presents – except my father only ever gets three, Husband has about six, my mother, me and the children might have about twenty between us and Jenny, Dan and the kids have another seventy-five to unwrap. My poor father is up and down on his knees, scrabbling in and under the tree for at least an hour, while the pile of torn paper mounts up in the middle of the sitting room carpet. While the rest of us have generic presents – pants, socks, a jumper or two – plus a few gems from my post-coital shopping trip, Jen's gang just don't stop and not only are the presents plentiful, worse, they are also "thoughtful". The oohs, the aaahs, the tears, the hugs: it's worse than watching the Oscars. By the end of it all, Dan and Jen are glowing with love and affection, while the rest of us are a little bit more drunk, and a hell of a lot more bitter.

Even Claire's done better than us. She's been pity-gifted by everyone in the room and the pile on her chair looks like it's about to collapse.

"Honestly, Jacqueline," she coos, as she opens another Clarins gift box. "You shouldn't have."

"No woman can ever have too much leg cream," shares Mum.

"Or too many scarves," adds Husband. "Claire's got at least three."

"Four," corrects Ella. "Which is about as many bath hats Gran has given me over the years and we don't even have a bath."

When we finally sit down to lunch, my mouth is so dry from drinking champagne I can barely swallow a thing.

Everyone else piles their plates as high as Jacqueline can bear, before she says curtly to both Sam and Dan that they can always have seconds if they can get through what they have on their plates. Bottles of red are opened, and Husband drinks so much that his eyes disappear and his lips and teeth turn maroon. Ella and Sam disappear off to watch a Bond film, while Coral and Josh hear all about how Stilton is made and Jen and Dan help clear up, after which Jacqueline and Claire contemplate opening another bottle of Baileys.

"We shouldn't," says Claire, a squiffy smile already gliding across her face.

"Why not?" asks Jacqueline. "I think we should. It's Christmas! For goodness' sake."

December 26th

Boxing Day is all about tidying up, throwing away, eating leftovers and going for a walk through the grey British countryside.

In the olden days, before children, when Husband and I had smaller suitcases and better-fitting clothes, we'd have been in and out of Rose Cottage as quickly as the M40 would allow. There was something about the low ceilings and poor lighting that would bring Husband out in hives. He found the small, flickering telly about as annoying as my mother's endless critique of his life and as mind-numbingly irritating as the high-pitched voice she used to talk to her dogs. He used to say that she was more interested in her dogs than she was in her children, which would be true, although Jen was the exception. And with Jen mostly in absentia, due to her residing in Australia, the shadow of Jen's perfection loomed large.

She was marvellous, intelligent and so beautiful she moved in slow motion, like a shampoo advert lit with a golden glow of brilliance. So about thirty-six hours of parents was all Husband could tolerate.

These days, however, he's worked out that the great big tumbleweed week between Christmas and New Year, when the world grinds to a halt and no one is available for a beer, is better spent horizontal in my old teenage bedroom. He's got a good enough internet signal to while away the hours looking at other people's Christmases on Instagram, while totally opting out of his own. He also knows that I'm too preoccupied trying to please my mother or corralling my own children into saying please and thank you and taking their elbows off the table, to have the energy to berate or argue with him. He once described the experience to me as being akin to a long-haul flight, where he'd drink sufficient alcohol to manage his naps and mealtimes and the rest of the time he'd spend horizontal, dozing, snoozing or seeing if he could make it the whole way through a film.

Meanwhile, I'm downstairs taking it for the team. And this year is no exception. So far, Ella is "worryingly vain" with her obsession with Snapchat and taking photographs of herself all the time. Sam is "worryingly lazy" in his desire not to play football with Josh, who as far as I am concerned is "worryingly good at sport" and Coral is "worryingly bloody too good at bloody everything".

At 11.30am I have had enough and suggest that Claire and I go for a walk in the slate-coloured countryside. Jacqueline insists that we take the dogs.

"Keep them on the lead, darling," she says, handing over two diamanté-studded leads. "And careful of Chow's little back legs, they are not as good as they were."

"I will."

"Good, because I know what you're like with the dogs. Not very responsible."

"If you're going to say I took the dogs on a bike ride, and made them run alongside the bike and one of them was so exhausted it had to go to the vet . . .?"

"At vast expense."

"At vast expense," I confirm.

"Yes?"

"Well, I'd like to remind you that was in 1987 and it was a different dog and I was probably twelve years old."

"Thirteen. Still," she smiles, tightly and firmly. "Stick to the lanes if I were you. And don't go into the woods."

"They aren't woods, Mother. They are a copse at most."

"Don't be so pedantic, darling, you've always been so pedantic, no wonder you don't have any friends."

"I've got loads of friends, haven't I, Claire?"

Claire's by the back door, borrowing a pair of wellington boots that she is straining to fit into.

"Um, yes," she says. "Lots."

"And don't be long," adds my mother. "I don't want poor old Jenny to end up cooking all the lunch."

"Aren't we having leftovers?"

"There you are again, no need to be so pedantic!"

I inhale and exhale deeply as soon as we are outside. It's good to feel fresh air in the lungs after the stale air of Christmas. I start off down the short drive, dragging the dogs behind me. Claire trots alongside: her red wellington boots are a little tight and her blue coat is a little too large, but she seems delighted. Her single Christmas is clearly suiting her, even if she's dressed as Paddington.

"Your mum's fun," she begins.

"Is she?" I yank one of the dogs, who's sniffing the hedgerow. "Not that I have ever noticed."

"Oh, she is, you know she is."

"I've always thought she's a bit of a witch."

"That's hilarious," laughs Claire. "It's like talking to Jade!"

"That's not fair."

"Well, I'm enjoying her company."

"Good, at least someone is! Maybe because she's not your mother and she doesn't sigh every time you open your mouth, or looks like she feels sorry for you, or always asks about 'your little life' as if it's an abject failure, or constantly compare you to your older, more brilliant, more fabulous, bloody thinner sister."

"Maybe," agrees Claire, her head on one side. I can see her special "counsellor face" a mile off. She's got concerned eyes and a worried smile. And I'm not falling for it. "We all revert to our childhood roles as soon as we go home. As soon as we cross that threshold, the old habits return and old hurts and wounds are reopened."

"Are they indeed?" I am marching along the narrow lane in the middle of the road.

"That's why most of us find it so hard to go home. I know I would."

"How is your mum?"

"Barely there, I suppose. I went to see her just before Christmas. She didn't really remember who I was."

"Oh dear." I stop and look over at her. If I had a counsellor face, I might pop it on now.

"I'm fine, really I am. It's been going on for years, the steady decline, ever since Dad died. I think the shock of it hastened it all. Do you remember she had a stroke soon after?"

"I do."

"I thought she might die then and there, of a broken heart. You can do that, you know, actually die of a broken heart."

"You read about it in fairy tales."

"But it's medically proven, it's called Takotsubo Cardio-myopathy, named after the Japanese doctor who discovered it. The grief is too much for the heart to cope with."

"Amazing . . ." I tug at the dogs again. "Imagine being that in love . . ."

A car comes slowly around the corner; Claire and I pin ourselves to the hedge, I pull the dogs close to my legs. Its windows are steamed up, there are presents on the back ledge, a small child squashes its nose against the window and waves at the dogs.

"Time is so precious and family time is even more so . . ." she starts.

"If you tell me to hold onto those moments and enjoy my mother while I still have her, I shall shove you into that ditch," I say.

"At least I have made you smile!" she quips.

"It's just hard, you know. My mother is difficult, my sister is perfect, her children are more than perfect, mine are useless and my husband's a wanker! And that's about the sum of it."

"Actually, your children are interesting. Ella is funny and bright, and Sam has lots of charm. And your husband—"

"Is a wanker. I'd just wish he would do something, join in, be fun . . ."

"There is a male menopause as well, you know. Loss of testosterone."

"He's certainly got the breasts for it."

"Hair loss, loss of libido, we have loads of guys coming into the shop for it. To come and see the Chinese doctor at the back."

"I didn't know you had a clinic at the back of the shop?"

"You should come in one day . . . you might enjoy it."

"I have been in."

"Not when I've been working there."

"I'm sorry."

"Don't worry, we're all busy." She smiles.

Too busy to visit my friend. I suddenly feel awful. I've been so wrapped up in my own madness, my own "little life" that I have forgotten about my real friends, the people who make everything worthwhile.

"I'll come in the New Year."

"Is that a resolution?"

"Don't talk to me about those!" I laugh. "I don't think I've ever managed to get beyond the second week of January."

"Why give up alcohol and chocolate for the worst month of the year? It'll only make you more depressed and miserable."

"Technically we should have dry June, that would be much more successful."

I turn off the lane and onto the footpath that leads to the woods.

"Let's go down here," I say.

"Are you sure?" Claire hesitates.

"Let's live a little!"

And then, just to hammer home my point, I bend down and let the dogs off the lead. They bark and leap and hurl themselves into the undergrowth, one chasing the other, just as the sun comes out and bathes the trees in a pale winter light.

It's still and quiet in the woods. The air is damp despite the sun, and sound doesn't travel far, noises clatter and fall as they bounce against the damp bark of the trees. The undergrowth is flat, wintered, save for a few valiant brambles that forge towards the sky and a couple of sturdy ferns that block our path. There are some splashes of colour, red berries, a rowan tree yet to be stripped by the birds. High up above our heads there are nests of mistletoe still green against the patchy blue and grey sky. I used to play in these woods as a child. I know where the badgers dig their setts and the foxes build their dens. Jen and I used to pick armfuls of bluebells in the spring; we learnt how to roll cigarettes in our teens and drank copious amounts of cider with the local boys during the long summer months. I was raised in this wood, I suppose. Jen and I would lie for hours on the dry summer leaves, staring up at the canopy, the dappled sun on our faces, discussing life, love, boys and how to get the hell out of there as quickly as possible. It's only now, in middle age, that I can really see the beauty of the place.

"We could go down here to the stream if you like?" I ask Claire, who is picking her way along the narrow path behind me.

"Is it far? Only my feet are hurting. These boots . . ."

"Are a bit small?"

"You could say that."

"Sure, don't worry, let's head back, it's time for leftovers and ham in Coke anyway! Let's just get the dogs. Chow!

Mein!" I shout, my flat voice echoing around the woods. "Chow! Mein!" My voice bounces back again. I scan the undergrowth for bouncing heads and black faces and fluffy fur. "Chow! Mein!" Claire joins in. We are standing back-to-back, shouting in different directions. "Chow! Chow! Chow!" I am exuding childish enthusiasm. "Mein! Mein! Mein!" I glance across at Claire.

"Oh Christ!" she says.

"Dad will be pleased, he hates them."

"Really? Why?"

"My mother loves them more than anyone else, I suppose, him included."

"Even Jenny?"

"Even Jenny." We both look at each other again.

"Shit!"

"CHOOOOOOOW. MEEEEEEIN!"

Both our hearts are beating hard, my anxiety is through the roof. Why did I do that? What was I thinking? My palms are sweating. I shout. Claire shouts. I shout again. We spread out, combing the woods, yelling their names, staring blankly towards the horizon, hoping, praying, not breathing, stand-ing stock-still, scanning the forest floor for any movement.

"Shhhhhh!" hisses Claire. We strain our ears together. A small rabbit hops out of the undergrowth. "Oh fuck!" she says. "Can you whistle?"

I purse my lips. A pathetic level of noise comes out. "No," comes my reply.

"CHOOOOOOW! MEEEEEEIN!"

The level of panic in our voices is audible. I am sweating.

"I've lost Jacqueline's favourite children," I say.

"CHOOOOW!! MEEEEIN!!!"

"Do you think they're on the road?" asks Claire. She is not looking good; her face is white with panic and her mouth is visibly dry.

"CHOW!! MEIN!"

I am losing the will to live. I am seeing hysterics, and crying, and the finger of hell being pointed at me, and my mother never speaking to me again, which could be the silver lining. My phone in my pocket beeps. It's a message from Ella. "Where are you? Granny wants to start lunch. Don't keep Granny waiting. 😊 😊 😊."

"It's lunchtime," I say. "What shall we do?" I'm frozen with panic. I can't think. I move one way and then the other. "Claire, come on, say something."

"I think we should go back for lunch."

"Really?"

"I don't know!"

"CHOOOW MEEIN!" Bloody stupid names. Bloody stupid dogs.

"They are clearly not here," she says.

"Could they have been dognapped? For money?"

"How?"

"I don't know." I'm seriously worried now.

"I think we should go home and get help to look for them."

"Shit," I say and shake my head. "I think plucking my nasal hair would be more preferable."

We walk back in silence, intermittently shouting the dogs' names, looking in the hedgerows, over garden walls, scouring the fields. Finally, we reach the small wooden moss-covered gate to Rose Cottage. We both pause, wanting the other to go first. I feel sick.

"Come on then," I whisper. "Here goes."

Inside, the kitchen is hot and steamy, the pine table is laid and everyone is sitting down, except Jacqueline and Jenny who are carving the ham and putting baked potatoes in a bowl on the table.

"There you are!" snaps my mother. "What time do you call this?" She looks at the brass clock on the wall. "It's quarter to two. You've been hours."

"I am sorry, but . . ."

"Sit down." She points to a seat in the corner. "Are you alright, Claire? Why don't you take that coat off and sit next to me, and tell me all about tarot, I'm simply desperate for you to read my cards."

"I'm so sorry," says Claire, taking off the blue Paddington coat.

"And what did you do to the dogs?" She is sawing away at the ham with bristling efficiency.

"What do you mean?" I hear myself say.

"You're so irresponsible. Letting them off the lead like that."

"I didn't," I lie.

"Really?" She turns to look at me, her face puce from standing over the hot ham. In one hand she has a pointed fork that has a slither of flaccid ham hanging off the end, and in the other she has a sharp knife. "How do you explain the state of them, then?" She jabs at the air with the knife, in the vague direction of the dogs' beds to the left of the back door. "They came home in an awful state, poor Jenny's had to give them both baths and Coral and Josh have spent hours grooming all the brambles out of their fur. I am lost for words. Lost. It's extraordinary behaviour on your part," she continues, clearly having found some more words. "What did you think you were doing? That is your problem . . . You never think. Selfish, that's you. You've always been selfish. Ever since you were a child. You never shared anything. You never think about anyone else other than yourself. Does she, Dickie?"

"No," agrees Dad, because it is a lot easier than disagreeing. Although sometimes I wish he would.

"You owe me an apology, and Jenny and her children and your father."

"I don't need an apology," replies my father, before catching a look from my mother. "But everyone else clearly does."

"Mostly the dogs," adds my mother. "Poor things."

*   *   *

It's 6pm and I still have not been forgiven for dog-gate. The stony silences, the endless sighing, the patting, the petting, the muttering of "poor little things", it's enough to make me want to pack my bags and leave for London, anywhere, immediately. Unfortunately, I have to endure Boxing Day drinks.

My parents have hosted Boxing Day drinks every year since they moved into Rose Cottage well over forty years ago. They both hate doing it, but they do it anyway. So much so that Jen and I used to think that being an adult was all about doing things you hated doing. Cooking, cleaning, washing cars, paying tax, driving, shopping and hosting a drinks party on Boxing Day. And now I'm an adult, I know that both she and I were correct. Being a grown-up *is* about getting through a series of events you don't want to do, but you can't think of a good enough excuse to get out of them.

So every year my parents stuff their stuffy sitting room with stuffy people they mostly spend the rest of the year trying to avoid. Jacqueline rushes around topping up glasses with wine and handing out more Marks and Spencer vol-au-vents and trays of pigs in blankets. This year she does so repeating the story of how I lost the dogs in the woods, only for Jen to find them and rescue them and groom them back to life. Which wasn't strictly true, but my mother has never really let *that* get in the way of a good anecdote.

As children we would be forced to take people's coats on the way in and put up with the endless hideous pecks on the cheek by various dank, cold, sweaty or painted lips. The worst was Mr Bagshaw who lives in the Old Post Office, which was converted into a house during the great utilities cull of the 1980s. For not only did he have lengthy, tickly whiskers which contained half his lunch, but he also sweated aftershave, which he'd deposit like a cold slap on both our cheeks as he arrived in the hall, and the smell would stay on our faces for hours.

Mr Bagshaw is still alive and arrives bang on 6.30pm with his walking stick and hearing aid turned up to the max. I glance across at my sister who grimaces slightly as he approaches, only to greet him like a long-lost friend, the professional that she is. He kisses her. And from the expression on her face as he walks away, I can tell that he's planted a sweaty, aftershave kiss on her cheek that no amount of rubbing with the back of her hand will efface. He has his sights set on me. I make a run for the door. The Bowens have arrived, she's tiny and thin and as brown as a vanilla stick, due to her permanently being on holiday, and he's as large as a wardrobe, eight months pregnant and hasn't seen his own feet since 1976. My father calls them Flesh and Bone, only not to their faces.

"Dennis!" says my father as I open the door. "Merry Christmas."

"You remember Adam?" says Dennis.

He steps aside to reveal a tall, rather good-looking figure, with a full head of dark hair. Wearing a crisp white shirt, a dark jacket and jeans, Adam has the sort of gentle suntan that only graces the affluent and a physique that exudes the well-massaged, well-oiled, super-toned feel of wagyu beef.

Adam Bowen. I glance over at Jenny. Adam Bowen. She hasn't seen him. We both remember Adam Bowen. Two years older than me, and a year younger than Jenny, he had a terrible crush on my sister, and we used to tease him mercilessly. He was always a little plump, poor at sport and spent most of his teens in braces. Visibly uncoordinated, he was the sort of boy you tried to avoid dancing with at parties. Not that we went to many of those.

"Amanda," says my father, addressing the diminutive Bone. "How very lovely to see you, and Adam, what a surprise!"

"We've only got him for a day or so," replies Amanda/ Bone, gripping onto her son's arm. "Before he disappears back to Hong Kong."

"Hong Kong," nods my father. "Very impressive. Do you remember my daughter?"

"Of course I do," smiles Adam. "Who could forget?" He leans over and kisses me lightly on the cheek. He smells of vanilla. "I was always very keen to hang out with you and Jenny, but you'd never give me the time of day."

"Ha ha ha. I'm not sure that's true!" I laugh, feeling my cheeks flush.

"Oh, it is," he nods. "Kind might not be a word I'd use."

"Fun?" I suggest.

"Not very."

"I don't think we were that bad." I laugh again. It's sounding a little high.

"Merry Christmas, Jacqueline," waves Amanda. "Adam's just reminding your daughter how mean she was to him when growing up."

'It was both of them," adds Adam.

"Not Jenny," corrects Jacqueline. "But yes . . . can you believe what happened today, she only went and lost the dogs . . . poor little things . . . come and have a drink. What would you like?"

"So you found them then?" he asks. "The dogs?"

"Yes." I take a large sip of my red wine. "Eventually."

"I saw you and your friend walking up and down the lane, calling their names."

"Nice of you to help!" I joke.

"You looked like you'd got it covered," he says, plucking a glass of white wine from the tray by the vol-au-vents. "And anyway, it was quite entertaining."

"What?"

"Watching you both run around in your ill-fitting wellies."

"Are you in the habit of not helping women?" It comes out a little more abrasive than I intended.

"Not exactly, I was just reminded of you as a child, it was rather sweet, running about in wellington boots. I imagine you haven't worn those in a while."

"Not much call for them on the Kilburn High Road."

"Is that where you live? I imagine you're probably quite high up now in marketing."

"How do you know I did that? I mean do . . . do that?"

"You've always done that. Haven't you? I remember. So where are you now?"

"I'm still in marketing," I smile.

"Great. So where are you now then? TalkTalk? Barclays? A big FTSE 100?" He looks me up and down. "Chanel?"

"Ha, ha." I laugh. "I'm helping a, um, local firm."

"Local's good," he nods. "Local is great. What do they do?"

"Sports . . . stuff."

"Right . . ."

"You?"

"I'm CEO of an offshore investment company that specialises in green renewables. We also have a charity arm that is trying to help with the refugee crisis in Myanmar."

"Right," I nod. I take another sip of wine. Just then Husband walks over. "Adam, this is my husband."

"Hello," he says. "I was just telling your wife that I was madly in love with her when I was a teenager."

"You were?" replies Husband, still looking down at his phone and pressing send.

"I think it was Jenny," I smile.

"Everyone thought it was Jenny," he replies. "But they were wrong."

"Oh, there you are, Adam." Dennis walks over slowly; his breathing is audible due to his exertion. His cheeks are like shiny pink apples and his buttons look like they're planning their escape from his tight, red, brushed-cotton shirt at any moment. "I've just been telling Richard about your new thirty-million-dollar deal."

"Very impressive," my father nods from behind the total eclipse that is Dennis. "Very impressive."

"Dad, no one's interested in that."

Husband just stares at him, while he clutches his phone. His fist is illuminated by its pale blue light.

"Well, I am, and I am very proud of it and you," replies Dennis. "He has a fabulous house in Hong Kong, over-looking the South China Sea. Honestly, Richard, it's like another world."

"I can imagine," agrees my dad. He's always been a gener-ous soul. "Very impressive. You must be very proud."

"Wife? Kids?" barks Husband suddenly, like they were right at the very top of his list of priorities. His head is twitching a little from side to side. His bed hair and day-three stubble make him appear in need of a deep clean with a bottle of Cif.

"Both."

"How old are they?"

Interestingly, this is not a question that Husband would be able to answer with one hundred per cent accuracy himself. He did once, when we were in the market for having a nanny, and advertised the position and got both our children's ages wrong; Ella's by three years.

"The wife or the children?" Adam laughs. "I have two little girls who are five and seven years old, and just for the record Emma, my wife, is thirty-five."

"Thirty-five." Husband repeats it like the concept is a dim and distant dream. A mirage from another world.

"That's young." I sound terse . . . and bitter . . . and old.

"Bit of an age gap, I know," Adam smiles. When did he get so good-looking? I just remember him being irritating and annoying and a little bit dull. "So I really try and stay in shape."

"What – the gym!" Husband scoffs a little, as if his magnificent physique "just happens".

"I try not to."

"I try not to as well!" Husband chuckles.

"And you're very successful," I reply.

Adam laughs. Husband does not. A fug of tension wafts between them. "Well, I sail, actually, most weekends. I have a little boat."

"That sounds nice. A rubber dinghy?"

I am not sure why Husband wants to prolong the agony of this conversation. Adam doesn't look like a rubber dinghy bloke and anyway, you can't really sail a rubber dinghy. Adam smells of success, and vanilla, but mostly success.

"No, it's a yacht." Adam's looking a little uncomfortable.

"How big?"

"Oh . . . I don't know."

"You must know, you're the owner."

"A few metres.'

"How many?"

"Twenty-eight."

"How many berths?"

"It sleeps six, with four crew," he mumbles. Husband strains a little to hear.

"Crew?" he asks. "I thought it was for exercise?"

". . . And enjoyment."

"Oh . . . *and* enjoyment," Husband nods. "Exercise AND enjoyment. Glad we cleared that up."

'Hi, Adam," purrs Jenny, with all the confidence of a thirty-five-year unrequited crush under her belt. "Fancy seeing you here."

"My parents live here, why wouldn't I come and visit?"

"I thought you'd be off somewhere exotic, like Bali, for Christmas."

"It's full of Australians at Christmas."

"That's because they have excellent taste!" She throws back her fine blonde hair and gives it a little shake.

"Well, one of them married you," he replies.

"And he's right over there, before you get any ideas!"

Dan is standing by the door to the kitchen, helping himself to some pigs in blankets; he is pulling at his collar, it's clearly uncomfortable, tight and a little stiff. His chinos are also stretched over his well-worked-out thighs. He's definitely a baggies and trackies kind of a guy.

"I don't really have any ideas," says Adam, quietly. "I never really have."

Jenny just laughs and gives him a little shove on the chest. "Don't be silly!" she smiles. "Anyway, it's been lovely to see you. Don't leave it so long next time. Although we are hardly ever here either, as we are mostly in Australia, living on the beach, surfing . . . swimming, running, that sort of thing . . . I think Dan might like another beer."

It's about 10.30pm and Husband and I are getting changed for bed. He's hopping around trying to get his pyjamas on; the seven glasses of wine he's drunk have clearly gone to his legs.

"That guy's a bit of a prick." He hops onto the bed.

"Which guy?" I know full well who he is talking about.

"That guy from Hong Kong."

"Adam?"

"Adam the Arse." Both his legs are in the air as he pulls his pyjamas down. He raises his bare buttocks off the bed and in one swift move, pulls his pyjamas up to his waist. "I mean . . . fancy showing off about having a boat like that. For exercise *and* enjoyment," he mimics. "What a wanker. Also showing off that his wife is thirty-five years old! I mean, who says *that*. And how has he got that? A wife that young. What does he do anyway? The tosser!"

"He invests in green energy, I think."

"Wanker. I hate him even more now. How long have you known him?"

"Years."

"Is he the one who's been in love with Jenny his entire life?"

"So everyone thinks."

"I bet she's pissed off," he concludes, sighing and slowly expanding across the bed.

"Why?"

"Well, he's a hell of a better bet than Dan over there. The sports science teacher from Sydney. This Adam is the one that got away! She could be sailing for exercise *and* enjoyment, living the high life in Hong Kong. Going on exotic holidays. Wouldn't that be something?"

I sigh. "It really would."

December 27th

Choices. Choices. Choices. All the choices I made. All the choices I failed to make.

I lie in bed for hours, not sleeping, just staring at the peeling stars on the ceiling thinking about the things I have done, the decisions I have come to. The guilt and the regret are overwhelming. They come in waves, coursing through my body, my chest tightening, my breath shortening, my mouth dry. It feels devastating, the level of anxiety is out of control. It is sheer, unadulterated panic.

Have I just been sleepwalking my entire life? Do I live in a dull twilight of my own making?

Have I not really thought about anything?

Did I just blithely do things and not think about the consequences?

Am I just passive and inert? Am I destined to go through life like an odourless gas, leaving no trace at all? My insignificance is total.

What is so terrifying is that if I open Pandora's Box or take the elephant out of the room and sweep it from under the very lumpy carpet, what will I find?

An unbearable river of pain that would not, could not, stop flowing?

I cry a little, I shiver under the duvet. How could I have got life so horribly wrong? Am I impervious to signs, other people's thoughts and emotions? Was Adam really sitting and pining for me for all those years, or has he rewritten his own story? And who's writing mine, because I sure as hell am not. I'm the author of nothing. I'm not in charge of anything. I am about as proactive as a leaf on the wind; I can neither choose my own direction nor my final destination. I am forever destined to be buffeted along the street, growing increasingly brittle and frail until I am finally squashed underfoot and turned to dust.

The next morning, my fight with my subconscious has been so brutal, no amount of coffee could revive me. I pack in silence, say muted goodbyes to my parents and my sister and go and sit in the car. When Claire suggests she might stay on for an extra couple of days with my mother as she is going to a New Year's Eve party nearby, I can't be bothered to even react.

December 28th

"Was your Christmas as fucking shit as mine?"

Sally is driving around, shouting into her crotch, while trying to find a parking space. It's The Sales and seeing as she is having baby number four, she needs to "re-up on more shit", while spending as little money as possible as she "might need it in the divorce".

"Let me just share this . . ." she begins. I can hear her indicator clicking and her turning the wheel, I can also hear the squeaking of her brakes and the distant honking of other people's horns as she irritates and annoys all in her path. "So I had Will's mother over, plus his sister, her husband, their two children who are fourteen and sixteen and therefore monosyllabic and just stare at screens all day, plus I had my brother, Jolyon, the one you went out with, and his extremely boring wife; why didn't *you* marry him, I ask myself, my life would have been so much more fun and then, of course, his dreadful daughters, my nieces, who did nothing to help and should know better, plus my three, and Will, and all the while vomiting copiously, and not being able to drink a drop, not that I wanted to because wine smells so disgusting, and don't even mention cigarettes, it's instant vomiting, ah here's a space, oh PISS off! I've just given a bloke in a van the finger . . . oh shit . . . it might be a police van . . . it is. Bollocks, I'll call you back."

Five minutes later she calls back. She's parked the car and is walking into John Lewis.

"So the police were quite pissed off until they realised that if they arrested me I wouldn't stop talking and would give them all tinnitus . . . anyway . . . how was your Christmas? How was Claire?"

"Claire and Mum have become best friends."

"Stop it!" she squeals. "I'm going to have to sit down. Or I might pee. I'm incontinent already. How? When? How did you let that happen?"

"They just got on."

"Got on? That's against the law and if it isn't, it should be. How did they *just get on*?"

"They drank a bottle of Baileys."

"I'm sorry, run that by me again. Claire and Jacqueline sat down and drank a bottle of Baileys? What, between them?"

Poor Sally is so confused. She is stuttering and spluttering down the phone.

"A whole bottle?"

"And they cracked open a second one."

"The world, let me tell you, has gone mad." She inhales loudly into the receiver, clearly girding herself for breaking news. "And another thing, just to prove what I am saying, Kate's got a boyfriend."

"Really? That's exciting." I feel a little rush of joy, good news at last.

"Is it though? I saw her the other day and instead of the usual condoms rattling around in her bag, do you know what I found? A packet of Compeed. Corn plasters! She's got bloody corns! *And* a boyfriend."

"What's his name?"

"She won't say."

"Why?"

"God knows. Because she wants to be mysterious! Like I care. He was married, or is married, and had a marriage, still married and . . . I don't know. All I know is that my vicarious sex life is over – O-V-A-H – and all I am going to be hearing from now on is how lovely he is, and what a fabulous vongole he makes, and trust me, no one wants to hear about vongole! I kind of hate her."

"I'm calling her right away."

"Don't tell her I said anything," adds Sally. "The last thing I need is an irate Kate. Now, I've got to go and look at double buggies."

"A double . . ."

"Yup. Buggy."

I start to laugh. "What? The two pushchairs in one?"

"Yes."

"Those things that take up the whole pavement and look like they should be run by Transport for London! That sort of buggy?"

"How else am I supposed to move all these bloody children around? Listen." Her voice is tight. "If you don't stop laughing, I am going to hang up." I laugh more. "I am serious." I can't stop. "I don't think it's funny. Right . . . I'm hanging up!"

I sit chuckling at the kitchen table. I stare out of the window at the small muddy patch of lawn and the moribund flowerbed covered in rotting leaves. It's beginning to get dark and it's only about 3pm. This time of year, between Christmas and New Year, really is the worst. Thank God for girlfriends.

I call Kate.

"Hi!" she huffs. "How are you?! Happy Christmas." Sally's right, Kate is clearly getting laid, she's never sounded this jolly at 3pm on a Tuesday afternoon.

"Are you running?"

"Always!" she breezes.

"How was your Christmas?"

"Great," she says.

"How great?"

"Great, good, you know . . ."

"How good?"

"Have you been speaking to Sally?"

"I have been speaking to Sally."

"I'm never telling that woman anything ever again!"

Later that evening, I'm drinking wine, making some sort of soup/stew/curried dish which involves what's in the fridge mixed with stock and rice, while Husband is sitting at the table waiting to be served, which is marginally better than him sitting on the sofa waiting to be served, mainly because Ella is on the sofa, having taken over the best part of it, watching yet another morbid American drama where beautiful, over-made-up girls with super blow-dries and fabulous figures discuss how awful their suburban lives are, while driving around in open-top cars in the sunshine.

"Kate's got a boyfriend."

"Mmm?" Swoosh. "Who?"

"Kate."

"A what?"

"A boyfriend."

"That's a surprise."

"Really? Why?"

"Because."

"Because, what? She's not attractive?"

"Kate's hot," he says, putting down the iPad, for once.

"Is she?"

"Oh yeah," he adds, warming to his subject. "Very hot, she's one of your hottest friends, she's sexy. If I weren't married to you, I'd fancy her. Well, actually, I am married to you, and I still do fancy her! But I wouldn't go out with her."

"Really?"

"No."

"Why not?"

"I just wouldn't."

"Even if she's hot?"

"She's a nightmare."

I stop stirring whatever is in the saucepan. "Wow."

"She's attractive and clever, got her own money and a good job and a life, and all that stuff, but where's a bloke going to fit in? She doesn't need one. There's nothing for us to do. She's got a big life with lots going on, but what's a bloke to do, tag along behind, carrying the bags? The only person who can really go out with her is someone whose life is bigger than hers and they are hard to find." He shrugs and takes a sip of his wine. "She's an apex predator. Any bloke that comes near her would be eaten up and spat out within weeks."

"An apex predator?"

"Like a T-Rex."

"I know what an apex predator is."

"Basically, men are terrified of them. Unless she finds another apex predator. And then they might just tear each other apart."

"What, over the remains of a sabre-toothed tiger?"

"Something like that."

"Is Claire an apex predator?"

"No," he replies. "She is like a Triceratops, fierce and covered in armour, defensive, difficult to know. Sally's a screeching Pterodactyl."

"That's quite accurate," I laugh. "And what am I?"

"You?" He puts down his wine. "A Diplodocus."

"The huge one with the very small brain?"

"That's the one!" He clicks his fingers and picks up his wine. "They're vegetarian. You don't eat much meat. Anyway," he adds quickly. "Who's her boyfriend?"

December 31st

Was there ever a more appalling night out than New Year's Eve? It is the classic "I saw you coming" night of the year, an amateur night, where the prices are tripled, the menus are set, the fun is forced and the joy is in short supply. And the worst of it? It goes on forever. You have to stay awake beyond midnight. I never really want to stay awake anywhere beyond midnight. The old adage is that nothing happens after 2am, but I always think nothing really happens after 11pm. Nothing more than a terrible headache and a slap across the face the next morning with the wet fish of regret and the cold sweat of alcohol guilt.

But Husband loves New Year, and most of all he loves dressing up for New Year. There's nothing he likes more than a themed party, and possibly one where he's allowed to wear drag. He thinks *Rocky Horror* is hilarious. He can do the Time Warp, he knows the moves, and he has got an old, buckled leather necklace somewhere in a bedside drawer that he's kept from his university days where he'd need no excuse to pop on a Frank N. Furter costume and get down to it. Fortunately, I have only seen photographic evidence of this. Had I actually met him in his black panties and suspenders stage, dear reader, I would not have married him. He's packed away the panties but the force, the need, is still there. Tarts 'n' Vicars, Hoes 'n' Pimps, Devils 'n' Angels. He's the first to crack open the black lipstick.

And this year is no exception; he's shelled out for a table at the local children's charity fundraiser, The Bush Trust New Year's Eve Ball, where the theme is *Moulin Rouge*. It's supposed to be quite *the night*, with a cabaret and everything. There's a set menu, as much Prosecco as you can bear to drink and a band. He bought the tickets back in September, when everyone was very enthusiastic; now, of course, as the day/night approaches, there appears to be an awful lot of flu going around and babysitters are bailing by the dozen. I would almost feel sorry for him were it not that I am dreading the evening so much myself.

I have been to their events before. The Bush Trust have form.

They always take over the same municipal hall just next door to the Episcopal Church off the Shepherd's Bush roundabout. Quite apart from the appalling flickering neon strip lighting that no one knows how to dim, the slate-grey carpet tiles that give you an electric shock just by walking on them, and the general smell of bleach that hangs in the air, the music is always so loud that everyone spends the night shouting in each other's ear, so you wake up the next morning hung-over like a hound dog, hoarse, with tinnitus and a Eustachian tube full of spittle.

But we still appear to be going. Personally, I'd prefer a date on the sofa, where I could set up an IV of wine and a box of assorted chocolates (for interest and variety), and I would happily watch enough Graham Norton for me to pass out, slack-jawed, on my old sheepskin pillow. But no such luck.

Sadly, Husband's table of ten is now down to six, which means that Madison has been on the phone (did I not mention she was the chair of the NYE Committee? The theme was her idea, *Moulin Rouge* is her favourite film) asking if we'd accommodate some strays from her table which is naturally full to bursting!

Husband is excited, he's hired a ringmaster's outfit complete with red jacket and tight white breeches, which he is convinced makes him look just like Ewan McGregor, or even better, Hugh Jackman in *The Greatest Showman*. He's tickled pink and striding around the sitting room with his top hat in his hand, shouting: "Are you entertained?" at the children, which is a line from *Gladiator*, but they don't seem to mind. Pig is laughing with him, and Ella is laughing at him. I'm just delighted they are laughing. I'm not sure my expectations of a night out could be any lower. Two pairs of Spanx later and I have managed to squeeze into a sequin minidress that stops halfway up the thighs, it's too short and I feel too old to be wearing it. I've found a feather boa in the old dressing-up box that hasn't been opened for about five years, and that's the outfit I'm going with. I could have made more of an effort, I know. But I'm too English to dress up. I find it embarrassing and anyway, I'm driving, otherwise it's seventy-five quid on a taxi down the drain.

As soon as I walk into the hall, I realise I have made a mistake. Both costume-wise and with my lack of alcohol. Madison has thrown the kitchen sink plus a whole load of bespoke handcrafted, hand-finished units at the party. Gone is the terrible lighting, the carpet-squared floor and the back note of bleach: the place has been transformed, lock, stock and even the lavatories into a fabulous Big Top tent. The floor is covered in sawdust, the walls balloon with red silk and all the tables are covered in candy-striped cloths that form a circle to create a Ring, or a dance floor for later. There is even a stage for the band. There's a cocktail bar serving Prosecco and Green Fairy, a highly dangerous-sounding absinthe-based drink, and there's a photo booth right next to the bar. You have to hand it to her, Madison's talents are wasted on the school run, Pilates and brunch at Grainger's. She should have been a Hollywood set designer. Turns out she just hired one instead.

"Cost her ten grand," says Erica, who's already announced she's on our table, along with her ever-elusive husband, who I was placing bets on not existing at all. But then again, I don't think she's ever met mine, bearing in mind it's taken him two years to notice that Sam's moved school, and has never knowingly been seen on the school run. She's peering at me through the corkscrew curls of her ginger Nicole Kidman wig. "Which is more than the charity is making on the party," adds Erica, the curls quivering. "Why didn't she save us all the trouble and just donate it all to the charity? HEY!!!" she whoops suddenly. 'Great pardy! Yayyyyyy Madison! Happy New Years!" she says, even though she's not American.

"Thank you, guys, so much for coming, so sweet of you, to give up the best night of the year for the poor kids and young people in the area, I'm so proud to be part of this, I really am." Madison has clearly had her face immobilised for Christmas. Her long blonde hair is pulled so high and tight that her eyes appear feline and only her lips are capable of movement. She has a hand on each of our shoulders; this would normally imply camaraderie, but I think it's only to stop us from walking away. "I can't tell you guys how much work it's been. It's like a full-time job. I had to get rid of half the committee as they were useless." She rolls her eyes. "But it is for the poor children, and all those good causes. But the battles! Let me tell you. Some of the women around here are utter bitches." She pats us both on the shoulder and makes her way through the crowd. She is swinging her hips; she is wearing a tiny, shimmering showgirl costume that cantilevers the bust and disappears halfway up the buttocks. She looks sensational. It's no wonder she chose this theme – she looks utterly fabulous in the costume.

"Do you think she had that made specially?" asks Erica, through her poodle wig, as she follows my eyeline.

"Probably." I nod.

"I'm off to *go find* my husband," she says, even though she's from Surrey.

Right next to the bar, I come across Will who's had three Green Fairies and is pretending absinthe is hugely mind-altering and that, he indeed, has a mind to alter.

"Honestly, Sal," he says, squinting at the glass. "You can see why Van Gogh chopped his ear off. This stuff is lethal. I'd offer you a sip, but you know . . ." He looks down at her burgeoning belly.

Poor Sally is very much here under duress. There really is nowhere less she'd rather be than inhaling the hideous canapé breath of a whole load of drunk idiots while having to stay seated until midnight. But Will bought the tickets before she was pregnant and she is determined that this pregnancy won't "change a thing", as Will is so deeply against it, so she's out and about, smiling, pretending everything is fine. Kate is also here; she's resolutely refused to wear fancy dress, saying it's for children and office parties, but she looks fabulous in her tight black gown, her skin is glowing; she is clearly enjoying the fruits of a new boyfriend. How long he will last is a different matter.

"I haven't had this much sex in years," she says, checking out the party over the rim of her glass. Sally and I both smile, valiantly.

"I am very happy for you," I manage to say. "You really deserve it."

"You are so lovely." She kisses me. "Most of my friends are so jealous, I can't really talk to them about it."

"That's awful," I say.

"Yeah, awful," agrees Sally, sipping a ginger beer, which seems to be her new go-to drink of choice.

"They are not your real friends," I add.

"No," agrees Sally. "Not at all. Real friends are thrilled and delighted you're having so much sex."

"Oh yes, delighted," I add.

"And all their husbands keep coming on to me," says Kate. "It's driving me mad."

"It's the pheromones," says Sally. "It's like they know you're up for business."

"Business?" Kate looks a little appalled.

"You know what I mean," says Sally. "It's like when you're pregnant every man runs a mile, except the weird ones, that is. The ones with a milky boob fetish."

"With what?" I ask.

"A MILKY BOOB FETISH!" she shouts, just as Madison cuts the music. Half the room turns around and most of the men quickly glance at her chest. "Bollocks," says Sally under her breath.

Madison pops her finger hard on the microphone to regain the attention of the room.

"Welcome, welcome, welcome, one and all, to my little soirée. Well, it's technically not mine, it's the Bush Trust's Annual New Year's Eve party! As organised by me, and the committee." Her open palm pans the room, suggesting other committee members, but the lights are so brightly set on Madison that the rest of the room is dark. "Thanks, guys." She bobs a curtsy, doing namaste hands. "I couldn't have done it without you, and you couldn't have done it without me!" She laughs. She puts her hands in front of her and claps. "Go, Committee!" She claps again. "But you're not just here to have fun!" A couple of her acolytes moan. "Ha ha!" she laughs, the tassels on her costume swishing from side to side. "On your table you'll find a little plastic thing like this, with some buttons on it." She holds up what looks like a flat, square plastic calculator. "This is for the silent auction. So, there will be fabulous things, experiences that flash up on the screen over there and you are asked to bid on them here, and please be generous, the prizes are amazing, and remember!" She grins. "By pressing the buttons, you are giving to the poor children!" She pauses. Lips pursed. Sincere face. "Ladies and gentlemen, dinner is served!"

After plenty of milling around in the dark, we finally find our table which is predictably near both the lavatories and the kitchens, which means we are hit with the heady cocktail of gentlemen's urine and roast lamb for most of the evening. I'm opposite Kate and next to Erica's husband, Steve, who's a diminutive bald chap with bright blue eyes and a sharp sense of humour. He works in finance and spends most of his time in Switzerland which is, or so he points out, the secret to the perfect marriage. Distance. Erica is apparently very busy with the children and her sport and her lunches and he has no hobbies at all. They both met when they were working for the same firm; Erica was marginally his senior and he couldn't believe she'd given him a second glance. And now he spends all day working and the rest of it sitting in his studio flat in Geneva watching box sets on TV, if he's not out eating vast amounts of melted cheese off a fondue stick, that is.

Kate is sandwiched between my husband and Sally's, both of whom are trying to get her smashed on Green Fairies, as Sally can't drink them, and I have had one sip and was triggered into a Night Nurse flashback and retched slightly in my mouth. They are both competing for Kate's attention, which she is dishing out on a needs-must basis, while trying to ignore them both and speak across the table to Steve. Meanwhile, Sally is stuck in the corner listening to Erica's horrific birthing stories.

"What is it about other women?" hisses Sally, after Erica has gone to the extremely close toilet facilities. "As soon as someone is pregnant, every other bloody woman comes up to tell them how they nearly died giving birth. It's like a massive slap in the face. 'Don't have too much fun, don't be too relaxed because I nearly snuffed it and my best friend here, ended up having fifteen caesareans for one baby and was forced to sit down on a rubber ring for a whole seven months.' Quite apart from the fact that I've had three children already. Why don't they leave me alone? It's like a conspiracy. No one wants to hear it, and yet give them a few drinks and they can't wait to tell you how they lost thirty-seven pints of blood and can't sneeze in public ever again, for fear of their kidneys falling out of their vaginas. Bitches, the lot of them."

The cold lamb is cleared away and the chocolate mousse is served, followed by cups of thin Americano coffee and petits fours the size of rabbit droppings. Will, Kate and Husband are now well and truly smashed, so when Pretty Little Movers, the band, take to the stage, they are first on the dance floor. Husband prances around pretending to be a ringmaster, his arm in the air, cracking a fanciful whip; Kate pretends to be some sort of lion-type creature, snaking her hips and snarling with claws; while Will just trots around pointing at people. He zigzags from one side of the circle to another, his arm outstretched, his forefinger is rigid and his left eye is closed. He is in a state of perpetual motion, the main issue being if he stopped, he would probably keel over.

All the while the silent auction is flashing away on the screen behind me. I strain my head occasionally to view the lots.

"I am bidding for the day out at Silverstone," says Steve, looking above my head. "But there's lots of stuff, Madison has been working really hard. There's even a breakfast at that little café next door to the school and a free birthday party at the trampol . . ." he stops and stares, his mouth slowly opens and shuts, his eyes narrow. "Is that . . .?"

"Oh my God!" Erica giggles. "Look!" She's pointing above my head. "She looks a bit like you! Doesn't she? That woman in the advert. Actually, she looks *just* like you!"

"Is it you?" asks Steve. His hand is on my shoulder, he's looking concerned.

"Ha ha," I laugh. 'Noooo, that's happened before. It's like . . ."

"Her twin sister," says Sally. I look at her somewhat incredulously. "She keeps her well hidden."

"Very," I smile.

"A twin," he enthuses. "That's exciting. Where does she live? Close by?"

"Very close," says Sally. "Almost in the same house."

"Almost," I agree.

"Jesus Christ!" says Will, falling slightly onto the table. "What the hell are you doing bouncing in the air with a banana-yellow T-shirt on?"

"It's her twin sister," says Sally.

"Twin, my arse!" pronounces Will, before spinning around, following his pointed finger off in another direction. "Photo booth!"

"Do you want to dance?" Sally asks me.

"Me?"

"We may as well!"

And so, just as the clock strikes midnight and everyone else is hugging and kissing each other, I am dancing with my pregnant friend, wearing a ten-year-old frock that is bunching on my thighs, while my husband is high on absinthe, stuck in a photo booth with his equally drunk friend Will and my hot-as-hell pal Kate.

"Five! Four! Three! Two! ONEEEEEEEEEE!" Madison yells down the mike. "HAPPY NEW YEARS!"

Sally and I embrace. I am careful not to squash her belly in the mêlée.

"Let's hope next year's a whole lot better than the last one," I say, giving her a squeeze.

"I don't know what you're complaining about," she smiles. "At least you haven't got one of these." She looks down.

"Oh, I don't know, it looks rather sweet," I smile. "What do you think it is, a boy or a girl?"

"It's probably another boy." She shrugs.

"Are you going to find out?"

"I think it's one of life's last surprises, so no, not if I can help it. It's either one or the other, as far as I know, no one's yet given birth to a spider plant."

"Happy New Year," I raise a glass of warm Prosecco. "I think I'm going to go home."

Predictably enough, Husband wants to stay, the Green Fairies are going down a treat and he's loving the band and apparently some cancan dancers are coming on later. Also, he hasn't bid on enough stuff yet. But just as I am clicking the key by the car door he comes careering towards me, red jacket flapping in the breeze.

"Kate's gone," he announces. "And I thought I'd save myself seventy-five quid." Which I suppose is his polite and generous way of saying "let's go home together on New Year's Eve".

The percentage proof of his breath as he gets in the car is overwhelming.

"What did Madison put in those drinks?"

"Christ knows." He belches through the back of his teeth. "But they are bloody brilliant, if it's good enough for Van Gogh . . ." He's flopping around in his seat, his hands are large and sweaty, his fingers are fat and he misses every button he tries to press, as he alters the heating, the music, the volume, his chair and level of heat blasting up between his arse cheeks. "No wonder he chopped his ear off. Van Gogh. No wonder . . ." He belches again.

Mostly the streets are deserted, save for the occasional group of girls. Bare legs, high heels, jackets up around their chins, they are walking slowly, bent against the wind, arms linked, no stragglers, no woman left behind. There's the odd group of boys, in pairs, threes, they are loudly, boisterously laughing, throwing themselves at each other, zigzagging, walking in the middle of the road.

As we draw up outside our house, there's a gathering of urban youth sitting on the wall and another gaggle smoking by the light of the security camera next door; a thick fug hangs in the air above their heads. There's laughter and screams as we get out of the car. My heels immediately crunch on a puddle of silver gas canisters that have clearly been inhaled by the dozen and chucked into the road.

"Alrigh'," slurs Husband as he eases himself out of his seat and winks at the wall gang. "'Appy New Year," he sniffs, speaking Cab Driver, as they all appear to be under the age of thirty. "Don't 'ave too much fun!"

"Alright, geezer," laughs a young bloke in a hoodie, his cigarette pinched in his right hand.

"Steady as you go!" Sniggers ripple through the group as Husband makes an extra effort to stand upright before navigating the pavement. "One step at a time!"

"Enough of your cheek!" Husband replies, sounding like an ancient copper from the 1950s.

"Woooooooaaaaah," replies the bloke in the hoodie, his eyebrow ring glinting in the streetlight. "Alright, Grandpa."

"Come on," I hiss, placing my hand on his back and directing Husband towards the door. "Let's get you inside."

"And you can pack it in an' all," he says, brushing my hand off and staggering up the path.

Inside the house, he slams the door and falls back against it, clunking the back of his head. "Shit!" he says, wincing in pain. "That little twat next door has got to be given his marching orders."

"Marching orders? I'm not sure you can do that."

"Bloody can. Noise pollution . . ." He starts to tick the reasons off on his hand. "Noise pollution . . . Noise pollution should do it . . ."

"Are you OK, Dad?" Sam is standing on the stairs, staring at his staggering father with an air of sleepy bewilderment. "Are you drunk?"

"What are you bloody doing up?" asks Husband. "And where is Ella? She's getting fifty quid to babysit you tonight." He pokes his head around the sitting room door and the sofa is very much empty.

"She's around," says Sam.

"Where is she?" I ask.

"Very close by."

"Where the fuck is she?" barks Husband.

"Stop swearing!" I hiss.

"She's next door." Sam looks a little terrified.

"At Dex's?" I ask.

"Who the hell is that?" asks Husband.

"The new next-door neighbour," replies Sam.

"How on earth do you know his name?"

January 1st

Husband is so hung-over he is nil by mouth. He spends the whole day lying around and eliciting the sort of low-level self-pitying moans only ever really heard in a bovine birthing suite. He does speak occasionally, as he stumbles around the house in his well-ventilated pyjamas, mainly to marvel at the idea that Van Gogh could have ever had a career in painting, or even held a brush without his hand shaking, after a night out on the absinthe.

"I mean, Jesus," he mumbles, moving his head slowly as he squints at the light. "How the fuck . . .?"

Ella's also a little sheepish, after I found her sprawled out on the sofa in Dex's sitting room, with a can of Red Stripe in one hand and a fag in the other, an ashtray balanced on her chest, as she was snogging a bloke, whose huge tongue seemed to have missed her mouth entirely and was lapping her cheeks and chin as he licked her face like a Mr Whippy. She was a little belligerent as I pulled her off the sofa, but I think deep down, or perhaps not even that deeply, she was quite relieved to be taken out of the place. Dex, on the other hand, was a little confused.

"It's you?" His face scrunched as his brain ran through a thousand Snapchats trying to find an image that it could recall. "From . . .?"

"Next door." I smiled stiffly. "And this is my daughter."

"Daughter! Wow! Did you have her at, like, two?"

"Very sweet of you. Like, no. Happy New Year. And do keep it down," I replied, stepping over cans, bottles, bodies and ashtrays.

And just like that, I went from Mrs Robinson to Karen in one short, sharp speech.

"Alright lady," he replied. "Keep your hair on."

So, Sam and I are the only ones keen on a New Year's Day walk. Not that Sam is keen, but even he admits that there is only so much pointless zombie war shooting he can do before his eyes glaze over and he dribbles on his own T-shirt.

"Hampstead? Hyde? Regent's? Or Holland?" I suggest, as we crack open the door to the New Year and let a little light in.

"Queen's?" he asks, already knowing the answer.

"That's not a walk. That's a stroll, and we are walking."

"OK, Hampstead then," he says, his shoulders sagging. "If we really must."

It's crisp and the bright sun is low in the sky as I lock the car and head towards the Heath. The pavements glisten with hoar frost, the black branches of the trees glint with white feathered beards. Our clouded breath follows us as we climb the hill towards the park gate. We are clearly not alone in our plan to cleanse and purge after the excesses of last night. Although I have to say, it's hard not to exude a little hangover-free smugness as we approach the shuffling masses, their heads heavy, gloved hands carrying bottles of water, as they atone for their sins. Meanwhile Pig and I walk briskly past them, picking up snippets of conversation as we go.

"... I think she likes him ..."

"... violin, you say ..."

"... so he flew using his library pass ..."

"... turned vegan ..."

"... resolution ..."

"... his mother doesn't do it but his father does ..."

"... what was I thinking ..."

"... hi there!"

"Hi, there! GUYS!!"

"HI! Sam! SAM!"

We both finally turn around on the pavement, just by the gate to the park. There's a man sitting in a white, open-topped car, dressed in a thick coat and red (Christmas?) scarf, waving at us both.

"Who the hell is that?" I whisper, out of the side of my mouth, while smiling and nodding in his general direction.

"Rob?" ventures Sam.

"Can't be."

"Happy New Year!" he waves a leather driving glove.

"Hi!" I smile. Clearly my Botox is weakening as the man detects confusion on my face.

"It's Rob!" he laughs. "Rob! Claire's Rob, although not anymore!"

"Oh, Rob!" I laugh. "I didn't recognise you . . . it's the sun . . . my eyes . . . and you look so well . . ."

He does look well, very well, he looks, well, unrecognisable.

"It keeps happening to me," he chuckles. "It's the new hair."

"New?" asks Sam. "How can you have new hair?"

"I bought it! Transplant," he declares, with a small pat to the back of his head. "I just worked out I was too rich to be bald." He shrugs at the perfect sense of it all. "There's a cure. Why not use it? Five grand. Bulgaria. Bloody bargain."

A few of the passing walkers are staring. Some are admiring the bouffy fruits of the transplant, others are thinking he's been ripped off.

"It looks amazing," I say, for it is. His hair is so thick and fecund, it looks like he's borrowed it from Burt Reynolds for the afternoon. "You look great," I add for good measure.

"Gym," he nods, glad that I have acknowledged his buffness. "Every morning, 6am. Everyday damn fitness. I even have abs." He fumbles around at the front of his jacket, as if he might expose them in minus two.

"No need to show me, I believe you!" I say, approaching the car. "How was your Christmas? How is Jade?"

"Oh! We had much fun in the sun!" he declares. "You?"

"We had Claire."

"Oh yes." His eyes roll a little. "Don't tell me she was depressed the whole time, crying into her turkey, despite being the one who brought the whole thing crashing down all on her own, in the first place?"

"She was fine, actually."

"Oh. Mine was more than fine, I had FUN! Jade and I together, without her, we had a proper laugh. Cried laughing. Best Christmas I've ever had . . . actually." He sniffs and wipes his frosty nose with the back of his leather driving glove.

"Good," I smile. There's an awkward silence. "You look great, anyway."

"Good," he says. I clearly don't. "So, did your mother hate her then?" He laughs.

"Claire? No, they're best friends," I hear myself saying. "Really good friends; in fact, Claire's staying with Mum at the moment. She's been there since Christmas."

"Christ. It's your father I feel sorry for. All he needs is for Kate or Swearing Sally to turn up and he's got the opening scene of *Macbeth*!"

January 7th

When are these school holidays ever going to end? How much time off do these children need? It's interminable. What are you supposed to do during those endless grey days that follow Christmas and New Year? It starts getting dark almost as soon as you wake up. When Jenny and I were children, we would watch endless hours of TV. We'd have a sofa and a dog each and we'd stare until our eyes went square and spent the rest of the time upside down in our bedroom, gazing at the ceiling, with a skull full of blood, reading the Cathy & Claire problem pages from *Jackie* magazine: that was as good as it got.

Well, it was certainly more interesting than the afternoon I have spent looking at trainers in JD Sports. If either of my children did sports, this would make sense. But they don't. Apparently, they need all this support and traction and lift just to make it down the street to Nando's, where they can fill their half-litre bucket of unlimited fizzy pop in whatever hellish combination they like.

And that's the other thing: other than entertainment, it's the food. How many more lunches and suppers am I supposed to cook? Pig eats everything, obviously, and Ella will only eat some specially prepared vegan alternative, with bacon and extra cheese. While Husband had his head permanently in the cupboard, helping himself to biscuits, bagels and tubes of Pringles that have been bought for the kids. It's like having the bloody *Tiger Who Came to Tea*, only he's left the water in the tap and drunk all the gin in the cupboard, and hoovered up the peanuts, Hobnobs and Doritos.

Also, he just never seems to ever want to go back to work. Apparently, the insurance business takes a big old break over the Christmas period, so they can all put their trotters up and bond with their families. Meanwhile, I'm like a frazzled sous-chef, permanently on standby in the kitchen.

It's not so much the cooking that bothers me, it's the actual thinking about it, the planning. The endless menu choices you have to offer up to tempt their spoilt, jaded palates. Chicken? Eggs? Grilled bloody something or other? I couldn't care less, just tell me, I'll cook it and you can eat the stuff and I can go and lie down in a darkened room and cry or re-up my IV of wine that I have set up in the spare room, if only we had one, so I could escape the snoring!

Fortunately, they are both going back to school tomorrow, and I shall be back at Bounce! I'm only hoping I can still fit into my uniform.

January 8th

Everyone's got a suntan. How did they manage that? I am standing in the queue waiting to drop off Sam, and all the mothers are looking amazing. They are bright-eyed, bushy-tailed, dressed head-to-toe in fanny-firming athleisure and all appear to be dusted in a fine film of Ultra Glow. Did I miss the memo? The memo that said: "Smart glamorous holiday, this way." "Sexy skiing trips, this way." "Generous colonics just here." I appear to be the only one to turn up at the school gate looking like I've been doing the Morgan Spurlock McDonald's diet and lived under a rock for the past four weeks. I have embraced my inner slug, while they have all turned into Gwyneth Paltrow.

"Hey you!" says Erica, like she's still in *Friends* – even Ella doesn't watch that show anymore and she'll watch *anything*. "How was it? Looking good!" She's on autopilot. Had she given me anything more than a cursory glance, she would not have acknowledged me on the steps. She'd have stepped swiftly aside, for fear it was contagious. "We had such a lovely time at the Four Seasons, Kuda Huraa." She says the words like I should know what she is talking about and pronounces them as if they are some long-lost Costa Rican tribe. "The kids did everything, swam with turtles and sharks, windsurfed, scuba-dived, paraglided, they loved it. We're going back next year. How about you?" She is craning her head and looking over my shoulder, smiling and handing out little waves, willy-nilly.

"We sat at home, watched telly and the kids did absolutely nothing. I like to keep self-improvement to a minimum."

"Brilliant . . . go you!" she says. She's not listening, which is probably just as well.

"Happy New Year!" Dave walks up behind me and kisses me full on the cheek in front of everyone. My heart lurches in panic. What's he doing? What's he playing at? "Did you have a lovely time?" He smiles. I blush so severely I can feel the tops of my ears about to explode.

"Fine," I stammer. "Happy New Year to you too . . . What are you doing?" I whisper.

But he doesn't hear me. "Erica!" he begins, and kisses her on the cheek.

"Dave!" She hugs him. "Long time no see!" She squeezes his shoulders. "How was it? Looking good!"

"Did you have a lovely time?" he asks.

"We were at the Four Seasons, Kuda Huraa," she replies, still referencing the long-lost Costa Rican tribe.

"I know it," he says. He does?

"Get away!" says Erica, giving him a flirty shove on the chest.

"Honeymoon," he replies. "The most expensive week of my life."

"Oh, we loved it! We're going back next year, so much nicer than . . ." She links arms with him, and they wander down the road towards the red-checked café for a "Coffee Club" coffee/tea/hot water-flavoured tisane.

I hate them for leaving me on the pavement, on my own. I fluff the top of Pig's head and wish him luck on the first day of term and I slowly walk back to my poorly parked car and sit in the driver's seat and cry.

What am I doing? What the hell is wrong with me? What was I hoping for? Why didn't he link arms with me and walk down the street *with me*? Have I finally gone mad? I frantically search in the footwell of the passenger seat for a packet of cigarettes. It's 9.10am; a damp, bent Marlboro Gold would be just about heaven right now. But there's nothing but old sweet wrappers and a half-drunk bottle of flat Dr Pepper plus an inside-out, licked-clean packet of Chilli Heatwave Doritos.

I pick up my phone. My hands are shaking, I'm shivering. It's suddenly very cold. Or is it just me? I should call someone. Who? Kate? She's got a new man, she's at work, she'll be busy. Sally? She's got her own cross to bear and three children. Claire? She's still with Mum. Maybe they might have run out of things to talk about by now? Maybe she might answer? I call. After three rings it goes straight to answerphone. I contemplate leaving a message, but what's the point? Last I heard, Claire was trying to work out what the best crystals were to put in her bra to protect her chakras or stimulate her chi, and thinking of opening some sort of yoga/healing centre in my mother's barn. She's finding the whole experience so restorative that she is also thinking of never coming back. My mum is all for it, apparently. And Richard's only too delighted as well. Anything to keep Jacqueline occupied so he can have a pint and pie down the pub and a snooze in front of the golf of an afternoon. They've got it all worked out; Jade's in her last year at school, so what's the point in buying a flat in Kensal Rise when Claire can live in the Chilterns for free, teaching middle-aged ladies how to douse their yonis in fresh stream water while flogging them vagina-scented candles, and CBD capsules to help aid sleep. Mystique don't mind, or so they say, and her job is always open for her, in a non-judgemental way, if she still wants it. Or at least, that's what they said when she finally got through to them. I am not sure I really want to speak to her. And anyway, Claire will only ring me back and put on her special, soft counselling voice, with a concerned tip to her head, which I most certainly can hear, even if I can't actually see it.

I could go to work, I suppose. Put in a shift at Bounce! and listen to *The Final Countdown* on a loop all day, while staring helplessly at my computer, hoping that the Mums, Tums and Bums idea really takes off in the January rush to a "better you".

Or . . .

I just start driving. Sitting in the car, there's a debate on loneliness on LBC. Husband must have borrowed it, he's always changing the bloody radio channels, like a dog pissing on its territory. Why can't he leave my stuff alone!

"It's the elderly I am worried about," says the caller.

"Not the kids?" asks the presenter, James O'Brien. "They're stuck in their rooms on social media all day. They're addicted to likes and affirmation. They have more imaginary friends than real ones, and they don't live in the real world."

I'd give anything not to live in the real world. The real world is hard. It's cold and hard and miserable. Sometimes it would be easier to get off. It would carry on spinning regardless.

I'm listening to the to and fro on the radio; it's like a depressing tennis match, where the balls are loose and no one makes their opening serve. I have no idea why Husband is obsessed with listening to this radio station, it would be more edifying to sit in a transport caff all day and listen to the banter, than tune in to this torturous moanathon.

Suddenly, I find myself outside Mrs Rees's house. It's the morning, and a Wednesday; neither factor is conducive to my visit. I walk up the path and ring her bell. What will

I do if she doesn't answer? Where would I go? What would I do? I can hear shuffling. She is in. Thank God. Whether she lets me in is a different matter.

"Who is it?" she asks. I can see her shadow at the door, I feel her eye blinking at the spyhole.

"It's me." I move my head into the light, push my nose towards the spyhole. She can surely see me distorted in the glass. All nose and eyes, no chin or face.

"Who is it?"

"Me."

"Who's me?"

I know she can see me. But you don't make eighty-two-year-old bones around here without being a bit of a cantankerous witch.

"Jane."

"What do you want? A cup of tea and a biscuit and a chat about World War Two?"

"Something like that."

"Well, you'd better come in then . . ." She pulls back locks and chains and bolts and undoes the key. "Sorry," she says; her hair is wrapped up in a scarf and her normally bright pink nails are chipped. "Had I known you were coming I'd have been to the parlour." She's dressed in her usual floral tabard and a pair of fluffy green slippers, and she's not got a scrap of make-up on her face. Oddly, it makes her look younger. Her usual slash of pink on her lips always bleeds out from her mouth along the lines, thickened and deepened through decades of smoking. She walks down the short corridor towards the sitting room. I follow the cloud of cold cream and lavender. The room is stifling hot and airless, there's a heavily buttocked indentation in the white leather sofa and *This Morning* is on full blast.

"Tea?" she asks. "Kettle's just boiled."

"Yes please."

"Sit down. Move the cat."

Winston is flat on his back, legs outstretched, his white furry stomach facing the ceiling, like some sort of animal sacrifice. He looks dead.

"Give him a shove," she shouts from the kitchen. "He's been there all bloody morning; he should go out and do his business. I am bored of emptying the bloody litter tray."

"I could do it for you," I say, staring at the TV. "Empty the litter."

"Holly's grown her hair," she says, walking back into the room with a large, hot mug of tea. "I've put some sugar in, just in case," she says, handing me the cup. In case of what, I don't know.

"Thank you."

"Them two were in trouble." She nods at the TV.

"Who?" I take a sip of my very hot tea. I burn my lips. It tastes of sweets.

"That bloke, Philip, Philip Schofield. And the lovely Holly. They jumped the queue for the Queen's funeral. God rest her soul."

"Oh. Was that a thing?"

"It was a big thing," she nods again.

"Why?"

"Who knows . . . He came out recently, you know?"

"Did he?"

"I'm not sure why he bloody bothered, we all knew he was anyway."

"Did we?"

"Oh yeah. He's good-looking." She starts counting off on her pink-chipped fingers. "Funny, kind, nice, well-dressed, groomed, washed, slim, looks after himself and can tell a good story. Gay. Obviously. Name me one straight man like that? Lucky Holly," she adds. "She's got a mate for life, right there. Anyway . . ." She sniffs and drinks her tea.

Her unsaid question hangs in the air. Why am I here? Why *am* I here? This is not supposed to be how this relationship works. I am supposed to be helping *her*.

"Mrs Rees?"

"I think it's time for Pamela, love, don't you?"

"Pamela." I pause. It sounds weird. I think I preferred Mrs Rees. "Did you ever feel lonely in your marriage?"

"What do you mean?"

"You know, sad?"

"Sad?" she looks puzzled. "We've all been sad, love. You lot don't have a monopoly on sad."

"Entirely by yourself, even in a crowded room?"

"Is that what this is all about?"

"It's just this void, this void of silence. This terrible sadness. Right here." I touch my chest as I feel it tightening. A huge lump, a ball of emotion wells up, and it takes all my willpower to keep it trapped in my throat.

"Oh, I know that feeling." She nods. "I think we all have it, at a certain time in our lives."

"Really?"

"That's the weird thing about emotions, every generation thinks they are the first to feel them. They're not. We're all the same, it's just how we deal with them that's different. My husband and I didn't talk for years. We'd sit in the same room, this room, in fact, in silence, while I secretly hated him for even breathing." She laughs. "And then we sorted it out. I loved him, and he loved me and that was that. I miss him now, I really miss him now he's gone. I stare at his empty chair in the kitchen and remember the good times. Or at least, I try to. The last few years weren't great. Whatever you do, don't take a long time to die . . ."

"So, you didn't have an affair?"

"Oh, we *all* had affairs! Of course we did! What are you talking about? We were the first lot to get the Pill. It was only given to the married women to begin with." She giggles into her chest. "Big mistake, letting us all off the hook like that, you could meet up with a fella whenever you wanted. The single women got it later, but you know, it wasn't hard to get your hands on. There was always a friend of a friend who could help you out. You lot didn't invent sex and you didn't invent the sisterhood either." She laughs. "We always looked after each other. Always. No one ever needs to go back to those dark old days of tears and gin." She shivers and puffs her cheeks. She leans back into the sofa and rests her cup on her knees. "We were brave, we were fearless. We fought for our rights . . . we won quite a few of them in the end." She smiles and looks across at me. "So, is it a quickie? Or are you in love with him?" I turn and look at her. I must look overwhelmed by the question. "Oh dear. That bad, is it? Drink your tea." She pats my leg. "They're doing a makeover in a minute." She nods back at the telly. "Alison Hammond's presenting. You'll like her, she's funny, and she doesn't care what anyone thinks."

January 28th

I have spent the last three weeks or so with my head down, dropping Sam at the corner of the road for school, studiously avoiding the school gate. I can't face it. I don't want to see *him* and I certainly can't look at *them*. Let alone talk to them.

And anyway, the conversation is entirely centred on everyone's self-improvement or how their self-care is going and indeed how dry everyone's January is.

Erica hasn't tasted a drop since the New Year's Eve fireworks display at Kuda Huraa where she had her feet in the sand, a 'Skinny Sunrise' in her hand, and the rockets flew over the Milky Way. Meanwhile, Madison has banned herself from hotel bars. Who knew such a problem existed? But apparently she's saved herself a fortune since she WhatsApped her own photo to the doorman of Claridge's and told him to refuse her entry, no matter how insistent she is. So far, she's only tested it once when she was drunk after dinner at Sexy Fish, and she turned up wanting a nightcap. He refused, she became obstreperous and called the man a cunt, so he finally let her in. Fortunately, she can't quite remember all the details; safe to say, she didn't shower herself in glory and she lost her earrings.

Dave and I, thankfully, keep missing each other. If I do catch a glimpse of him, he is always in a rush, he's got a new client, or account, or something like that. Either way he's very important and busy – all of which I am not.

I have seen Sally a bit, who is bemoaning her ever-increasing size, as if it's all a complete surprise that she can no longer see the tips of her toes or bend down to put on her socks. When you've had as many children as she has, or so she says, the stomach muscles have more or less given up the ghost and can't be bothered to contain the bump/baby, so it's all hanging out. She also has a vagina like a clown's pocket, or so she insists on sharing.

"It's not actually a technical term, Clown's Pocket, they don't put it on your form, unlike Crone mother, which they do," she says, her feet up, an Ole and Steen cinnamon bun in hand. "But all I know is this one is going to be enormous. Over ten pounds, they keep telling me. I'm not looking forward to it. Like giving birth to Boris Johnson. Just my luck to be genitally mutilated at the fourth attempt."

When I haven't been squeezing into my tight yellow T-shirt at Bounce!, wishing the day away, watching the other ladies in their exercise class, I have mostly been smoking on Pamela's white leather sofa. We started off drinking tea, but now we're on to the hard stuff. She likes a Dubonnet and black, just like the Queen, and I try to stick to the gin. She's filled me in on the complicated plot line of *EastEnders* and I am sort of managing to keep up. In short, Mrs Rees is keeping me sane and she's only a few minutes' walk from home.

It's dark, as I am wandering up my street, after a glass of sherry and a gripping episode of *Pointless*, where the final pairing actually won, which both Pamela and I agreed was a first, for a while at least. I'm standing at the foot of the path, bracing myself before opening my own front door, when my phone vibrates. It's a text from Dave, asking me if I am free for a "cup of tea" tomorrow at four.

Tea? At 4pm? Tomorrow? "A cup of tea?" Does he mean sex, or actual hot liquid? Does he even know the "cup of tea" consent thing? I can't remember. It's hard to tell. My heart is racing. I need a fag. I rattle around in my bag and pull out a squashed packet of cigarettes and sit on the wall. I spark up, I look down at my phone and inhale. What do I say? How do I reply? He's barely spoken to me since before Christmas, and now he wants afternoon sex? Does he? Or have I gone mad? A booty call at 4pm? I exhale.

Wouldn't that be amazing? Even if he does weep and snot afterwards. Sex. Some sort of attention, physical contact, something to make me think I am still alive, visible, in this dark and dreary world . . .

"I'd love one," I reply. I press send. I hold my breath. I close my eyes. Please let it be sex, please let it be sex. There's a ping, I look down, it's the thumbs-up emoji. That tells me nothing. Absolutely nothing. I pause. I could live in a limbo-like bliss for a while, thinking, hoping, he means a shag, or I could press him further . . .

"What on earth are you doing there?" asks Husband, standing on the pavement in his suit and tie, holding his briefcase, his face orange in the streetlight.

I quickly put my mobile in my pocket. "Nothing. Just having a quickie, a cigarette, before the fun-sponges tell me off for shortening my life by five minutes. Although why anyone would want to hang around after the age of eighty is anyone's guess."

"Well, that's where you're wrong," he says, picking his way past me, a little revolted by the *eau de sherry*-infused with *tabac* that I appear to be emanating. "Eighty is only old when you are under sixty, and the closer you get to it, the more acceptable and desirable it is, and if you're eighty-five, eighty is positively young. Ask your mother. If you only spoke to her instead of that old bat you insist on getting wrecked with three times a week."

"She's not an old bat."

"You've changed your tune." He opens the front door and turns around, backlit by the row of dusty spotlights in the hall. "What's for supper?"

"No idea." I throw my arms in the air like a petulant child.

"By the way, have you seen the Amex bill? Someone had a good Christmas. I hope you've got some money saved from that job of yours, because I'm not paying for all that shit."

January 29th

I've showered and shaved my legs and washed my hair. I've even had a go with the tongs that Kate gave me from an old goodie bag she'd been given at the Advertising Awards about ten years ago, when companies were rich enough to give stuff away for free. To be honest, as I look at myself in the mirror – skirt, boots, push-up bra, white shirt, unbuttoned just a little bit too much, cinched bouclé jacket (thank you Zara), I don't look too bad. I could even say good, were it not for the puffiness around my eyes from lack of sleep, due to the constant snoring. I am even wearing silk knickers.

I take a deep breath, I run my hands through my hair and look at my phone. The message is an hour old. How did I miss it?

"See you at the red and white café near the school, looking forward to it."

It's like a kick in the gut, it's painful as hell. I stagger backwards and slowly sit down on my bed. It is tea: a drink with jam and bread. How dare he? Raise my hopes only to dash them just like that.

I march out to the car as another text comes in. "I'm in the corner table. Do you want a cake?" Do I want a bloody cake? Yes, I do, mate. I want a bloody cake and I want to bloody eat it. I'm driving fast. I know I'll end up getting points for this. I jump a red light and take two speed cameras. Six at the very least, but I don't care. I need to get there before I change my mind and lose my nerve.

I pull up outside the café, slam the car door and stride right in. They can give me a parking ticket if they want.

He's sitting there, both hands cupping a cappuccino, he has a little carrot cake in front of him, that he's already taken the corner off. He is wearing a thick clotted cream-coloured cable-knit jumper and baggy trackie bottoms.

"Hi." He smiles. He looks nervous, like he has something to say.

Frankly, I am in no mood to hear it. "Come with me, now." I grab his hand and pull him up sharply from behind the table. There's a terrible scraping noise of the chair being dragged across the floor; several pinch-faced ladies stare.

"But . . . I've ordered you a Victoria sponge," he stammers.

I don't reply, instead, I walk him out of the front of the café and down a small alleyway to the side. I push him up against the rough brick wall and, taking my jacket off, I hurl it to the ground as I start to kiss him, full and hard on the mouth. He mumbles a vague protest, but he can't speak; his protest dies quickly enough and soon his tongue is probing my mouth. I rip my own shirt off. I am standing in the alley in my pale pink push-up bra, and he can't help himself. His hands immediately plunge in, cupping my bosom, burying his head between them. He starts to moan, he gasps for air, he pushes me back a little and looks me in the eyes.

"What are you doing?" he whispers.

"Just get on with it," I reply.

"But there are children and parents." He glances up the alleyway.

"All the more fun." I smile.

I pull my own pants down and step out of them, leaving them in a puddle on the cobbles, next to the pointed high heel of my boots. I move my back against the wall; I am standing in my bra, my skirt and my boots. He looks at me, he glances once more up the narrow alley and I pull him towards me. He fumbles around with his baggy trackie bottoms and lifts me high against the wall, holding me by the buttocks.

The first thrust is so powerful, I cry out with joy and desire.

"Shhhhhh," he says, covering my mouth with his lips.

His trousers are around his ankles as his bare buttocks pummel me against the wall. It's dirty, it's dangerous and it's utterly thrilling.

I can hear the children talking, I can hear the nannies nattering, the scooters coming. I'm coming. He's coming.

Five minutes later, we are both standing in line, ready for pick-up, stinking of sex.

"Hi Dave," says Erica, elbowing her way to the front. She pauses and looks him up and down. "Been to the gym again?"

"You could say that," he replies.

"And I've just run here from the bus," I add, not that she's asked, not that she's even noticed me.

She looks down. "In those boots?"

"They're quite comfortable, actually."

"Really?" Her thick collagen lips curl. "I don't think I've seen those stocked in a while."

"There you are!" says Madison, with a swish of her blonde ponytail and a lightning strike of her white teeth. "If you're quick you can stop them, there's a warden about to ticket your car!"

I run, pretending it's easy as pie to sprint in a four-inch stiletto heel.

"Hey, hey, hey!" I am waving. "I'm sorry, I'm just collecting, I won't be long. Please . . ." And for some reason, maybe it's the bouncing boobs in my low-cut shirt, maybe it's because I'm apologising, not screaming, I'm smiling and I'm beaming, I say, "I'm sorry."

The warden puts away his pad of misery and shrugs and says: "Five minutes."

And I can't believe my luck. This never happens to me.

"Coco! Coco!" shouts a woman behind me. She's calling a child, or a dog, I am not sure which. "Jesus Christ, Coco, what the hell is that?" I turn around to see a fluffy ginger cockapoo running along the cobbled alley behind me, my silk knickers in its mouth. "Coco! Drop! Coco, drop! DROP!" My La Perla are on the pavement for all to see. "What on earth . . .?" The mother leans in.

"Let's see," says Erica, stepping forward to inspect them. "Oh my God!" she exclaims.

"Underwear!"

"How disgusting!" adds Madison, having a good, long look. "*And* they're a large."

February 3rd

It's Sunday lunch and I am sitting opposite Husband who is eating his pudding like he's having sex. It's chocolate mousse, his favourite, and every time he puts his spoon in his mouth, he lets go of a little moan, his eyelids quiver and his nostrils flare. It's hideous to watch.

"I bumped into Rob yesterday," he says, between orgasms. "He's had a hair transplant and lost ten pounds and his business is doing really well . . . mmmmm . . . Divorce suits him."

"It normally does," I reply.

"What?"

"Suit the blokes."

"Really?" he asks, adding a moan.

"Always. They walk out, leaving the children, the goldfish, a litany of broken hearts and promises and the ex-wife ends up doing everything."

"That's a bit seventies of you," he replies, putting down his spoon. "I know loads of blokes who are desperate to see their kids, and who were the ones who tried to keep the marriage together in the first place. It's the *women* who are walking out these days. The *women* who are leaving!"

"Oh, boo-hoo-hoo for the patriarchy. You've been at the top of the tree for last two thousand years and now, budge up, babe, it's our turn." Ella smiles; her braces glint in the weak afternoon sun. I'm reminded of Jaws in *The Spy Who Loved Me*. "No one cares about your little pity party . . . Dinosaur."

"What's the patriarchy again?" asks Pig, looking up from his bowl, his face covered in chocolate.

"YOU!" yells Ella and, shoving her untouched pudding across the table, she announces, "I'm out of here. I can't sit around listening to *this* all day. It's tragic. Men complaining about their wives . . . lives. I'm going to meet my mates in the park."

"Which park?" I ask.

I don't blame her, frankly. I only wish I could leave too, with her, to spend the afternoon sitting under the trees, devoid of responsibility, ignoring the cold, plucking up the courage to flirt with the boys, my whole life ahead of me, plump with promise.

"Hyde," she replies, shoving her chair back under the kitchen table.

"Put your stuff in the dishwasher," I say as she walks out of the room.

"I laid the table!" she replies, her hand in the air, about to give us all the finger.

"Don't you dare!" says Husband, ahead of the game for once. She slams the door. "You spoil that child," he says.

"Our child."

"Whatever . . ." He looks down at his chocolate mousse. He's gone off the idea.

February 10th

It's been almost a week since side-alley sex-gate and I have been avoiding Dave's calls. God knows what he thinks. I don't know what I think myself. I don't want to have to explain myself, I don't want to see him, I don't know what'd I say. I am not sure I have ever been so forward in my life. Kate's always banging on about her sexual needs; she's got half the Goop website in her bedside drawer. I remember one night, when we were particularly drunk, staying together on a girls' weekend in a cottage in Cornwall, she arrived in my bedroom with some enormous purple vibrator the size of a baby's arm and told me "to have a go on that". When I baulked at the idea of using her second-hand, shop-soiled sex toy, she told me it was "fine" as it had been through her dishwasher.

Who on earth puts their dildos in a dishwasher?

"Knock, knock?" Deborah Day's shiny, happy face pokes around my office door, filling the room with the smell of sweat, sweets and Monster Energy drinks. "Can I have a word?"

That never bodes well. "Sure," I say, fighting a wave of nervous trepidation. Am I about to be fired? I'm worried. Could I possibly be enjoying this job?

"Well," she pauses on the threshold. "It's *only* the best January we've ever had!" She squeals and jumps and waves some sort of paper/spreadsheets in the air. "I had you there, didn't I?!' She grins, pointing a fluoro-pink acrylic nail in my direction. "I was being Simon Cowell in *The X Factor*!"

"You did," I laugh half-heartedly.

"That idea of yours to get the mums in during the day has been *amazing*. The classes are growing week on week. We're going to have to hire another trainer, we've got so much work on. I mean . . ."

"That's great news." I have a feeling it was actually her idea, but if she's offering, I'm accepting.

"Isn't it," she nods. "So . . ." She rubs her hands together. "Can I take you out to lunch to say thank you?"

"Really?"

"My pleasure."

"That would be lovely."

"No time like the present."

"Today?"

"Yes, today. Not yesterday." She laughs. "Today."

"But I've only come in my uniform," I say, suddenly conscious of my tight yellow T-shirt and blue fanny-grabbing tracksuit bottoms 'n' trainers.

"No one cares," she says. "Look at me!" I am. She looks great. "Just shove your coat on and no one will notice a thing."

Wow, Debbie drives fast. She nips in and out of the traffic in her immaculately cleaned and vacuumed-twice-a-week Mini, while blaring loud pop music on the car stereo. As she spins around each corner, I get another waft of pine from the Magic Tree swinging off her rear-view mirror. She pulls expertly into a narrow space outside a swanky new brasserie that's just opened around the corner from Pig's school. My heart sinks into my trainers. I quickly pray to the Lunch God that the harpies from Sam's class are all still playing tennis or shagging the delivery boy from Freddie's Flowers and are not yet having lunch at 12.30pm on a Tuesday.

"Have you been here before?" asks Debbie, as she slams her car door. "Jay and I came last week and loved it – they do a great steak and tiramisu."

We walk into the mostly empty, panelled dining room. It's smart, the tablecloths are linen and the waiters stand, alert as meerkats, pre-empting the diners' every move. It is cavernously quiet. Our trainers squeak on the parquet floor as we make our way to a far corner table. The waiter is effusive and charming and flaps out our napkins, while pretending not to notice we are dressed for the gym.

"Isn't it glam?" whispers Debbie from behind her enormous menu. "Someone told me that Myleene Klass was in here just last week. Shall we have a glass of Prosecco to celebrate?" she asks. "I never drink at lunchtime, but, you know . . ."

Debbie and I are sitting eating our steaks, and we're dipping our chips into ketchup and mayonnaise and reminiscing about the Christmas party when I think I see Erica out of the corner of my eye. Well, at least it looks like her, they are dressed like her, and yet, it's not quite, or is it? I hunch my shoulders, hoping to disappear, as she glances around the room to see if there is anyone who she should wave to. She gives our table the briefest of looks and sits down, and, with a rattle of gold bracelets, picks up the menu. I can tell by the birdlike hands and pale pink nails that it is her, yet she's done something extremely odd to her face. Her eyes are feline, her cheeks are pure hamster and the skin around her jaw is so tight, she has a permanent uplift to her smile, a bit like The Joker. In short, she looks like she's been panic-buying plastic surgery. She's been stockpiling in the wake of Brexit, in case it runs out. The result is weird. She doesn't look younger. She could be any age, anything from thirty to sixty-five. She just looks done. She's gone total Tussauds. I know I look like a melted candle and I am all for a tweakment, but that . . . that's Madonna without the Instagram filter.

"See that woman over there," I ask.

Debbie glances over. "Yes," she whispers.

"How old do you think she is?"

"Sixty-something? I dunno," says Debbie. "She's had a lot of work, I can see that. I've got this mate who works as a receptionist in Harley Street, and she's had everything. They play around with injectables when they're closed. She's got lips like you can't believe. She can barely close her mouth. They get all sorts in that clinic. I had my lips done there the other day. Mate's rates." She taps her bouncy bottom lip. "Do you fancy another glass?"

Fortunately, Erica leaves after less than an hour of three glasses of water and flicking some greenery around her plate, having failed to notice that the woman in the yellow T-shirt in the corner of the room is known to her SIM card. I heave a sigh of relief and accept Debbie's tentative yet hopeful offer of a third glass of Prosecco.

"So how long have you and Jay been married?"

"Nearly twenty years this spring. And I love him as much as the day we met over the Lancashire hotpot in the school canteen."

"Is that really where you met?"

"More or less. I was in the food queue, holding my tray, and he came up and talked to me. He was in the lower sixth and I was just about to do my GCSEs."

"At Carlton Academy?"

"It was Carlton College back then."

"And how long after did you get married?"

"Immediately. I got married at eighteen years old. Straight out of school. Jay was doing well, and I wanted to start a family right away. I wanted a big family . . . loads of kids . . ." Her voice trails off.

"And you've got Danny. He's lovely."

"I have." She smiles. "Lovely, sweet Danny. He's the light of my life."

"I bet."

"And you've got your two."

"Ella and Sam."

"You're *so* lucky. To have a boy and a girl. I've always wanted a girl . . . I've got so many shoes she could have!" She laughs and takes another swig from her glass. Debbie's cheeks are a little flushed and her eyes are rheumy; it's dark outside. "But it wasn't meant to be." She sighs and starts to play with the stem of her glass. "Sadly."

I don't know what to say. I don't want to pry. "Yes," I say, for want of something to fill the silence.

"I just couldn't." She shifts uncomfortably in her seat. "We did rounds and rounds of it." She sniffs. "IVF. But we just couldn't get pregnant."

"I'm sorry."

"Don't be. I'm over it now. But it took years of pain and waiting and hoping and money. Don't forget the money.

SO much money." She looks towards the heavens. "We could have at least six gyms by now if it weren't for the IVF. It's such a horrible thing, you know. Like being in a long, dark tunnel with a tiny little light at the end. It's this small." She puts her finger and thumb together. "And you keep hoping that you'll get there. They promise you the world, they pump you full of drugs. It's hell. In the meantime, my mates were popping them out like rabbits. Left and right. They'd meet a guy, fall pregnant. I can't tell you how bad *that* is. You feel so jealous, so angry, that your best mate is having a baby and you're not. You can't even see them, let alone be happy for them. You feel like such a bitch. You can't even pretend. Oh God." She shivers. "It's awful. I had nine miscarriages. Nine." She takes a large glug from her glass. "Nine."

"I had no idea."

"Why would you?" She shrugs. "I don't like talking about it, I never talk about it, really. It's one of those things you don't talk about, isn't it? Not being able to have a baby. Being barren. It's supposed to be easy, so easy you spend your whole life trying hard *not* to get knocked up. Except it's not. It's one of the hardest things in the world . . . I thought you could get pregnant by sitting in a Jacuzzi, can you imagine. In your bikini and everything, shows how much I knew!" She takes a sip of her Prosecco. "I was jealous of my own *sister*. I remember crying on her wedding day, thinking if she had a baby before me, I'd

345

fucking kill her!" She laughs. "And let me tell you, that's not a good look when you're dressed in the vicarage curtains and you've got eyeliner all down your face."

"But you've got Danny."

"The twenty-five grand baby!" She smiles. "And he's worth every penny."

"I bet he is."

"But we couldn't have any more. I tried. I did a couple more rounds. I froze my embryos. I had them put back in two at a time, but nothing. The last time we did three. I was terrified. God! Imagine three kids at once! I'd have managed, I know I would. But nothing happened. Except a lot of crying. There was so much crying. I think in the end we ran out of tears. Still." She smiles. "You have to be happy with what you've got, haven't you? I have Jay and Danny and they are my world."

"They are."

"That's why I was so fat, by the way!" She giggles. I must look puzzled. "Before Bounce! I was about two stone heavier. All the hormones, the jabs, the steroids, the sadness, everything. Awful. At least that's all gone now. I'm glad that's all over." She grins and picks up her glass again. "Shall we make a little toast?" She looks at the dregs in the flute. "And I mean little." I smile. "Be thankful for what you've got." She raises her glass and taps it against mine. "And to the best January we've ever had!"

"To January," I say and drain my glass.

February 14th

It's Valentine's Day and I am having dinner with love's young dream: my mother and Claire.

Husband left this morning after a terse rant about the "commercialisation of romance", arguing that Valentine's Day was a basic "Hallmark Event", along with Father's Day and Mother's Day, and all those other hideously "over-promoted days", which are quite frankly "up there with Halloween and Christmas".

"In fact, the only day they haven't managed to fuck up entirely," or so he opined as he stood in his pants at 7.30am, pointing his frothy toothbrush at me, "is Pancake Day. That's yet to be bloody Hallmarked. Although," he pauses. "They did try to make it into Jif Lemon Day, once. Thank God that never bloody took off."

So, I was left with a hastily scribbled heart on a piece of paper that Pig managed to cobble together with a wax crayon, just before I drove him to school. Which is probably more than I deserve, anyway. Needless to say, Dave has done nothing. Not that I was expecting him to. Although it would have been nice to have received a random something. Anything. He has been sending me a few texts, mainly of cobbled streets with #thinkingofyou. I am presuming it's supposed to be romantic, or a little sexy, but all I feel is the sweaty, hot flush of embarrassment.

"It's a shame your husband isn't here," exclaims my mother, somewhat unexpectedly, as we sit down.

"Really?"

"For you, that is." She smiles.

We're in a not-so-newfangled Asian Fusion restaurant, where you fool yourself you are eating healthy, coriander-infused salads, until you realise you've necked nothing but lychee Martinis and buckets of fried food, and consumed more sugar than a Mars bar. This place is normally packed with women shouting at each other over the chronic acoustics, however tonight it's as quiet as the grave. It's full. It's just packed with hand-holders, gazing at each other over the battery-powered tea lights, mute with familiarity, as they work their way through an overpriced set-menu dinner with complimentary champagne.

"He's in Bracknell."

"Bracknell?" she repeats, a characteristic curl to her nose. "Where on earth is that?"

"Berkshire," says Claire, sitting down next to her. "It's not very far away."

"He's got two days of meetings," I reply. "With Fujitsu, which is why he is staying over."

"Jiu-jitsu?" asks Jacqueline, cupping her right ear.

"Fujitsu," corrects Claire, giving her a little pat on the knee. "It's a Japanese company."

"Oh, right." My mother nods and grins at Claire.

Their relationship has moved on to the symbiotic stage since I last saw them.

"How are you?" I ask Claire.

"Well." She nods.

"Doesn't she look well?" adds my mother. She does. I have to admit. She looks lighter, brighter and altogether more alive since Christmas. "A few months in the country has made the world of difference. You should try it, darling. Rural life. Get out of the city. There really is nothing better."

"I am quite happy here, thank you," I reply.

It comes out a little more sharply than I intended, but there is nothing more irritating than people who live in the country extolling the virtues of the country, while about to tuck into some fancy food, in a fancy restaurant, in a relatively fancy part of town. It's right up there with expats commenting on Brexit while sipping *vin rouge* and chomping on Comté from their spacious homes in the Dordogne.

"Gooooood, just so long as *you're* enjoying your life, that's all that matters," she says, while perusing the menu down the length of her lengthy nose. Two months with Claire discussing tarot, her chakras and the healing power of rose quartz clearly hasn't made the blindest bit of difference. Jacqueline is still reassuringly offensive. "What on earth does one eat here?" she asks, placing her menu on the table with evident confusion. "Claire, darling, why don't you order for me, you know what I like."

After much back and forth with the under-informed, half-attentive waitress, fielding questions about gluten intolerance and cooking methods and sustainability, Claire finally orders for the table, while I slowly suck down my cocktail, which is by no means punchy enough.

"Excuse me," I say, waving my empty glass. "Can I have the same again, but double?"

"That was a double," she replies.

"Then a triple."

"Darling!" declares Jacqueline, over her half-moon glasses. "A triple? Are you sure? It is not very attractive."

"A triple," I confirm.

The waitress smiles weakly and backs away.

Claire starts talking about life in the Chilterns and living with my mother as if it's as bucolically beautiful as glamping in the Healing Fields at the height of the Glastonbury Festival. I simply had no idea there were so many beekeepers, organic perfume makers and fabulous candle people in such a small patch of the countryside. Or the commuter belt, as it is sometimes referred to. The cheeses are incredible, the dairy is out of this world, and simply everyone is making their own sourdough. Except my mother. Richard can't stand the stuff, so what's the point?

Anyway, Claire is smitten, and my mother loves Claire, like she's "the daughter she never had", even though she has got two others to choose from. But Claire's business plan has secured a business loan, and they are developing the back field into some sort of yurt sanctuary and nature spa. Or is it the other way around? And Jade is coming to run Reception in her year off and staying in my old room.

"Your mother said you wouldn't mind," says Claire. "As you hardly ever use it and if you do come for Christmas, you can always stay in a yurt!"

I laugh. "Nothing I'd like more than a yurt in December!"

"They are super-cosy and waterproof and there are loads of throws!" assures Claire.

"Ella would love it," adds my mother, popping a dumpling in her mouth. "It would do her the world of good."

"I saw Rob the other day," I say, mainly out of spite.

"Oh yes. How is he?" There's barely a flicker from Claire. A tattooed eyebrow rises, and she's quickly found her counsellor's face and is exuding benign concern/interest.

"Well. He's had a hair transplant." I laugh.

She doesn't. "He needed to."

"He's lost ten pounds!"

"That too." She smiles. "And he's got a girlfriend, I hear."

"Has he?" She beats me there.

"Jade told me, apparently she's lovely."

"Is that code for twenty-six years old?"

"No, seriously. Jade says she's lovely and he's really happy. Which is good."

"Is it?"

"Darling, what's wrong with you?" my mother chips in. "Of course it is good news. When I was young, we all wanted to stay friends with our exes. It was important for us *all* to stay happy families."

"That's mainly because you were *all* sleeping with each other."

"No, we weren't." She looks at me with deep disappointment writ large on her face; it's an expression I have seen before. "And anyway, darling," she adds. "Revenge is just bourgeois."

Fortunately, the silence is broken by the arrival of some chilli squid and a black cod that we all want to eat but are too polite to do so. We pick off little bits, leaving the bulk of it to go cold, until eventually, after much encouragement, Claire finally finishes it off.

"Have you spoken to Kate?" asks Claire.

"A bit," I reply. "But she's quite involved with her new man."

"I know!" Claire's pale eyes open wide. "She told me she's moving in with him."

"That's a terrible idea," says Jacqueline, like anyone asked her.

"Actually, I think it's the other way around," corrects Claire.

"No, I think you're right," agrees Jacqueline, nodding away. Her big golden doorknob earrings glimmer in the battery-powered light. "That's what she said last time she called. Wasn't it? I seem to recall. So much better him moving in with her than the other way around. Don't you think? If you've got property, you don't want to lose it or give it up over a man, let me tell you."

"The only problem is then you have to kick the bloke out at the end of it all," I say. "And what happens if he refuses to leave?"

"Far better that than you end up homeless yourself."

Jacqueline has all the answers, especially after two lychee Martinis.

"She sounds very happy, though," says Claire. "Do you think this is *The One*?"

"I do hope so," says Jacqueline.

"In so far as there is 'The One' over the age of forty-five," I add. They stare across the table. "But yes, yes, fingers crossed!" I cross my fingers. Perhaps a little less cocktail for me.

"I think we should all go on a big night out," suggests Claire. "All of us. It's been ages. A big girls' night out before Sally's baby is due, I move to the country and Kate buys herself a pressure cooker and starts cutting recipes out of magazines. D'you think she'd be up for it?"

I'm looking at her. Am I the only one without a plan? She doesn't notice.

"What do you think? How about Sally?"

"You could ask her. I'm pretty sure if it involves terrible karaoke, she'd be up for it."

March 14th

It's taken so long to organise, but finally we are all in a taxi on our way to the Karaoke Rooms in Soho.

"This is my kind of place," says Kate, scrolling through her phone. She's dressed in a black silk shirt and black velvet jeans, her long legs stretching across the cab in front of her. "There are fifteen pages of cocktails and only one of food."

"Lucky I've eaten already then," yawns Sally from the corner of the cab. "I've had all the pies available on the Portobello Road and am not sure I can stop farting."

"Jesus, Sally," winces Kate, crossing her high black boots. "You are the most appalling advert for pregnancy I've ever come across. You make it sound so deeply unpleasant, I'm glad I'm never doing it."

"I think she's doing brilliantly, she's out, out-out," I reply. "When I was pregnant all I ever did was lie on the sofa troughing Mini Magnums."

"And pregnancy yoga, don't forget," chips in Claire.

"We *all* did pregnancy yoga," Sally and I say at the same time.

"Are you downward-dogging with that one?" asks Kate, glancing down at Sally's large belly that is spilling over her jeans and onto her thighs as she lies back in the seat.

"Of course I'm fucking not," she replies, with an exhausted fly-swatting wave. "It'll be lucky if it's ever picked up, or fed. It'll spend most of its life licking the bloody pavement. Child-rearing is the law of diminishing neglect. The first one gets organic sweet potatoes sifted through angel's wings and the last one is lucky to get a can of Irn-Bru and twenty Marlboro Reds. How much longer till we get there? I think I need to pee."

Pulling up outside the Karaoke Rooms on Dean Street, Sally has to steady herself as she gets out of the cab.

"God!" She retches a little. "I'd forgotten how much Soho smells, it's like a whore's knickers." She coughs. "Old booze and fags and sex. If I upchucked here, no one would even notice."

We are straight inside and into our scarlet-red padded cell, so designed that your neighbours can't hear you scream. The lighting is low, the microphone is live and there's a jug of Long Island Iced Tea on the diminutive bar, along with two ready-sliced margarita pizzas that are slowly congealing and seeping over their respective paper plates.

"This looks fabulous," says Sally, collapsing onto the red banquette. "Is there anything soft to drink?"

"Are you alright?' asks Claire, sitting down next to her and slurping her cocktail.

"Can you hear the depression in my voice?" questions Sally. "I am so bloody fed up with being the size of a house, actually a marquee. You know how some pregnancies fly by, and others just seem to last forever? This is a forever pregnancy. It's been going on since the dawn of time. It's Jurassic."

"Do you know what it is?" asks Claire.

"I bet it's another fucking boy. It's bound to be. I only do boys." She shakes her head with irritation. "Anyway, who's going first?"

Of the four of us, the only person who can really sing is Sally. The rest of us sound like cats in various stages of strangulation. I'm a garrotted cat, Claire is a throttled cat and Kate is a feline in the last stages of asphyxiation. Not that it appears to stop her. I remember going to a wedding once, when we'd had a few sherries before the service, and I was standing next to Kate while she belted out "Jerusalem". She'd only got to "the holy lamb of God" before the whole of the right side of the church was corpsing. She was apparently oblivious and, chin in the air, she finished the hymn only to be told by some old trout in the row in front to "never sing again".

"Me?" volunteers Kate. "Let me just down this drink to get the vocal cords working." She necks it in one long professional gulp and wipes her mouth on the back of her hand, like a darts player sinking a pint. "Anyone have any suggestions?"

"'Single Ladies'?" says Claire.

"Fuck off! And anyway, I'm not," says Kate, with a little shimmie. "For the first time in, like, a thousand years."

"Britney?" I offer up, as I have a sudden flashback to the last time Kate was rolling around the floor, crawling on her hands and knees, trying to look incredibly sexy while screeching "I'm A Slave 4 U".

"Perfect!" she replies, touching her nose, like she's playing charades. "'Baby One More Time', it is."

And so it begins, two hours (oh, yes, we double-booked the room) of dreadful singing and drinking, all except for Sally, who does good singing and no drinking. Kate is having a whale of a time wailing. Her Britney is terrible, and it is swiftly followed by Adele. As I watch her "setting fire to the rain", I can't help but think she suffers from reverse self-doubt; maybe her mother was one of those parents who told her she could do "anything and everything". And she still believes her.

"One more!" she says, her finger in the air. "Just a quick Spice Girls and I promise I'll sit down." And she's off, complete with some half-remembered dance moves, high-kicking her slim legs, embracing her inner Posh Spice. Claire's giggling at the dance moves and Sally is wincing slightly at the sound, sipping a Diet Coke. "Phew!"

says Kate at the end of her set, flopping down on the red leather. "I really enjoyed that! Who's next?"

Sally steps up and nails "Jolene" and follows it with a quick "9 To 5" and a "Holly Jolly Christmas" just to show us all how it's done.

"So, when am I going to meet your new man?" I ask Kate, while Sally sings.

"You sound like my mother," smiles Kate, draining her cocktail through the melting ice. "She keeps asking me the same question. Truth is, I don't really want to share him just yet. I like keeping him under wraps!" She hunches her shoulders. "That way you lot don't get to discuss him when we've left the room. I know what you are like. You'll be sweetness and light and then as soon as our backs are turned you'll be saying he's fat and bald and has no sense of humour."

"That's not true, or fair!" I laugh.

"It is true and fair, and accurate. You all eviscerated the last one."

"Is he fat and bald with no sense of humour?"

"No, he's divine," she smiles, stretching like a cat. "He's introducing me to his mum at the weekend."

"That *is* serious."

"He's moving in, so that's about as serious as it gets in my book."

"When?"

"A couple of weeks."

"I'm really happy for you."

"I'm really happy for me too. And once he's in the flat, and he can't run away, then you must all come round for supper."

"I'd love to."

"Cheers." She clinks my glass. "I think it's time for some Abba – no karaoke night is complete without Abba."

"And 'My Way'," I add. 'Don't forget 'My Way'."

As the jug of Long Island Iced Tea slowly disappears, so the murdering of tunes continues. Claire destroys Karen Carpenter, Kate has a go at some Queen tracks, I inevitably shuffle about and point my finger a lot during "Dancing Queen". We all do the "Crocodile Rock" and finish, via "My Way", on the full-length version of "Let It Be", which does frankly go on for hours and hours, and finally we are deposited laughing and singing into the street.

It's almost 11pm by the time I have dropped everyone home in the cab, as I am the last port of call, as usual. As I pull up outside my house I spot Dex, on the pavement, who is also wending his way home.

"Good evening!" I'm a little more than ebullient, to be fair. "And how was your evening?"

"Not as good as yours by the looks of things," he replies.

"Mine was fantastic!" I throw my arms in the air. "Excellent singing, excellent dancing."

"Excellent!" He smiles. "Fancy a drink?"

"The night is young, and I can sing you some songs if you want."

"I'm alright, thanks," he says, opening his door. "Do you want gin or whisky? That's all I've got."

Twenty minutes later, I'm horizontal on Dex's mattress/sofa listening to The Doors, smoking a joint, nursing a whisky on my chest, which I haven't drunk in about twenty-five years.

"Don't you just love Jim Morrison?" says Dex, taking baby tokes on the joint, his right eye closed to the smoke, his face lit up with the red glow of his lava lamp. "I've been to see his grave in Paris. There's an inscription on it in Greek which says: 'According to his own demon'." He nods. "Cool." He adds, "Don't you think? I'd like something like that on mine."

"I'm not sure you should really be thinking like that," I laugh and have a sip of my whisky. I wince. "It's a bit negative."

"He died at twenty-seven years old, did you know that?" he asks. I smile. "That's me. Next year. Twenty-seven. There's a club, you know, the 27 Club, where they all die at twenty-seven. All the greats. Dead. At twenty-seven."

"Not *all* of them, exactly. Bowie? He lived a long life. Christ, Jagger's still alive!"

"But these were The Greats. Winehouse, Hendrix, Cobain, Joplin, they all died at twenty-seven, there's this conspiracy . . ."

And as he carries on with his conspiracy, I can't help but think how very young he is, how very sweet his smile is, and how much millennials bloody love a conspiracy theory – the Queen is a lizard, Prince Charles is a vampire and there's a cannibalistic paedophile ring that operates an international child sex trafficking network involving most of the world leaders. But then again, I suppose, we had fake moon landings and Elvis living long after he died on the lav eating a fried banana sandwich.

"So, do you want to go and have sex upstairs?" he asks.

I am suddenly seized by a rush of panic. "Gosh." I inhale rapidly and burn the back of my throat with the spliff. I cough and cough and my eyes start watering.

"I mean, I don't see why not? Bit of a MILF moment? Most of my mates have fucked a middle-aged woman. It's a thing."

"Is it? A thing? Wow. Um. Thank you for the, er, kind offer, but I think under the circumstances . . ." My phone starts vibrating in my coat pocket next to me on the sofa. I grab it. "Saved by the bell," I smile.

"What are you doing next door?" barks a very familiar voice.

"I'm not!" I lie, a little too easily.

"You are. I can see you on Find My Phone."

"Oh? Are you sure?"

"Yes. Oh. I am *very* sure. And you've been there a while, according to this. Quite a while."

"Well, I can explain . . ."

"You can sleep in the spare room." His voice is cold, extremely cold.

"We don't have one." I try to lighten the moment, but my voice is dry and my throat is killing me.

"The sofa then. I'm sure you'll find it comfortable enough, and then . . . you and I need to have a serious conversation. Not now. I'm very busy for the rest of the week, but . . . at the weekend. Let's wait till then."

March 15th

Husband has already left by the time I wake up, stiff, dry-mouthed, anxious, awful and a little terrified on the downstairs sofa. I'm cold as well. The small crocheted blanket that I'd bought at some overpriced "pop up" where I'd been invited by a friend and couldn't leave until I paid for something proved to be as useless at keeping me warm as it was expensive. My neck hurts, my head is pounding, a parrot has clearly shat in my mouth and I am late to get Sam to school.

Poor child, it's not his fault, it's mine. I'm all over the place and furious at the same time. There is nothing worse than a delayed argument. "At the weekend." How dare he? If he wants to shout at me, or say something, or throw things at me, it would be so much better to get it over and done with now, than having to go through the next two days with the sword of Damocles swinging gently above my rather sore head. I feel sick. It could be the whisky or the spliff, or indeed both. I can only hope it's cold, draughty and bloody miserable up there for him, on the moral high ground.

I drop Sam at school; he's only twenty minutes late. The school door is already locked and I have to make up some crap excuse about having to find our missing dog as it ran away this morning, scared by the builders who'd let it out. All I can see is Sam looking up at me, fascinated at the elaborate lying web I am spinning. The fact that "We don't even have a dog, or builders for that matter" look is plastered all over his face. I give him a little shove on the shoulder past Mrs Barnes and apologise profusely, saying it won't ever happen again. Sam is marked down as late, regardless. Mrs Barnes is not a very nice person.

Arriving at Bounce! suddenly feels like a bit of a sanctuary. Even the terrible looped music and the aroma of rubber-soled socks and aspartame don't really affect me anymore. I also think Debbie and I have turned a corner, ever since our Prosecco lunch; we have developed a rapport and a mutual understanding that goes beyond trampolines and fitness classes.

It's super quiet as I walk up the stairs to the office. I can hear the pop music ricocheting off the walls in the jump pits, and there's about an hour to go before the first fitness class. The café is not open yet and there's only one feather moustached teen on the Formica reception. I am a little relieved, as I don't want to talk to anyone; I want to sit quietly in my office and slowly work my way through my large cup of coffee and almond croissant. One dry bolus at a time. I'm definitely feeling the worse for two glasses of whisky and my millennial proposition. Not that Dex really seemed to care that much as I grabbed my coat, made my excuses and left. In fact, I think he muttered something like "another time", like he was asking for a new smashed-avocado recipe rather than extramarital sex with his significantly older next-door neighbour. I half wonder if he will remember it this morning.

I sip my coffee and scroll through the various mini films of our terrible singing that Kate, Claire and Sally have been sharing on our "Harlots on the Town" group WhatsApp. The films, the pics, the crying-with-laughter emojis are flying back and forth. I'm afraid I don't really feel like laughing. I feel profoundly miserable. However, listening to Kate's terrible singing is a welcome distraction from emails and exercise class application forms.

There's a loud knock on my door. I leap out of my skin like a teenager caught watching porn. Through the glass I can see their faces. It's Debbie and the teenager and two police officers. Police officers . . .? Two? What are they doing here? My head is scrambling, my heart is beating. Why are they here? What have I done? Our singing last night was criminal, but . . . Debbie opens the door. She looks worried, white, like she knows something.

"Are you sitting down?" she asks bizarrely, as I am very obviously sitting down, at my desk, behind my desk, on my low spinning chair. "These two officers would like a word."

Parking? Speeding? Jumping a red light?

I sit, I stare, I wait for the "this-is-nothing-to-worry-about" line, the one where they tell me "everything's OK", but they don't. Instead, they walk slowly towards me, so slowly it's like a dream where they're trapped in treacle, and I can't move, or hear, or scream, or talk or run. I am rooted to my chair, my now tepid cup of coffee still in my hand, crumbs of almond croissant in my crotch.

"Excuse me, madam, are you the mother of Ella . . ."

Ella! I think I scream. I drop my coffee, I know that for sure, as it spills all over my desk and dribbles onto the carpet tiles at my feet.

"Can you come with us, please . . .?"

I am shaking so much I can barely walk down the stairs. My head darts back and forth from one policeman to the other.

"Is she OK?"

"Where is she?"

"What's she done?"

"What's happened?"

"Is she alright? Please say she is alright!"

Neither of them has any detailed information, or maybe they just don't want to share it.

"Hit-and-run."

Is all I hear.

"Hit-and-run."

Why would someone hit my daughter and run off? What sort of person would do that? *Why* would they do that? *How* could they do that? My beautiful daughter, my little girl.

I sit in the back of the police car, my forehead against the cold window, my breath fogging the glass; the whole of Ella's life flashes before me. It's so fast and quick, the highlights. From her screaming birth, her newborn smell, so clean and fresh, untouched by the world. I see her crawling, laughing, blowing out birthday candles; I see her in the nativity, dressed as a star. Riding her bike, swimming, laughing, reading, drawing me a birthday card. She's in the school play, she's reading in assembly, she's dyeing her hair. She's dressed for a party. She's dancing, she's running towards a light. The tunnel is dark. Her face is smiling, it's white, she's white, she's wearing white, a long dress with a silver sheen . . .

"It's serious, isn't it?" I whisper.

"She is in ICU," nods the policeman, sitting next to me.

I call Husband. He drops my call. I ring back. It goes straight to answerphone. I call him again. He just lets it ring. I text him, my hands can barely move, I can't spell, I can't think. Where is he when I need him most?

"Where are we going?" I ask the policeman.

"St Mary's Paddington," he replies.

I text Husband again, I stare at the phone, waiting for him to read it. He doesn't. Nothing I have to say is of any interest to him. He's ghosting me, ignoring me. This is not the time. I call Claire. Of all of us, she is the best in a crisis. She picks up and immediately launches into the joys of last night. She's laughing and chatting away, giggling at Kate, marvelling at Sally, recalling the revolting cocktails.

"Don't you think? So, so good! Such a great evening." She chuckles. I am silent. I can't speak, because if I do, I don't know what will happen. So far, none of this is real and if I talk, if I say a word, anything, then it becomes reality. "Are you there? Is the phone dead? Hello? Can you hear me? Can you hear me now?"

"Yes," I whisper. My mouth is soundless, I am gripping onto the door handle of the police car, my knuckles are white.

"Are you alright?"

"No." I can't say any more.

"What's the matter? Where are you?" There's a rising panic in her voice. "Speak to me. Speak to me. If you don't speak to me, I can't help you."

"It's Ella . . ." That's it. That's all I needed to say, and I am crying, I can't stop crying. I can't breathe, I can't inhale, I can't exhale. I'm panicking, I'm gasping for air, all I can do is sob inconsolably. My shoulders are rocking, my nose is running. The policeman sitting next to me has no idea what to do.

"Stop, breathe, please tell me slowly what's happened. I can't help you if I don't know ... talk to me, slowly ... talk."

"I'm sorry, Claire, I'm sorry," I stammer. "I'm fine, she's ... not, she's not fine ... she's ... in hospital."

"Which one?"

"Paddington."

"I'm on my way."

The next half hour is a blur. I arrive, I am escorted through swing doors, up lifts and along corridors with strip lights and trolleys and endless masked faces, white plastic ponchos crackling with efficiency. I'm surrounded by people, all being kind, patting my arm, touching my shoulder, offering me tea. I don't know where I am, what I'm doing, then I'm led to a window and there she is ...

I know it's her by the soles of her feet, poking out from under the covers. I know those soles. I've kissed them. I have tickled them. I've checked them for splinters. I can't see her face, she's covered in tubes, but I know that hair, I know the orange highlights we did the other Sunday afternoon with plastic gloves on in the garden. She didn't care that I messed it up, that I left a lump of bleach the size of an egg at one side of her parting. She thought it was funny. We laughed.

"You are many things, Mum," she said. "But one of them is really not a hairdresser!"

Her right hand hangs limp over the side of the trolley. Her silver ring collection is dull against her waxy white skin, her fingernails are bitten and painted with chipped blue nail varnish. All I want to do is push through the swing doors and grab her hand. Hold it to my cheek. To squeeze her palm and tell her I love her and she'll be OK.

"At about 10am this morning." Another policeman is talking, mumbling through his thick dark combed beard. "Ella was knocked over on the zebra crossing outside school. The car was speeding. It was part of a police chase, and she collided with it, throwing her high up in the air. She landed on her back, her head hitting the road. The police van stopped immediately and called an ambulance, and she was brought here. We are currently tracing the car . . ."

I look at him. He has a kind face; it is contorted with concern. "Why wasn't she in school?"

"Why wasn't she what . . .?"

". . . In school?" I'm looking through the window into ICU. "She should have been in school. Why wasn't she at school?" I look back at him.

"I can't help you with that, I'm afraid."

"That's what I want to know. That's where she should have been. In school. Safe. Learning. Not lying run over in the middle of the road."

I'm escorted to the family room at the end of the corridor. It's hot and airless, with red furniture, bright neon lighting, an out-of-order coffee machine and an array of pamphlets on a low table in the middle of the room. I glance down at their covers: words like grief, counselling, funeral, organ donorship, death certificate leap out from the pages. This is not a place to receive good news. I sit down in the corner, hunched over in my coat. A nurse comes in dressed in blue scrubs; she has her name around her neck on a lanyard and a selection of pens in her top pocket. She is wearing white plastic Crocs.

"Ella is being prepped for surgery, there's some swelling on her brain, where her skull smacked the road. A surgeon will be here in a minute to explain what is happening, but in the meantime, I need you to sign some forms, as next of kin. Would you be OK to do that?"

Where is my husband? Where is he? Why isn't he here? I rummage around in my handbag, looking for my phone. There's no signal.

I am trying to read the forms but I can't focus. I can't really see. My hands are shaking.

"Can you just tell me where to sign?"

I scribble, my writing is illegible, I can't even remember my address.

"Don't worry," says the nurse, holding my trembling arm. "It's the shock, most people find this impossible. Would you like some tea? The surgeon will be along in a minute."

I just wish everyone would stop being so nice. I wish people would stop offering me tea. I hate tea. I wish it would all stop. I wish I could wind back the clock and start all over again. I sit, my shoulders slumped, staring at the floor, rocking, waiting, twitching, scratching my hand, hoping, hardly breathing, praying that she will be alright.

"Oh my God!" Claire bursts into room; her cheeks are red and she's panting and short of breath. She throws her arms around me, encircling me entirely. She smells of soap, toothpaste and fresh air. "We came as quickly as we could!"

"Thank you." I hold onto her for dear life; I bury my face into her neck. "Thank you for coming. Thank you. Thank you for being here."

"This is not a time to be on your own." I look up and over Claire's shoulder.

"Oh Kate, thank you. You are both such amazing friends. What would I do without you?"

"Sally's on her way." Claire squeezes me tighter. "She's just getting someone to look after the children."

"Thank you." I kiss Claire on the cheek, I am so grateful for her presence, and I feel the tight grip on my heart loosen, just a little.

"Dave and I came as soon as we heard," Kate announces.
"Dave?"

"Dave," smiles Kate. "Not an ideal way to introduce him to you all, but he insisted on driving me. He's so lovely like that."

Through the haze and the tears and the raw, terrified emotion, I see Dave, *my* Dave, standing there, in the doorway, dressed in his blue trackie bottoms and his cream cable-knit jumper. A look of cold horror creeps across his face; the colour slowly drains from his cheeks and his lips turn a pale shade of blue. He looks like he is about to have a cardiac arrest. At least he's in the right place for it.

"I should go," he mumbles. His eyes are spherical.

"Stay!" insists Claire.

"Make yourself useful," adds Kate. "Do you want something?" she asks me. "Water? Coffee?" She glances at the machine in the corner. "Of course, it's out of order. Some proper coffee? Anything? How long have you been here?"

"I have no idea," I reply, staring at Dave. How long has this been going on?

"Dave, go to that Caffè Nero place we saw on the way, will you, darling? And get us all something, we're going to need our strength." She dismisses him with a confident wave, without so much as a backward glance; she knows he'll do exactly as he's told. And she called him "darling". A while then. Of course it's been a while. What am I thinking? I am not thinking.

I sit slowly back down on the unforgiving red sofa, with Kate and Claire either side of me. I look up at the clock on the wall and watch the noiseless seconds tick by. It's not even 11am and my whole life has been turned upside down. Kate and Claire are talking, saying kind platitudes, like she'll be fine, and they're sure she'll pull through. They both periodically pat my knee. I keep looking at the door. I don't know who I am hoping will walk in. Husband? The surgeon? My daughter, laughing, flicking her long hair, explaining that all this is an elaborate, foolish, silly joke and that she is perfectly fine?

And then, suddenly, there he is: my husband. *My husband.* His face is as broken as I feel, his shoulders are as hunched as mine, his eyes are as anguished as my heart. His voice is cracking with emotion.

"Christ!" he says, running towards me. "What the hell happened? How is she?" He grabs me by the shoulders and looks into my eyes. "Tell me she's going to be OK?"

"She's going to be OK," I mumble, staring at his familiar face, looking into those soft yellow-brown eyes.

"Is she?" He sounds so desperate to believe me.

"I don't know!"

The wail is guttural, the emotion so raw that Kate and Claire inch off the sofa and walk quietly out of the room. I am sobbing, he is weeping, and we are both clinging to each other like drowning men without a raft. Over my husband's shoulder I see Dave arrive: he pauses for a second, unsure what to do, and then, slowly, blushing with embarrassment, he puts his tray of coffees on the table and silently leaves the room.

"Thank God you're here," I say, my head on his shoulder.

"Thank God you are too," he replies.

March 17th

Time stands still when you're in hospital. It stops altogether. A giant hiatus. There is no day, no night. It's hot and airless and stultifying, and the atmosphere hangs like a headache. You're parched, you're hungry, you can't eat, can't leave, you want to move, you sit in the same position holding your breath, aching with wait. Waiting for the doctor, waiting for the results, waiting for the anaesthetic to wear off, waiting for Ella to open her eyes.

I sat for two days in the same chair. I slept in my coat. My teeth and face unwashed, my clothes unchanged. I was so scared that if I left something would happen. Something worse. I made a pact with God, you see, that if I didn't move, she would live. HE must be so bored of it. People like me who don't bother HIM their entire lives, except at weddings, funerals and the odd carol service, suddenly knocking on his pearled gates asking for a favour. As if HE cares what

I do, where I go, if I leave Ella's bedside. But that's what I told myself, through the waves of terror and grief. If I sit here and don't move a muscle, God will make sure she's OK.

The nurses were amazing. People always say that, but until you've been there, rigid with anxiety, staring into the abyss, you don't know how extraordinary they are. They have seen all of life: the very depths to which we can sink and the mountains to which we can soar. To you this is the worst moment of your life; to them it *is* their life. And yet they were never not understanding, they were never jaded or too knowing, and they were always unfailingly kind. They were never flustered, or rushed; they moved as if in slow motion, silent as the night, gentle as the dove, wise as the serpent wrapped around a caduceus – checking, watching, taking notes, while the monitors bleeped and the bags dripped liquid, chemicals, drugs, sedatives, anti-inflammatories, cocktails of compounds I have never heard of, into Ella's arms, her veins, her body.

By Monday morning I know all of their names and they know more about Ella than her closest friends. They ask what food she likes, what TV shows she watches, what are her favourite shoes, and all the while they check on the oxygen going up her nose and the liquids going into the back of her hand, making sure they dab the spittle at the corner of her mouth and empty the bag of urine that hangs off the side of the bed. Weirdly, the body keeps on working, even while the brain is asleep.

My husband comes and goes. He brings news of the outside. He's called my mother, she is looking after Sam; he's contacted Ella's school and Sam's school and told them what's happened. He spoke to Debbie at work and most of my friends. He's been busy keeping Sam amused, trying to keep the balls in the air, while I just sit here, unable to move.

As dawn breaks on Monday, he arrives at my side, carrying a small bag.

"How are you?" he asks, pulling up a grey plastic chair and sitting down next to me in the corridor.

"I'm alright." I smile. He looks as exhausted as I feel. His dark hair is a mess, and he hasn't shaved.

"How is she?" He looks across at the glass-panelled doors that divide us from our daughter in ICU.

"Better, I think. The swelling is coming down and they're beginning to sound a little more hopeful."

"That's a massive relief," he says, handing me a hot paper cup of coffee. "Here. I've put a shot of vanilla in it. I know you only have that in an absolute emergency, and as this is one . . ."

"It is." I nod. "Thank you." I take a sip. It is strong and sweet and delicious. I feel it trickle down my throat, and a warm glow slowly emanates from the pit of my stomach.

"So, the doctors are more hopeful?" he asks, his hand resting on my leg.

"They seem to be."

"Thank God."

"Thank God indeed."

"And no more bleeding?"

"No more."

"Gosh." He leans back, his head resting against the wall. A small frisson of relief. "And they are definitely more hopeful?"

"I think so . . . How's Sam?"

"Worried. Obviously. Missing you. Obviously. We all are. But he's enjoying being spoilt by your mum."

"She's spoiling him? That's a first."

"She's discovered Deliveroo and can't believe all this food arrives at your door in a matter of minutes. She's astonished!"

I laugh. It sounds weird. It's the first time I've made that sound in days. It's the idea of my mother, embracing Nando's, miracles . . . and all that . . .

"And I brought you some clothes." He picks up the bag and unzips it on his lap. "Pants, deodorant, a toothbrush, those baggy comfy trousers you like and the new jumper I got you for Christmas. I thought they might make you feel a little better. You know, clean stuff." I look at the bag; he sees my reticence. "I can sit here while you change if you want, so she is not alone. Oh, and this . . ." He digs out the small white paddle brush I have had for years. He starts to clean it, pulling out the stray hairs as he is talking. "Everyone always feels better after they've brushed their hair."

"Do they?"

"It's famous." He carries on, removing the last few strands.

"Is it?"

I watch him. He looks up at me and smiles. I can feel the tears welling up, stinging my eyes. I try hard to stop them, biting my bottom lip, but slowly, quietly, they run down my cheeks.

"It'll be OK," he says, taking hold of my shoulders. He still has my hairbrush in his hand. "I promise. Everything will be OK." He pulls me towards him and gives me a hug.

May 29th

It takes two months for Ella to learn to walk, talk, smile and laugh again. And my husband and I are there every step of the way. From the moment she woke from the eight-hour operation to fix her impacted vertebrae and stem the bleed at the back of her skull, to her rehab, her convalescence and eventually, finally, thankfully her return home. Our world simply stopped spinning, and we both got off. Nothing else mattered; there was nowhere else to go and nothing else to think about. We tried. We tried to do other things. Occasionally. But somehow, sitting around a supper table, laughing at someone else's jokes, drinking their wine, just made me ill. I couldn't concentrate. I felt that if I relaxed and took my eye off the ball, Fate, God, would intervene again and deal me another, even more horrific card. It's control, apparently, and trust. Or at least that's what Ella's doctor told me when I confided in her one afternoon about the pact I'd made, and that I found it almost impossible to think about anything else and if I did, for a second, lose concentration, I was terrified that the Universe, God, would punish me for it, again. Not that the Universe, or God, isn't very busy elsewhere, of course. But feelings aren't logical. Especially the ones that stalk your head between the hours of three and five in the morning.

I bumped into Dave about three weeks after Ella's accident, just after I had dropped Sam at school. He insisted on taking me to the red-checked café to explain himself. I told him I wasn't interested, but he almost prostrated himself in front of me on the steps, and Madison was trying to raise her eyebrows when she saw us, so I went just to keep the man quiet.

"I did try to tell you," he mumbled like a teenager, cupping his cappuccino. "But you had other ideas."

"Right," I nodded, my cheeks flushing a little with embarrassment.

"I wanted to tell you that I had a girlfriend, and that it was serious, but . . ."

"And she was my best friend?"

"I didn't know that at the time."

"Really? Not even a tiny bit?"

"Well, um." He paused. He glanced around, hoping to pluck some sort of alternative story from the ether. "I did see a photograph." He failed.

"Oh." I sat back and crossed my arms. "But you still had sex with me anyway?"

"I don't think I had much choice in the matter."

"Poor you."

"I'm sorry." He looked abject.

"The thing is." I leant over the table, and glancing right and left, I whispered, "She must never know. Do you understand?" He nodded. "Never. Ever."

"Alright."

"No one must ever know. I'd rather die than upset my friend, who I love, by the way. All I want is for her to be happy. And amazingly, she is, with you. Who knew! *You*, of all people!"

"Really?" He sat up straight.

"Amazing." I smiled. "And the last thing I want is to destroy that. Ever. Do you understand?"

"Yes."

"Are we clear?"

"Crystal."

One week later he proposed. To Kate.

And now we are all dressed up for the day we never thought would happen. Kate is getting married, and Ella is following her down the aisle as her chief bridesmaid, and my husband and I could not be happier. Our daughter is walking, our daughter is well, and my very best friend is getting married.

"I thought Sally was your best friend," says my husband, as he gets out of the taxi in front of the church.

"She is." I smile.

"But you just said it was Kate?"

"I have lots of best friends."

"But you're only supposed to have one best friend," says Sam, tugging at his shirt collar. "And why do I have to wear this?"

"Because it's a wedding," says my husband.

"Do you *have* to be uncomfortable at a wedding?"

"It's the law," replies Ella, stepping out of the car, wearing a pale blue floor-length silk dress with shoestring straps and a cowl neck and matching silk-satin kitten heels.

"It certainly is," agrees Sam, who has never seen Ella in such an outfit in his life.

Kate is confounding all her nearest and dearest and, instead of tying the knot in an edgy registry office, followed by tequila slammers down the pub, she's opted for the full Country Wedding Experience with flowers, bridesmaids, a big frock, a big tent, speeches and a disco and her father, the sweet, poor old sod that he is, is so delighted that his forty-something seemingly-never-going-to-settle-down daughter is finally making the commitment that he's agreed to pay for half of it.

So we've all driven, for hours, down the A303, past Stonehenge to the beautiful honey-stoned village of Mells in Somerset where Kate grew up. Walking up the path towards the fifteenth-century St Andrew's Church with its imposing tower and glorious stained-glass windows, we are confronted by a sea of hats and floral frocks billowing in the breeze. Sally's standing at the entrance to the church, waving, wearing a white power suit, her three boys at her feet all dressed in the same pale blue silk as Ella. Poor Ella's job is to corral them like kittens down the aisle behind the fragrant bride.

"Hi!" she waves, brand new babe in arms. Expertly wrapped in a soft white blanket, it's fast asleep, its smooth pink cheeks, soft as a peach, poking out from underneath a neat white hat with a frilled edge.

"How are you?" I ask, kissing her.

"Well, fine, fabulous." She offers up the baby. "Look at her! Just. Look. At. Her!" she smiles. "Not a squeak in the car, as good as gold, girls are SO much better than boys. Girls are brilliant."

"You really do need to stop saying that," smiles Will, giving his daughter the lightest kiss on her cheek. "But you are right, they are."

"She's adorable," I say, giving Will a kiss.

"Everything alright now at home?" he asks.

"Much better." I smile.

"You must be so relieved. It was touch and go. A real white-knuckle ride."

"I am. It was." I nod.

"He nearly lost everything, you know."

"Who?" What *is* he on about?

Will glances furtively across at my husband. "The whole company nearly went under." I'm confused. "I thought you knew? He clawed it back from the brink."

"He never said anything."

"What did you think he was doing? Working all the bloody time. Sweating his bollocks off. Having a laugh?" Drinks with his mates?

I look across. My husband is organising Sally and her boys into a photograph with Ella and Sam. He is ushering, cajoling, getting them all to say "cheese"; he grins over at me. I smile back. He never said a bloody word.

"Right, I'm handing all this lot over to you, Ella," says Sally, looking at the mêlée at her feet.

"If that's OK? But come and grab me if you need any help. I'm going inside."

"Sure," says Ella, looking down at the boys. "Now listen here, you lot, you need to do exactly what I tell you."

"Are you OK, darling?" I ask, touching her arm.

"Mum, stop fussing, I am not made of glass. I can cope with this lot easily."

"If you're sure?"

"I'm sure, now go inside and let me get on with it."

Rob is on the door. "Bride on the right, groom on the left," he says, repeatedly, handing out the order of service.

His hair transplant is looking lush, and he has the remains of a well-worn tan. He's dressed in a well-cut navy suit, sporting a bright blue cornflower in his lapel and is clearly getting laid.

"I wonder who is with the groom?" asks my husband, plucking an order of service out of Rob's hand.

We walk down the aisle towards the front of the church. Each pew is loaded with flowers: blousy peonies, pale pink roses, sweet peas, anemones – it must have cost a fortune. Kate's side is packed already with a wild and varied-looking crew. Most of them I have seen, or met, at various stages and at parties or drinks. They all look excited for her, even the ones who are hung-over. Dave's side is much more sparsely populated. They appear stiffer, a little rigid, more upright, but they are significantly better dressed. There's nobody there I recognise, except, suddenly, the outline and the shoulders look familiar – near the front, two rows back – it's Madison. And her husband, Rick "at it like a dawg" who is looking decidedly bored. She turns and smiles at me. She is bizarrely wearing a small black pillbox hat with a veil, the sort of thing you'd wear to a funeral. She holds up a tiny white lace hanky.

"I'm ready!" she stage-whispers.

"Good." I nod.

Sam, my husband and I settle into the third row back. We're next to Claire and my mother, who has somehow managed to wangle an invitation. Richard politely declined to accompany her on the grounds that he would not know anyone and could barely pick the bride out in an identity parade; my mother had no such compunction.

Dave is standing at the altar, dressed in a neatly pressed morning suit with a cornflower in his lapel. He is twitching with nerves, fiddling with his shiny gold cufflinks, whispering to his best man and constantly glancing up the aisle, anxiously awaiting the arrival of his bride. He spots me in the crowd, a weak smiles flickers across his face and he looks straight back up the aisle.

Finally, the organ strikes up with the opening chords of Handel's "Arrival of the Queen of Sheba" and the whole of the congregation turns around. Kate and her father walk into the church. He looks like he's about to burst with pride, right out of his morning suit, and cry with uncontainable joy. She looks beautiful, so happy, serene and about fifteen years younger. I glance back at the altar. Dave's face has lit up and he doesn't take his eyes off her.

Kate had threatened to wear a large meringue dress with acres of tulle and a silhouette like a lavatory brush concealer, but instead, she's gone for something altogether more glamorous and sophisticated: a long, cream evening dress with three-quarter sleeves and covered buttons down the front. She has a small bouquet of white sweet peas in her hands and her hair is swept up and tousled all at the same time. Sally's boys in blue are right behind her, and Ella is standing behind them. She is smiling and looking so beautiful and I could not be more proud. *My Ella.* A bridesmaid. Alive. Walking. Wearing, uncharacteristically, a pretty, long, baby-blue dress and kitten heels.

As they slowly process down the aisle towards the altar, I reach over, searching for my husband's hand resting on his lap. I want to hold it, savour this moment. I'm not looking, my eyes are on Ella. But I can't find his hand. It's not where I think it is. I panic a little. Then suddenly I feel his warm, soft skin against mine as he takes hold of my hand and gives it the gentlest of squeezes.

Acknowledgements

With very grateful thanks to the wonderful Eugenie Furniss, who kept the faith, and to the marvellous Jon Elek and all at Welbeck who have made this whole process so delightfully enjoyable. Thank you.

Also, to my very dear friends Daisy, Sarah, Santa, Candace and Claude whose time and patience, I have called upon endlessly as I have sat on their sofas, drunk their wine and bored for Britain. I salute you! To the Witches Katya, Eleanor, Angela, Susanna, Sarah, Delphine, Susan, Alex, Simon, Pippa, Jonny and Nick, may we please be together again soon!

And my font of fun and wit and wine and wisdom -Sean, Claire, Jennifer, Katie, Joanne, Peter, Seb, Tina, Charlotte, Anna, Max, Charles, Celia, Mike and Michele.

Lastly to my family Scarlett, Marcus and Leonie and to *my* family Kenton, Allegra and Rafe thank you for letting me do this, every day, without a huge amount of complaint. But especially to my husband, who doesn't resemble Husband, at all . . .

About the Author

Imogen Edwards-Jones is the author of over 20 books (including several *Sunday Times* bestsellers). She was responsible for the hugely successful Babylon series, which sold over one million copies in the UK alone, has been translated into twenty different languages worldwide and was made into two BBC primetime TV shows.

Imogen has worked for over 25 years as a writer and columnist on Fleet Street. She has written and presented numerous television and radio shows and podcasts. She is an honorary Cossack and a member of the London College of Psychic Studies.

www.imogenedwardsjones.com

WELBECK

PUBLISHING GROUP

Love books? Join the club.

Sign up and choose your preferred genres to receive tailored news, deals, extracts, author interviews and more about your next favourite read.

From heart-racing thrillers to award-winning historical fiction, through to must-read music tomes, beautiful picture books and delightful gift ideas, Welbeck is proud to publish titles that suit every taste.

bit.ly/welbeckpublishing

WELBECK

ANDRE DEUTSCH

MORTIMER

MORTIMER

WELBECK

OH!

October 2016

Turns out there is lots of parking, shitloads of it, in fact; then again, who wants to come to an industrial estate at 2pm on a wet, grey, dank, dismal, bloody awful Tuesday. No wonder *Fifty Shades of Grey* did so well in the UK, I think, as I slam my car door; we're masters of the colour. And today is peak grey. The sky, the clouds, the clouds within the clouds, the pavements, the roads, the drizzle, the people, even the sodding building. Frankly, thank God for the Bounce sign. It's scrawled across the corrugated iron building (pale grey) like someone has ripped open a packet of sweets in virulent colours and toothache flavours. BOUNCE! It even has an exclamation mark after its name – so it must be fun.

I pause a little on the threshold, breathe deeply and then push my way through the heavy swing doors. I am met by a young man dressed in a pale yellow T-shirt. He is the other side of the navy Formica counter, looking down, and his hair is stiff and gelled solid in a centre parting, which then tapers into a carefully constructed rat's tail finge that must take at least twenty minutes in the morning to achieve. He looks up; every pimple and blemish on his face is highlighted by an orange concealer that is fifteen shades darker than the rest of his face. He must be about seventeen years old and in the full throes of that spoiler of hopes and dreams of ever getting laid: puberty.

'Welcome to Bounce, how can I help you? You're a bit early for the 3pm session, if you'd like to take a seat.' He mumbles this at breakneck speed and then points to a row of empty chairs.

'A session?'

He nods helpfully and glances at his watch. '3pm?'

I am not sure whether I love him or want to throw myself across the counter and slap him across his heavily pimpled face. I have had two children and I'm hurtling towards the precipice that is fifty years old. The idea that I could possibly leap up and down on a trampoline without a Tena Lady the thickness of a double mattress is inconceivable. In fact, the last time I did venture onto one of those things (one child down) in an attempt to flirt with a friend of mine's stepson (eighteen years old), I had to leave at a sprint and then spend the next twenty minutes trying to dry the huge damp stain in my trousers using her hairdryer in the toilet. It was mortifying.